JENNY BUNTING

Editing: Lopt & Cropt Editing

Cover: Kari March Designs

BOOKS BY JENNY BUNTING

Here in Lillyvale

Happiness (Caroline and Brady)

Here (Zoey and Jonathan)

Hustle (Taylor and Malcolm)

Home (Addison and Kirk)

Hubby (Makenna and Dan)

Stuck in Love

Please Be Seated (Erin and Landon)

In Case of Emergency (Cassie and Smith)

For Your Safety (Raegan and Henry)

Finch Family

Fool's Gold (Annie and Cameron)

Gold Rush (Whitney and Reid)

Golden Hour (Shiloh and Jackson)

Standalones

Safe with You (Izzie and Eugene "Thumper")

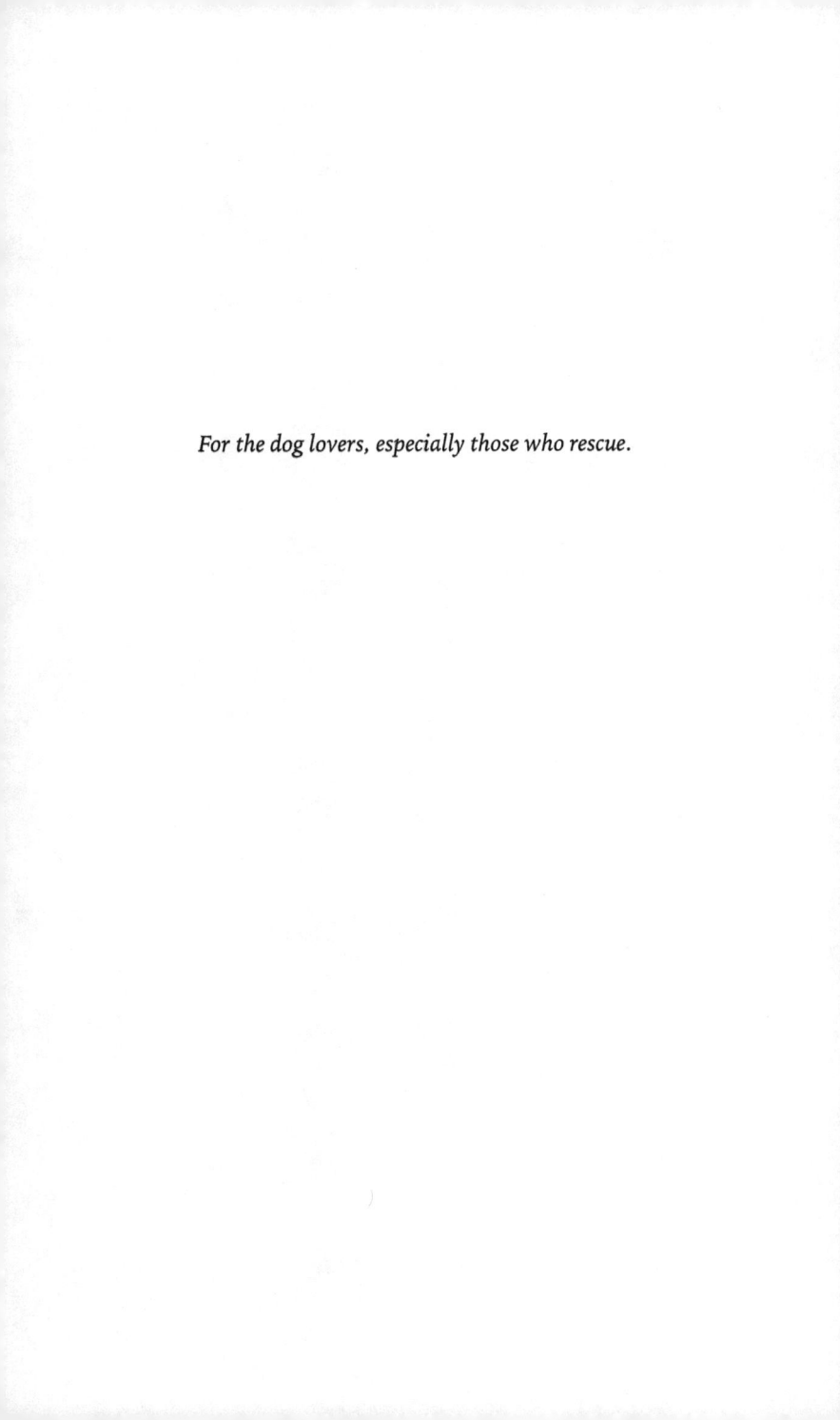

For the dog lovers, especially those who rescue.

A NOTE FROM JENNY

Thank you so much for reading *Golden Hour*! I hope you enjoy it.

This book deals with themes of death of a loved one to cancer, pet loss, pet abandonment, alcoholism in a parent, poverty, and depictions of complicated grief.

If you are sensitive, please take care of yourself.

1

SHILOH

"Today is going to be a great day."

I smooth down my new Woody Finch polo shirt, turning to inspect myself in the mirror. The sound of rustling comes from outside my room. My grandpa must be up. Showtime.

I leave my room quietly and sneak down the short hall to see Papa stationed and comfy in his trusty recliner.

Once I'm in view of the living room, I fan my hands out like I'm Judy Garland and kick. Got to give him the razzle-dazzle.

He hides a smile as he takes a sip of coffee. The book I lent him sits in his lap, so he closes it and puts it to the side. He's humoring me and reading a thriller, my favorite genre.

"What are you doing?" he asks.

"Entertaining you," I say, flailing my feet to tap dance. We live on the bottom floor, thankfully, because my tap dancing sounds like stomping.

"Girlie, you are too much." He points to the kitchen. "There's some coffee left."

"You're too good to me."

I kiss him on the cheek and scamper to find my favorite

tumbler, a shiny mint one, and pour in my favorite creamer and then fill it to the brim with coffee. It's the perfect color, my preferred ratio of creamer to coffee reached.

The first sip is heavenly.

"There's also some muffins," he says.

"Ooh, did you bake?"

My grandpa has never baked a day in his life. "Hell no. Costco. Those double chocolate muffins. Before you give me a hard time, I only allow myself half. I saved the other half for you."

"Yum, thanks, Papa." I find the other half, a knife resting on the crumbly wrapper. My grandpa doesn't eat the best, and his stroke earlier this year indicates we need to do better. However, my stomach churns with nerves right now, so that conversation is best for later.

Besides, those muffins are delicious.

"Who took you to Costco?" I pop a bite in my mouth. Chocolate explosions are always the best way to start a day.

"No one." My grandpa just shed sixty years with how red his cheeks are.

"What's her name?" I tease.

"Are you getting used to the bed?"

I guess we'll add "my papa's lady friend" to the list of conversations to have later.

"Yes," I say with a smile although a spring in the hide-away bed is bound and determined to kill me. "I had the strangest dream last night."

"Clowns get you again? I couldn't shake Bozo for five years."

I shake my head. "The dream was very calming. A woman was trying to show me something. A man, I think." I pop another bite of muffin and shrug. "Could mean nothing."

"Dreams are like that. Mean nothing or something." He goes back to reading his hardcover, and I sip my coffee.

Images from my dream float back to me. We're at Tin Lake, I think, the sun setting and reflecting against the water, creating shards of light. The woman points across the beach at a sitting man, with no face.

"You ready for your first day, girlie?"

"Yes. I can already tell it will be a great day." I take another bite and swallow. "What are you going to do while I'm gone?"

"Pete is coming over to watch the baseball game, and then we're going to the lake, I think."

My nerves calm. The main reason I'm here is to help my grandfather, who can't get around like he used to. My grandmother passed some years ago, so my mom, sister, and I are all he's got. His friends have volunteered to help too, so I felt comfortable getting a job.

"Don't you dare watch the next *Blue Bloods* episode without me."

"I wouldn't dream of it," he says. "It's sure nice having you here. It feels like it's been longer than a week."

I throw my arms around him and kiss his cheek. "I just love you, Papa."

"I love you too, girlie." He looks down, and his face softens. "The Finches are lucky to have you."

"Even if I don't drink?"

"Your personality more than makes up for it. Go get 'em."

"Oh, I will. Have a great day, Papa," I say, kissing him one last time and grabbing the last of the muffin and my packed lunch.

The drive to Woody Finch Brewery is so whimsical and lovely. The sun is shining, everyone smiles and waves, the birds are singing. It doesn't get much better than that. First-day nerves are still present, but the day is too beautiful to let them get to me.

I feel light again for the first time in a long time. This move was the right choice.

I park in the employee parking and check my phone. One missed call from *Bad News!*

There goes my great mood.

Thank goodness he didn't leave a message. "Don't you dare talk to him for six months," my sister Summer whispered in my ear before I drove off in my car a week ago. A voicemail is tough to ignore, but a missed call is okay, I think.

Pulling my shoulders back, I walk to the entrance, the same time as an olive-skinned man with dark hair walks in. He holds the door open.

"Hey, we match." I point to his shirt and then mine.

"You must be new," he says.

"Shiloh Abbott."

"Ramon Veracruz," he says, shaking my hand.

"I'm so nervous. Were you nervous when you started?"

Ramon chuckles. "You don't have anything to worry about. The family is very nice, and it's a great place to work. Emily will do your orientation. Once you're done, I'll show you around."

"I can't wait," I say, shaking my fists. Ramon looks at me like I'm nuts, but I get that a lot. Most people don't know how to take my energy as first. Teachers called me exuberant. *Bad News!* asked why I got excited about everything.

I touch Ramon's shoulder. "What are the rest of the siblings like?"

"Reid is a little serious, but an overall nice guy. Cameron is fun. He plans all the events, and he's good at it."

"What about the oldest? Jackson is his name?"

Ramon stops and turns. "It's best to avoid him."

"Why?"

He shakes his head. "He grunts at people. Seriously, just don't talk to him."

"I'm sure a little conversation won't hurt me. Or him."

"No, really. He's a dick. Just leave him alone."

We walk into the taproom area, and I take a deep breath. Now that I'm here, all the nerves float away. A smile crosses my lips, and I huff out a breath.

Today is going to be a great day.

"Shiloh, hey," Emily says, walking from behind the bar.

Emily is older and taller than me. At our interview, her hair was sleek and smooth but today, in a ponytail with a similar frizz to mine. Aw, a fellow curly girl. She shakes my hand again. I hold myself back from tackling her in a hug. *Bad News!* used to get annoyed that I had to hug everyone.

"I see you met our star employee, Ramon. He can change a keg in fifteen seconds flat."

He places his hand on his chest. "I'm gifted."

"You are," Emily says. "Shiloh, let's go meet the family."

"Excellent," I say. I already feel right at home. The Dog Hall of Fame in the hallway calms me. I stopped in my tracks when I left my interview and saw it. It was a sign that Woody Finch Brewery was the place for me.

Growing up, I was the weird girl who had to pet every dog. Big, small, young, old, it didn't matter to me. The minute I got a house with a yard, I rescued Rory, a ten-year-old mutt who was my soul dog.

I miss him terribly.

Emily humors me when I stop at the wall to admire all the dog photos. There's a large portrait in the middle of the entire family, with a German shepherd in the middle. I didn't see this before, but I'm glad they're a dog family. Another great sign.

I point and ask, "Who's that handsome boy? Or girl?"

"Boy. That was my parents' dog. Woody." Emily's lips straighten to a line. "He passed away around New Year's."

My heart is squished. "I'm so sorry. My dog died a couple months ago too. Rory."

"I'm sorry to hear that. It's so hard to lose a pet." She nods. "Woody was definitely my dad's dog, but the whole family misses him." Emily notices my chin droop but adds, "There's plenty of dogs that come through here so my dad can get his fix."

Lots of dogs come here. Heaven.

We pass by an open office where a man sits at a computer screen. His oak-colored hair sweeps his broad shoulders.

"Don't mind him," Emily whispers. I stop anyway.

"Who is that?" I whisper.

"Jackson. You don't need to meet him."

"He's your sibling, isn't he?"

"Yes, but…"

I just walk in. Even if everyone says to stay away, he deserves a *Hello, nice to meet you, good morning*.

"Hi," I say in my most cheerful voice. He stops typing, and the air shifts. Emily makes a tiny intake of breath, and I just keep smiling although he hasn't turned to face me yet.

"I'm Shiloh. Today is my first day. I love the Dog Hall of Fame. Emily says lots of dogs come in and I just love dogs."

You are such a nerd crosses my brain, but then I replace the thought with *Loving dogs makes you you, Shiloh. You're the best.*

He grumbles and turns around. His eyebrows crease as he looks me up and down, taking in the braids and the polo shirt. He is more handsome than I expected with light green eyes, like peridots, behind thick-rimmed glasses. He's wearing the same polo shirt I am, but it fits him so well, I gulp air. This gorgeous man now sees me as the dog-loving psycho who's saying hi to him when everyone told her not to.

This awkward train is already moving so I shoot my hand out toward him. He studies it, and I bite my lip.

"She comes highly recommended. Say hi," Emily whispers.

Jackson doesn't look at me, but stares at my shoes. I try not to fidget, although it's growing more awkward as I stand there like a mannequin, modeling a bracelet. The longer I stand here, the higher chance I'll turn to mush.

After what feels like ages, he takes my hand and shakes it. His hand is warm and smooth as it engulfs mine. Touching him feels like the one time in middle school I square-danced with my crush, Aaron Hanson. Aaron looked at me similarly to how Jackson is eyeing me now.

"Hi," he says. "Jackson Finch."

My heart quickens as he drops my hand. He studies me for a beat longer before he swings his chair back to the computer, resuming his typing.

"Pleasure to meet you," I say as Emily coaxes me out of the office. She closes it quickly and rushes off.

We both exhale. Hers must be relief. Mine is to try and cool down.

He is the handsomest man I've seen in a good while. Some people avoid closed-off people, but after a lifetime of seeking others' approval, I see it as a challenge. I've been called weird enough in my life so it doesn't faze me.

"That went better than I expected," Emily says as we reach the end of the hallway.

"It's now my mission to say hi to him every morning."

"You don't have to."

"I want to. He seems lonely."

"He's not. He likes to be alone. He's just…"

"Grumpy?"

"Yes, that's a great word."

"I love grumpy," I say. "He just needs sunshine."

"My brother needs the Sahara Desert if that's the case. Come on, I'll introduce you to my other brother Cameron, who is much more outgoing. He'll talk your ear off."

"Can't wait," I say. I hear something and turn to see the door close to Jackson's office. My heart drops, but I still smile.

Jackson Finch is my new project. I will *make* him like me.

2

JACKSON

I wake up to vigorous knocking at my door.

"Oh shit," I say, sitting up, the headache hitting me in my temples like a sledgehammer. When I stand, I stumble, bracing against the wall.

I don't remember falling asleep on my couch, but it happened. Sundays are my day off from the brewery, so I stayed up late drinking whiskey and going down Internet rabbit holes. It's ten o'clock, and I wanted to get to our garage gym by at least nine.

Fuck me.

I open the door to find my mother. Scowling.

When I first moved home, I rented a small apartment off Main, while this apartment stood empty. My mother wore me down, and I eventually moved into their refurbished garage apartment this summer. It's less than ideal because my mother knocks on my door several times a week. I usually answer, because if I don't, she uses her key. Or calls the police.

"Jackson Rollins." She used my two names. I'm in deep shit.

"What's up, Mom?" It hurts to open my eyes completely.

"The monthly employee barbecue is today. Did you forget?"

"I tried to," I say, shaking my finger. "Thank you for reminding me."

"Are you going to grace us with your presence?"

While many businesses try to say their employees are family, my parents took that dare and said "hold my beer" this year. We've become one of the best places in Goldheart to work because my dad treats his employees well, and one of his tactics is lots of free food and alcohol. After a suggestion from Emily, we now have monthly events (sometimes more) that I bob and weave away from like I'm an elite dodgeball player.

It's amazing what has happened to this business this year.

After my dad almost ran the family craft brewery into the ground, my siblings and I stepped in and saved it from catastrophe. All four of us went all in, quitting our jobs to make this dream for my dad happen. I needed the most coaxing.

He called me one day and begged me to come home. "Please, Jackson, you haven't been home in years. Please help me fix this. Please turn this around." I knew I could, and I wanted to. Although this town dials my anxiety up to an eleven, I agreed begrudgingly.

Within two months, I left my finance job, my apartment, and a quiet existence in Seattle to move back here. With my guidance, my dad pulled his beer from distribution, stopped chasing large-scale money-pit ideas, and focused on the taproom and building community within our small town founded during the California gold rush.

My dad listened to me too well.

"Our business is only as good as how happy our employees are," he said once when he put another event on the schedule.

Hence all the barbecues.

I prefer not to attend. Every chance I get I try to get out of them. The employees-only ones aren't so bad, especially because many of the employees weren't around ten years ago. I would rather stick pins underneath my fingernails than go to the Goldheart events. Between a group of women Reid now calls the "Bad Biddies" and friends who are now strangers, I just avoid them all together.

"Jackson, are you coming to the barbecue?" my mom repeats.

"Aren't your other kids going?" I ask.

"Yes, and you're one of my kids."

"Allegedly."

"Jackson Rollins Finch."

"Katherine Rollins Finch."

My mother runs her hands down her face. "Don't be a smartass. Take a shower and make an appearance. We have a couple new hires coming. Clover and Shiloh."

"I met Shiloh already," I say, punching a finger in the air. My parents, especially my mother, love when I'm social. I deserve credit for meeting that girl.

Shiloh is the type of person darkness dwellers like me hiss at. Sunny, bubbly, wears braids unironically. Her shoes have a hole in them, and she wore them on her first day with us.

My mother should be excited I shook her hand and that I didn't make her cry.

"Emily says you're avoiding her."

I grumble. After her first two shifts where she went out of her way to say hi to me, I looked up her schedule so I could hide the next time she was on.

When I went back to my desk after hiding, she left a sticky note: *Hey Jackson! Sorry I missed ya! Shiloh*

A heart replaced the dot above the i in her name.

"Are you going to come, Jackson?"

My head pounds; my stomach churns. I have no food in my fridge, and the food my dad orders for these things is usually amazing. I can eat, drink some of the special edition beer my dad pulls out, and put in enough face time to get out of the next few events. Also, I could stop Shiloh from being so fixated on me. The pros outweigh the cons this time.

"Fine," I agree.

"Great. It starts in a half hour."

"Oh shit. Gotta go, Mom, shower time," I say, closing the door in my mom's face.

"Hey!" she shouts, and I open the door.

"Sorry, Mom. See you soon," I say, before closing the door gently.

Forty-five minutes later, I'm showered, and the pain in my head is now a dull ache behind my eyebrows. I take some of my kitchen Ibuprofen, chug some water, and leave.

My sister, Emily, zones in on me within seconds of being at the party, and I contemplate launching myself into the bushes.

Her kid Olive plows into my legs. She's eight and the only child I can tolerate. She trolls her mother. Literally me in a small person's body.

My sister walks over, tightening Olive's ponytail. Olive swats her mother's hand away.

"Hi, Uncle Jackson. It's been sooo long," she says, flapping her arms. She also has a flair of drama. Just like her mother. She's a cute little stinker, at least.

"What is up, Martini?" I pick her up by the armpits so she's face-to-face with me. She giggles.

"I wish you all would stop calling her that," Emily grumbles. Cameron started it and it stuck, especially after we found out how much it pisses Emily off.

"Nothing much, Uncle Jackson. Look at my shirt."

I put her down so she can show me. It's a cartoon raccoon with the words "Cute but Trashy."

"I love it, Martini." I palm her head like a basketball, and she giggles.

My sister is a single mom and doing a phenomenal job, but the raccoon fixation is getting out of hand.

First it was a pair of raccoons they named Thelma and Louise who ate the cat food for the cat my sister does not have. Then, it was a raccoon-themed birthday party, and then, Olive let in a raccoon who got into the grain at the brewery. Now, we have "raccoon loss" as a line item on our loss report.

"How's my little raccoon?" my brother Cam asks, picking up Olive and throwing her on his shoulder. More giggling. Cameron's smile drops when he sees me. "Nice of you to join us, Jackson. Are you already counting down the minutes?"

"I've started the timer." I flash him my phone. I'm going to be here a half hour, tops. I'll make sure my mother and father see me, make a round with my scowl, then retreat back to my space and dread the next event in three weeks.

"Hi, Jackson," that voice that haunts my nightmares says behind me.

When I turn, I can't help scanning Shiloh, head to toe. Her lavender crop top ends at her ribcage, showing a hint of taut stomach from the side. She's wearing those braids again. I look away. Her adorableness does something to me, and I hate it.

"Who is this beautiful and obviously very smart lady?" Shiloh rests her hands on her hips, and it shifts her overalls, so I see more of her smooth stomach. My jaw clenches involuntarily.

"Olive Jean Finch." Olive gives a serious handshake, and Shiloh smiles widely.

"What a firm handshake! My name is Shiloh Louise Abbott."

"Shiloh, like the dog in that book?" my niece asks.

"Yes, the very one," Shiloh says.

"Louise. That's a nice middle name."

"Thank you. Louise was my grandmother's name."

Louise. My face feels tingly and numb, all at once. My breath is shallow, so I try to get a deep one, but it's not working.

"I need a beer," I mutter. I walk to the cooler, and I feel a person next to me. I'm racing toward my people limit for today, and this might put me over the edge.

"Jackson," Shiloh says behind me. Why is she bugging me? I stand up straight, cracking the beer. I take a long swig, the hops scratching the back of my throat. I turn around with a scowl.

"Everything okay?" Shiloh asks.

"Fine." I take another drink of beer. "Do you want a drink?"

"Sure, I'll take a soda."

"No beer?"

"I don't drink."

I almost drop my beer. "And my dad hired you?"

"Yep," she says. Her exuberant smile disarms me, and I suppress my own. I'm losing my edge. She shoves her hands in her pockets, teetering on her sneakers. I see a hole near the pinkie toe. Why doesn't she get new shoes?

"How can you sell our beer if you don't drink?"

"I'm *very* outgoing," she says.

"I'm shocked." I hand her an off-brand root beer. "Is this okay?"

"Perfect," she says like I offered her ten thousand dollars. She opens it and takes a sip, her eyes closed in bliss. Who the fuck is this girl? "I love root beer with my whole heart."

"I prefer the real thing," I say, taking a big gulp, wincing a little bit. The hops overpower this one, but the faster I drink this, the more tolerable everyone becomes, including Shiloh. She unnerves me. It's more than Shiloh sharing her middle name.

Shiloh is too sunny, too positive. She acts like the world is full of wonder and possibilities. She probably believes everything happens for a reason, that what happened was meant to happen. She doesn't know yet that this life is one long string of endless coincidences until you die into nothingness.

I've given her zero reason to invest what short time she has on this earth into me. Why is she even bothering? I should leave, but I stand here, watching her drink a soda while I chug this beer. It's so pure the way she closes her eyes, savoring the taste of the soft drink.

We stand there, uncomfortably, as I watch her.

Shoot me. Shoot me now.

"Why do you talk to me? No one else talks to me," I ask.

"I want to." She hesitates for a moment before she says, "You're obviously a stunning conversationalist."

I chuckle from deep inside my chest. That's a new one.

Shiloh takes another sip of her drink and shakes her finger at me. "I was warned about you, but you don't seem that bad. I think there's a big squishy heart in that stone-cold façade."

I laugh again. My body doesn't know how to react. It's been so long since I've genuinely laughed. I guess the gall from a tiny woman who wears overalls would do it.

"I'm all machine under this."

She laughs, and her smile is cute. "Jackson Finch, I will make you like me."

"That's quite a challenge. Because I don't like anyone."

"What about your niece? You seemed somewhat fond of her."

"Spunky raccoon-loving children I'm blood-related to don't count."

"Hmm," she says, taking another sip. "Challenge accepted."

"It's an impossible challenge. Are you up for it?" I cross my arms.

Shiloh rests her hands on her hips and looks up at me. "Yes. I don't know why you have a chip on your shoulder, but I intend to find out."

I clench my jaw. If she asks around enough, she'll find out what happened. Why this whole town feels like a minefield of excruciating conversations. Why I shop right before closing, why I see the two delivery guys in my town more than my siblings. Why there are only three places I can go in this town without seeing someone who will give me doe eyes.

It makes my skin crawl if I think about it.

The whispers. The pity. *Jackson, the oldest Finch son. So sad. So tragic.*

I could barely handle it when Shiloh said her full name.

"Ask around," I say, crossing my arms tighter, the beer warming in between my arm and my body. "This town loves to talk about me."

"I would rather you tell me," Shiloh says, turning away, holding her root beer to her chest.

"You'll be waiting forever."

"That will make that much more special when it happens. Have a good day, Jackson."

"You're not going to stay here and annoy me some more?"

"I'm playing the long game. Toodaloo."

Toodaloo? She walks off so I open the ice chest again, searching for a less hoppy choice. I look at her again, walking toward an old man.

My mother approaches with a smile on her face. "I see

you were talking to Shiloh. That makes me very happy."

"Who's the old guy?"

"Her grandpa, Earl Abbott. Used to come to the brewery all the time before his stroke."

"She doesn't drink, you know."

"We know. That's doesn't matter to us. She's sweet and a great worker."

"She's obnoxious if you ask me." Cracking another beer, I down half of it as I look at the clock. "I'm here...for another nine minutes." Mom knows about my timers.

"That's fine," she says, her voice cracking. "I'm just glad you're out and..."

My mom, crying. The thing I hate the most, and it happens every time I show my face. Like it means a lot to her that I come, but the emotion just makes my skin crawl.

Just because I like to be left alone doesn't mean a damn thing. Plenty of people are homebodies and prefer their own company. Two months alone in the woods has never sounded more appealing. No brewery events or small blond girls saying hello to me or writing me notes.

"I'm fine, Mom. I just hate these things."

"I know." She opens her arms, and here it goes. The sentimental hug. Once my mom gets a hug from me, it's okay to leave; I've done my duty. She cups my cheek, and I can't look at her.

"My baby. I'm so sorry."

"For what?"

"That you want to live your life like this. Shutting out the whole world."

The saliva coating my throat grows thick, and I grind my teeth. I've lived a full life. More life than anyone could dream of. I don't know why anyone feels sorry for me. They shouldn't.

At one time, I had everything.

3

JACKSON

I shove my key in the lock of my office and turn, just to feel no resistance.

My office is unlocked.

I'm very good at locking my computer and locking my files, after years of compliance officers breathing down my neck. My desk is usually clean and my trash empty.

However, when I open my office slowly, inch by inch, something isn't as it should be.

In the middle of my large calendar sits a to-go coffee cup and a Danish on a paper plate.

I look around for someone to catch me smile, to record my reaction as a prank.

I inspect the breakfast like it's a bomb.

I open the coffee lid and sniff, noticing the coffee is the exact color I want, the perfect distribution of creamer to coffee. Taking one sip, I can confirm it's my order. Americano from Gold Roast with half an inch of cream, one pump of caramel.

If he found out I like one pump of caramel, Cameron wouldn't let me live it down.

Pressing my fingers into the Danish, I confirm it's warmed and my mouth waters.

Who found out my Wednesday order? Who is responsible?

I put the investigation to the side to take a large bite of the Danish, letting my eyes roll to the back of my head. I drank way too much bourbon last night, and my stomach is so hollow and empty it creaks.

Damn, these pastries are good.

My Wednesday order is usually reserved as a mid-week reward for busting out a pain-in-the-ass task. I wait for the breakfast rush to pass, when Gold Roast naturally has a lull around nine-thirty, and I walk behind the buildings on Main Street to avoid prying eyes.

Now I don't have to, because of a coffee guardian angel. This breakfast gets at least two groans from me, because I don't have to go out in public and because it's free.

"Did I get your order right?" a light voice asks from behind me. I jump at least a foot off my chair.

It's eight o'clock, well before Shiloh's scheduled shift at eleven. Who let her in? What traitor divulged my order?

"What are you doing here?" I ask.

"I decided to get you breakfast. I know Wednesday is your usual day and you don't go until nine, so I made sure to get here before you."

"How did you get in?"

"A coffee fairy godmother never reveals her secrets," Shiloh says, folding her arms. "Is it good? I didn't know you got a pump of caramel in your Americano. I should try it."

I point a finger before I realize it's rude, and I lower it immediately. "Please don't tell anyone."

"Just because you like something sweet?"

"It'll ruin my image." I have one bite left in my pastry, and I shove it in my mouth. *Don't groan, it'll give her some satisfaction.* "You didn't have to do this."

"I know. I just thought it would be nice. Bribe you into liking me."

"It's a little try-hard, don't you think?" I brace for a scoff, a reaction that I offended her when she so kindly provided me with my Wednesday breakfast.

I'm such an asshole.

"No, it's try-just-hard-enough. You're a tough nut to crack," she says, shaking her head. "But I'm going to bust that shell wide open."

I wipe the crumbs from my mouth with the napkin she left for me. I'm fully aware I'm playing into her spiderweb. "Not today, coffee fairy godmother. I'm not your Cinderella."

"At least you're talking to me. My access point said that my plan would not work. But I make small goals. Reasonable goals. I was hoping for three sentences."

Dammit, she won.

"I've said too much," I say, spinning my chair back to my computer. I will never admit this out loud, but I love a good swivel chair.

"Your swivel chair is so smooth. I love swivel chairs."

This is getting creepy.

"Shiloh, I mean this in the nicest way possible: Thank you for the Danish and the coffee, but please get out of my office."

"Are you going to the end-of-season party?"

God, another party. This one planned for the day after Labor Day to say thank you to the staff and close early. They usually get way too much pizza from Booker's Pizza and let the beer flow from the tap. It's an accounting nightmare, especially when I come into my office with a mound of greasy receipts and tallies that look like chicken scratch.

I also saw an invoice for a karaoke machine.

"There will be karaoke, so absolutely not."

"Oh, you won't get to hear my singing voice."

"What a shame," I say sarcastically.

"I'll have you know I'm an excellent singer."

I swivel again, with a deliberate stiffness and no head sweep, which is my signature move. I can't be wrangled into a duet. Crossing my arms, I look up to this wide-eyed happiness monster who is currently the bane of existence. My rudeness is not fazing her at all.

She opens her mouth, and everything shifts to slow motion. If she sings a cappella, I will cringe so hard, I might sprain something. I wave my hands at her, and the "No" barely crosses my lips before a bright smile burst through hers.

"Gotcha," Shiloh says. "I know how to torture you now."

"You're doing such a good job already." I close my eyes and bring my hands together in a praying motion. I tap the tips of my fingers against my forehead.

"Come on, come! I'll keep you company!"

"All the more reason not to go." I look at her. "How about getting out of my office?"

"Sure." She knocks the door frame and almost leaves but then peeks her head in, like she's leaning back at an ungodly angle.

"Have a lovely Wednesday!"

"Goodbye, Shiloh," I say, and dammit, it almost sounds encouraging.

I'm alone for mere seconds before my sister strolls in and sits down on my desk without an invitation.

"Christ, what do *you* want?"

"One pump of caramel, huh?" Emily asks.

I point my finger at my sister because it's not rude, it's called interacting with a sibling.

"You don't tell anyone," I say.

Emily crosses her arms. "Shiloh impresses me. She's not scared of you like the others."

"I prefer the fear." I take another sip and try not to groan.

"Come to the end-of-season party. I swear you'll be off-limits for karaoke."

I look up at her and point in the direction of Shiloh's trajectory. "She will pull me up for a duet. I just know it."

"Karaoke isn't the worst thing you can do," Emily says. "Seriously, be nice to Shiloh. She's only trying to get to know you. She's a hoot."

"I have to get back to work." I swivel back to my computer, dragging my feet along the floor.

Emily leaves, but stalls in the doorframe. "You can't hide in the brewery forever."

"Watch me. One more year, and I can leave this place," I say.

"It must be tiring," she says. "Hiding."

The numbers swirl on the screen as her words hang in the air like a children's mobile.

"Did you and Mom come up with a script to follow to get me to come to these things?"

"No," Emily says. "I guess we just wonder if you're lonely."

Just because I don't run towards forced business get-togethers or I don't become buddy-buddy with an employee doesn't mean I'm lonely. My dad asked for a favor, and I'm here. I'm fighting like hell to get this family out of debt so my dad can live his dream. That should be enough.

There's no way in hell I'm going to that party.

4

SHILOH

I freaking love karaoke.

"Jolene" by Dolly Parton is my go-to, and I killed it. Riding a high, I leave the stage and hand the microphone to Cameron. I scan the room, looking for that too-long hair and a sour attitude.

All the other siblings are here, of course. Cameron has done a few songs, including a very sexual version of "I Want It That Way" by the Backstreet Boys. Even Annie, his girlfriend, sang a decent version of Mariah Carey. Reid, the other brother, just watched. Emily even took a couple turns, singing "The Right Kind of Wrong" with her daughter.

I find my cup, full of Sprite, and I take a long sip. Gosh, I love the sugary, lemon-lime flavor. Heaven.

Ramon walks next to me, his red Solo cup full of beer. "He didn't show, huh?"

I shake my head. "Nope."

"I'm not sure why you try with him. I said hi to him my first two days here, and he just groaned."

"He talks to me," I say, although most of it is snarky. I refuse to believe Jackson is mean, though. He's just grumpy, and even grumps need kindness. "I swear there's a warm center there."

"Meanwhile, I think if you peel back his skin, it's all machine. He's a manbunned robot."

"He made the same joke," I say with a smile. I grab another glorious piece of Hawaiian pizza.

I wonder what Jackson is having for dinner.

"Do you think I should bring him some leftover pizza? There're tons."

"He has five family members who can make sure he's fed," Ramon says, his eyes narrowing as he takes a sip. "You like him."

I scoff and my mouth hangs open. "I do not, Ramon."

"You do," Ramon says. "All the Finch men are incredibly good-looking, but Jackson is damaged goods. You, my dear, deserve a prince, not the ogre."

"I'm not looking for a prince right now." My heart clenches when I think about Bad News! trying to call me and leaving a text. *I miss you.*

He doesn't love me. I know I need to stop hoping for it from him.

To like me is a different story. That's rather easy because I don't give up.

"All I'm saying is put your energy elsewhere. Your dog-walking business, the rescue."

"Thanks for connecting me, by the way. Your aunt is so nice." Working Buddies' Rescue takes in German shepherds, Belgian Malinoises, and other working breeds to ensure they go to good homes, ones can handle a high-energy, prey-driven dog. I hope to learn as much as I can from Ramon's aunt, Priscilla, so I can open my own rescue one day.

It will be my mission to save as many as I can.

"You're welcome. They're always looking for volunteers." Ramon kisses my head, and I giggle.

"Are you getting up there?"

"If Cameron ever gets off the mic."

"Seriously."

"You were great though. Did Dolly proud."

"To Dolly." We cheers and take a sip. Ramon wanders away, and I breathe in and out deeply. Sometimes when I feel uncomfortable in a social setting, I just take deep breaths and sit in the uncomfortable. Most of the time, it goes away, and I can be present. Smiling helps.

Emily walks toward me with a big smile. Out of the all the Finch siblings, she's my favorite. I admire the heck out of her.

She has raised her eight-year-old daughter, Olive, all by herself. Her daughter couldn't be sweeter. Alongside doing some of the human resources and employee training, Emily also has a jewelry side business that does well, but she doesn't brag. According to Ramon and other employees, she's the only sibling who owns her own property. Cameron parks his tiny home on it.

"Hey Shiloh, how are you? You were super good up there," Emily compliments.

I try not to blush. "Thank you. I love to sing."

I pause because I want to ask about him so bad. Something about Jackson stings me, inspires the tiny voice in me not to give up. To keep trying. "Is Jackson coming?"

Emily looks toward the entrance. "I think Reid is trying to convince him over the phone. But my gut tells me probably not."

I bite my lip. I've said too much. I can't explain why I want to see him, why I want him to participate.

"You don't know what happened to Jackson, do you?" she asks.

I wave my hand. "I want Jackson to tell me himself. It's only fair. I hate gossip."

Emily nods. "That is fair. It just may be a while until he does. Like, never."

"I'm willing to wait," I say.

"Are you dating anyone?"

I shake my head. "Single. You?"

She laughs out one-note. "*Very* single."

I almost ask why, but I clamp my mouth shut. Emily's beautiful, with rosy cheeks and eyes the color of clover, and she's funny and personable. Any man would be lucky to have her.

"Where is Olive's dad?" I ask.

She shrugs one shoulder to her ear. "He didn't want us."

I can feel how uncomfortable this makes her, so I blurt, "I'm sorry I asked."

"No, it's fine," she says. "I can't be mad at him. He gave me the best girl in the world."

"I want to be a mom. You know, someday." I want that most of all. I want my family to come from everywhere—me and my husband's genes and foster care. It's scary how close I was to foster care so many times.

"I recommend doing parenting with someone. Definitely. I think she's turning out alright, though."

"She is. You know, I was raised by a single mom, and I turned out okay. Olive has such a strong family there for her."

"Thanks, Shiloh. That makes me feel good."

"You're doing a great job." I pull her in for a hug and she returns it, wrapping her arms around me. "He's not coming, is he?"

"Probably not," Emily says.

"Too bad he's missing all of this. The food and decorations and the *music.*"

Cameron steps on the stage again, motioning for Annie to

join him. He twirls his finger to start the opening bars of "I Got You, Babe" by Sonny and Cher.

"It's probably for the best he's missing this." Cameron starts singing off-key.

A thought pops up in my head. "What do you plan to do with the decorations?"

"Put them in storage for the next inevitable party. Why?"

"I have an idea."

5

JACKSON

The day after the party, my office door doesn't budge. I can hear plastic squeaking, and when I shove the door open, a large pop makes me jump a foot off the floor.

"What the hell?" I ask, looking around my office.

It's full of balloons. The tinsel my parents obnoxiously put around the brewery for every event hangs from my binders full of procedures. My diploma is defaced with stickers, all saying, "I Survived a Tourist Summer at Woody Finch Brewery." I check, and they're attached with Scotch tape. An inflatable dog sits in the corner. My chair is wrapped in streamers, in the way we used to TP the principal's car in high school.

My jaw clenches, and my blood boils over.

A card is propped on my keyboard, the edges tucked into the grooves.

I open it, half-expecting glitter to fall out.

Since you couldn't make it, I thought I would bring the celebration to you! xoxo, Shiloh

There's nothing I hate more than people who can't be confrontational, who use roundabout ways to be petty and infuriating. I crumble the note in my hands and toss it into the garbage.

There are streamers from the *ceiling*?

Emily leans against my door frame.

"Did you help?" I swirl my finger to all the decorations.

"Yes, I helped."

"I can't fucking work like this!" I yell, my forehead creased, my face probably red as a tomato. "I didn't want to go to another fucking party after another stupid party was two weeks ago. There're too many goddamn parties, Emily."

"I agree."

I gnash my teeth together. "Shiloh is pushing too far. Why does she do this?"

"I don't know," Emily says, crossing her arms. "She just wanted to bring some of the party to you and make you happy. It comes from a good place." She walks to the door and turns around. "Not everyone is out to get you, you know, Jackson."

Emily leaves me alone with my thoughts. I was able to clear most of the decorations and I folded up the ones we reuse for parties. I sat on the streamers on the chair, typing away, trying not to think.

I check the schedule. Shiloh doesn't come in until one.

At one-fifteen, I leave my chair to find her.

6

SHILOH

"And he just stopped calling me. Like, I thought we had a great time, and then he doesn't say good morning anymore," Ingrid says, dabbing her eyes. "What should I do?"

Biting my lip, I rehearse what I'm going to say in my mind before I open my mouth. "I think you move on. Maybe try not dating for a while. Go out with your friends. Do things you enjoy. Don't worry about him. You are wonderful, and if he can't see that, he wasn't worth it in the first place."

Ingrid's face breaks into a grin. "Thanks, Shiloh. You're totally right." she says, turning away from the bar.

I kind of started a thing.

I was called "The Therapist" in high school because everyone came to me with their problems and I always knew what to say. It took a little bit for Goldheart to catch on, but now I get one to two advice-seekers each shift.

Ingrid is two years younger than I am and trying the apps in a small town with no big city close, which means the men are scarce and the good men even scarcer.

I don't want to know how bleak it is.

Ingrid reappears. "Okay, so should I..."

"Enough," Jackson says, stepping up to the bar. I didn't see him come in, but now he's mere feet away from me. He studies me, and I let out an audible breath.

He found the decorations, and he's not happy about it.

"Jackson, hi," Ingrid says, turning toward him. I get it, he's a good-looking guy, but she's looking at him like she's a German shepherd and he's a pizza box she wants to destroy.

"Are you going to order?" he asks Ingrid.

"I, um, I..."

"Shiloh, why don't you help that person over there? I'll finish up with Ingrid," Jackson says, straightening his arms as he leans into the bar top. His position causes his triceps to bulge, and my eyelashes flutter. Does he find Ingrid attractive? She has the longest, most toned legs I've ever seen, and dark, silky hair. She fills out those jeans, while mine always gap at the waist because I have no curves whatsoever.

I'm nothing like Ingrid.

Turning, I help a customer, pulling a beer just as I was taught, tilting the glass to the side to avoid too much foam. Ingrid is gone when I turn back, and Jackson still stands there. After I smile and start a tab for the customer, Jackson is still staring.

I made a big mistake.

"Where did Ingrid go? Did she order a beer?" I ask.

"No. She was just wasting your time."

"She wasn't wasting my time," I whisper. My cheeks heat. *You can do this. It's just confrontation.*

"Why do you do this?" he asks, his chin tight.

"What?"

"Decorate my office. *Bug* me."

My mouth doesn't work; the saliva has dried up.

"What do you want from me?"

"Nothing."

"People aren't nice. Not really. Unless they want something."

"No, I…" I couldn't stand up for myself in the past, but there's always new chances to change. Direct course. Be different. I take a deep breath. "I like being nice. It makes me feel good."

"Well, stop it. There's a mess in my office right now because of you."

Tears threaten my eyes, and I sniffle them back. Holding my chin high, I look at him directly.

"Let's go into the office." I turn toward Tyson, who is helping a customer and point to the hallway. Tyson nods once.

I follow Jackson to his office like a kid caught cheating in class. Fifty percent of the decorations are down, except for the tinsel on the bookshelf and the streamers hanging from the ceiling.

This reaction wasn't what I wanted. I just wanted to cheer him up. Instead, it's gone so, so wrong.

We stand across from one another, and I cross my arms as a reflex. I can't meet his eyes. If I do, I will cry.

"Why won't you give up?" Jackson asks. "I've made it very clear I don't need anything from you."

"I…just wanted to bring some of the party to you," I say. "That's all. It was a fun time. I had a blast. I wish you were there."

"You shouldn't," Jackson says. "I'm not fixable. I am the way I am, and no amount of Danishes or streamers will change that. You're wasting your time. Got it?"

"Got it," I say.

"Someone told you what happened, didn't they?"

"No." My voice quivers. "Like I said, I wanted to hear it from you."

When we catch eyes, I see the truth. His eyes are soft

around the edges, looking at me. There's pain there, simmering under the surface.

"I'll put this away," I say, seconds away from free-flowing tears. I take down the remaining decorations and fill my arms.

After I leave his office, I tuck the reusable decorations back in the supply closet, making sure they're stashed neatly under the various holiday banners. I keep it together long enough to go to the bathroom, a single room marked Employees Only.

I sit down on the toilet lid and drop my head in my hands to cry, but stop myself.

Shiloh in Goldheart doesn't cry. She holds it together.

"Today is a great day," I say to myself. It's just enough to tilt my chin high and pull myself together.

7

SHILOH

"Sweetie, what are you doing back here by yourself?"

I came back to change out a keg, but I found the youngest Finch peeking outside the back door. A back door I was told should be always closed.

"Nothing." Her voice is too high to be nothing.

Besides Jackson, the rest of the family has been open and welcoming. Olive always says hi to me when she hangs out at the brewery. She's usually a good kid, reading in the corner or harassing Cameron for snacks.

Olive rarely leaves her small table in the corner, but now she's looking out the back door like she's trying to sneak people into the movies from the exit.

I knew Olive would be hanging out at the brewery tonight while Emily worked on her jewelry orders at home. Cameron and Reid are off tonight, so it's just me and Ramon out front. I have no idea where Kit, Olive's grandmother, is. It's slow for a Wednesday in September since the tourists left with the Labor Day holiday.

I walk up behind her. "Where's your grandma?"

"Shh. You'll scare her."

"Who?"

Olive pulls her head from behind the door and the frame. "She's here."

"Who?"

Olive opens the door wider and in saunters a raccoon.

A humongous raccoon.

My saliva evaporates, and a squeak comes out of my mouth. Ramon warned me about this, but I honestly thought it was a joke. *Under any circumstances, please keep the back door closed since a gang of raccoons will take advantage of access. If a small child tries to lure a raccoon in, you stop it.*

I'm realizing the small child I was warned about is Olive.

Now, a raccoon has breached the back door, on my watch. I am letting this happen. I'm so getting fired.

"Olive, that is a wild animal. It shouldn't be in here."

"She's not a wild animal. Her name is Lena, and she's a mama. Where are her babies?" Olive sticks her head out again.

I can be assertive with a child.

"Close the door, Olive."

"But the babies!" she cries.

We have bigger problems in the shape of a giant raccoon. It moves slowly, toward the grain.

"See! Lena is friendly."

Lena is friendly because she's getting what she wants.

I shake my head. "Raccoons can't be in here, Olive. Just because Thelma and Louise are cool..." Cameron told me about Thelma and Louise, a raccoon duo, who are infamous in Goldheart for attacking Annie's ex, exacting raccoon vigilante justice.

This animal is not Thelma or Louise.

This animal needs to get out of there. Not only do raccoons carry a lot of diseases, they can be nasty. Even meaner than Jackson. One once attacked my dog, and I've never forgiven them. Although Rory wasn't hurt and he was vaccinated, I still don't like them.

The door is still open, and I pray it gets spooked and escapes.

Olive pulls her face back in, pale with lips parted. She freezes, and I could pee myself I'm so scared. What else is out there? A bear? A mountain lion? This raccoon's hundred raccoon friends?

"What?" I scan the storage room for a weapon.

"That's not Lena right there." Her little finger shakes as she points to the raccoon. "That's *Darryl*."

"Who?" I ask.

"Thelma's husband. Darryl is a meanie. Oh no. Mom's going to be mad. I let Lena in a month ago, but she needed to feed her babies…"

"The raccoons are married?" I ask.

"We named them from the movie. Lena is the waitress at the Silver Bullet. Darryl is Thelma's husband. You really need to see *Thelma and Louise*, Shiloh."

"I've seen it, Olive. We'll talk about how you've seen that movie later," I say. "We need to get Darryl out."

"Darryl will not go nicely," Olive says, her hands pin-straight at her sides, like she's a Nutcracker. Her chin quivers. I can't handle a crying child right now.

"It's okay, Olive. Help me get him out. What should we use?"

I scan the room again because the raccoon is now touching the bag of grain. I'm not sure if we can use it if a critter has touched it, but I really don't want the mess to be on my hands and Jackson to know I'm the reason we had a loss in product.

He hates me enough as it is.

"Do you see a broom or something?"

Olive points, and I see one hidden between the shelves. I grab it slowly, to avoid spooking the raccoon.

"We shouldn't make any sudden movements. Stay behind me, sweetie," I say, holding the broom out. I nudge Darryl with the bristles, and he looks back at me with teeth bared.

I move slowly, trying to hook its body and usher it closer to the open door, and I'm just praying Darryl's buddies don't come charging in.

The gentle suggestion of exit angers the raccoon even more. Its beady eyes focus on me, and my heartbeat quickens.

"Olive, I'm going to need you to go get your grandma."

"No, I can't do that, I'll get in trouble. Please don't tell on me, Shiloh. I will do anything," Olive says, fat tears dripping down her cheeks. She sniffles and backs away, her eyes squeezed tight.

Between the raccoon in our back room and the child tears, I don't know what to do.

"Just get out of here, slowly. I'll handle this," I whisper, in the most soothing voice possible.

The raccoon goes back to molesting the grain, instead of lunging at Olive as she leaves. She closes the door to the hallway, and I breathe out a sigh of relief. At least, it's contained now.

A raccoon loose in Woody Finch's main taproom would make the paper. Again.

My next broom nudge is to the ribs as the raccoon sticks its little black hands into the bag, but once it touches its fur, it flashes its teeth at me, absolutely pissed off.

It happens so fast.

The ball of fear launches at my bare legs. I try to pivot out of the way, but I'm not quick enough and I feel a hot sear on my thigh. I drop to the ground, landing hard on my knees. I'm now face-to-face with Darryl the raccoon.

He looks at me.

I look at him.

He's closer to the door, but still stares at me.

"Get out of here!" I scream. The raccoon hisses, his hackles raised. My hand grabs for the nearest item, a roll of toilet paper. It doesn't have the necessary force, but it surprises the animal enough when it bops him in the head. The roll startles the demon creature, so I launch another one, and another one. The animal is stunned.

My toilet paper bombs give me enough time to stand up to grab the broom, an all-around better weapon.

I take a stance, and the raccoon looks at me, unimpressed. "Come and get me," I yell, posturing with open arms.

The raccoon figures it's not worth it and scampers outside. I walk to the back door, slam it closed, and lock it.

Leaning on the door, I scan the area to see nothing out of place or distorted.

My head becomes woozy when I look down at my leg. There's a bright red gash I can't look at it for too long or I will fall to the ground.

I don't know how I get to the office, but I find Olive in Kit's lap.

"Um, I think I need to get checked out," I say in the doorway, and I walk in, careful not to get blood on the doorframe. "And I need to sit down."

"Let me call Jackson," Kit says, pulling out her phone.

"Why him?" I ask. Then, the lightheadedness hits me, and my head drops between my legs.

8

JACKSON

"Where are you?" Mom asks, panicked.

"In the brewery," I say, pinning my phone between my shoulder and ear. I now take my laptop into our tiny storage closet that keeps the cleaning supplies. I turned over a bucket and have been happily working here when I know Shiloh is on shift. She hasn't caught on yet.

"Good," Mom says, not questioning why I'm working at eight p.m. on a Wednesday. "You need to take Shiloh to urgent care."

"Why, is she okay?" I slam my laptop shut and stick it on one of the shelves, next to the window cleaner. My mind races to life-threatening situations, like an aneurysm or accident. My heart clinches that she's hurt. I'm not sure why I care.

"I think she was bit. She has a gash on her leg. It's not too bad."

"Bit by what?"

"A raccoon attacked her."

Now, that's funny. Of course, Shiloh would try to be friends with a trash panda.

Then, I remember rabies. I hope she's okay.

"Emily puts her phone on Do Not Disturb when she works on orders, I'm watching Olive, and Ramon is still out front. I need to stay here. Cameron is out with Annie, and Reid isn't picking up his phone. Your dad is taking a much-needed night off. You're it."

I almost offer to watch Olive so Mom can take her, but the last time I was alone with my niece, I ended up with a horrific smoky eye and pearl clip-on earrings.

"Okay, I'll do it."

"Come soon. She looks green."

My pulse quickens as I close the closet and walk down the hall to my parents' office. It's at the rear of the hallway, past the bathrooms and the joint office my siblings use.

Why was Shiloh close to a raccoon?

I've seen her with the dogs that come into the brewery. When she's not looking, I watch her pet every dog aggressively, talking to the owners. She baby-talks every goddamn one, and they lick her face like she's a T-bone steak. My dad does the same thing, and Fitzgerald the resident Golden-doodle has never been more thrilled. That dog freaks every time he sees my dad and now every time he sees Shiloh.

She seems like the type to want to cuddle anything, diseases be damned.

When I reach the office, I expect the typical Shiloh— bubbly and excited to see me and saying hi, even if she's shaken up. Pretending like our incident in the office didn't happen.

Instead, I'm met with Shiloh's pale face and a large gash on her thigh.

"Oh shit," I say, covering my mouth.

"Uncle Jackson, it was Darryl!" Olive shouts. "Shiloh was so brave!"

"Who is Darryl?" I ask.

"I think it's one of the raccoons. I can't keep them all straight," Mom says.

"He's the big one who likes to trick me…"

"Olive, I would love to hear everything about the raccoons later, but I have to get Shiloh to the doctor."

"Yes, yes, yes," Olive says. "Shiloh saved me."

Shiloh's eyes drift closed, and my heart stops. She's as white as the tissues on my mom's desk, and who knows what she's been exposed to. I drop down to a knee and place my hands on her forearm, without thinking. I can't remember the last time I touched a woman I wasn't related to.

Shiloh is not special. You would be this concerned about anyone.

I'm lying to myself. Shiloh is not just anyone.

"Are you okay?" I ask.

Shiloh's eyes flash open, and she rips her arm away from me. So she doesn't forgive me for how I acted when she decorated my office.

I honestly thought she would keep trying, bringing me coffee or leaving notes. Maybe up the ante with a singing telegram. However, over the last month, there's been nothing. She still says hi to me with a bright smile and a hand wave. I've lingered in her presence, in case she wants to say something. Greetings and hand waves are all I get now.

Now, Shiloh looks like she would rather let rabies ravage her body than go to any medical facility with me.

"Do you need help standing?"

"Maybe. I don't know." Shiloh braces her hands on the chair to stand up and winces.

"I can help you," I say, offering my arm. Shiloh hops over, and my arm slides around her waist. Her body presses against mine, and tingles I haven't felt in a long time rampage through me.

"Does the wound hurt?"

"Yes, a lot."

I point to Olive. "No more raccoons, Olive Jean. Promise?"

"Yes, Uncle Jackson."

We hobble to the side door, where my family parks their cars. I unlock my truck with the key fob and open the car door, holding her up while I do. She can't put any weight at all on her leg. Her hand sits on my shoulder as I hoist her into the truck.

I shake my hands as I walk to my side. Her waist is small but soft, and it felt great in my hands. My fingers still tingle from the contact.

When I start the car, Shiloh leans her head back on the headrest. "God, I hate raccoons."

"Really?" I ask. I'm stunned that she doesn't love all woodland creatures.

"I didn't like them before, but I really don't like them now."

This is the first time I've heard her say one negative thing. Everything is usually unicorns and rainbows with Shiloh. It's like I'm finally seeing the real her.

"You give off 'Snow White with all the critters' vibes. Especially with the brewery dogs."

"I do not feel the same about all God's creatures. Especially raccoons. And snakes."

"I understand the snake thing." I turn out of the brewery, and drum my fingers against the steering wheel. "I don't get why my niece is so fascinated with raccoons. Just because Thelma and Louise did one decent thing for Cameron and Annie does not speak for all raccoons."

Shiloh chuckles as she shifts in her seat. "They're so mean. I don't mind if they need to tip a trash can to eat, but they attacked my dog once so I've always been judgmental toward them."

"And that's why you were fighting one tonight?"

"Yes. I threw toilet paper rolls at it. I stunned it."

A laugh leaves my chest. "I feel like we should make you employee of the month."

"Not so fast. I think the racoon touched the grain. You might need to order some more."

I groan. Another tally for the raccoon loss line item. Trying to reconcile the prior raccoon grain incident was a nightmare for two days.

"I really wish I could've been a fly on the wall to see that," I say. Watching Shiloh fight off a raccoon would've made my whole year. Not much excites me nowadays, but the image of Shiloh pelting a raccoon with toilet paper rolls brings me joy.

"Are you smiling? Because I got attacked by a raccoon?" Her face is stone and unamused.

"It's an amusing image," I say, with a laugh. Shiloh's face is slack, and then she bursts into laughter and throws her head back. We laugh in unison, and then she quiets, turning her head. Her braid became loose with the attack and blond hairs stick out from the coils. I wonder what her hair looks like down.

"It was a disaster." She covers her eyes. "But we got the raccoon out and I didn't faint."

"There's a bright side to everything, I guess."

"I believe that with my whole heart." She grows quiet as we drive. "Why are you driving me, Jackson?"

"My mom asked me to."

"You could've said no."

One more block until Goldheart's only twenty-four-hour urgent care. It glows against the starless sky. I could respond with snark, but I just drive. Didn't feel right to fire back at her.

Shiloh looks back to the road. "I'm sorry. I shouldn't have decorated your office. That was too much."

I press my lips together and say, "It's fine. I overreacted."

"I know you hate me." Her voice is a soft whisper.

Do I hate her? I talk to her more than any other employee. If it was any other person from the brewery, I would've driven in silence. I wouldn't be admitting I was wrong.

"I'm out of practice. With people," I say. "I don't like people that much."

She continues to watch the businesses flash by; she sees a dog being walked and she perks up.

I continue, "It's just me. I'm like this. It's not you."

"It just…" She takes a deep breath. "Are you happy?"

What a question.

My life is quiet and uncomplicated. I spent eight years with lots of unknowns and variables dictating my whole life. Now, every day is the same, predictable. It's comforting to have so much control. I get to choose what happens to me.

I just didn't expect someone like Shiloh to barrel through and make me question everything.

"Don't worry about me," I say. "My life's perfect the way it is."

"What happened to you, Jackson?"

I shift in my seat, the car now stifling hot. My family won't ever bring it up because I react hotly, desperate to avoid any mention of it. Strangers whisper behind my back instead of to my face.

Shiloh's question hits me like a sword to the chest.

I breathe in and out slowly, letting my heart slow.

"I don't want to talk about it." My tone is curt and direct, and Shiloh flinches.

This is the first time I wish I could be my brother, Cameron, who laces his words with sugar so that even the harshest criticism goes down easy. I'm all thistle and thorns. Everything I touch hurts.

Shiloh presses her rosebud lips together and looks out the window again, away from me. "I'm sorry I asked."

"It's okay."

She folds into herself as we park close to the entrance and the engine is barely shut off before Shiloh opens the car door and hobbles out, toward the entrance.

I race after her, an apology thick on my tongue. "I'm sorry" has never been part of my vernacular, but it feels warranted. She apologized when she didn't need to, and now I can't even say it back.

"You can find out from anyone. Your grandpa can tell you if you really want to know."

"I said before, I want to hear from you. I don't like gossip," she says. She continues to the entrance, wincing and limping. She pauses and sticks her hands on her hips. "This really hurts."

"May I?" I ask with my arms out. She nods, and I scoop her up. She's light in my arms as I adjust her, her bad leg stretched out. She loops her arms around my neck, and I swallow, her vanilla scent hitting my nostrils.

She smells like a comforting bakery, the kind we used to go to as kids.

Her skin is soft and warm in my hands, and I feel her breath on my chin.

I breathe in and out again, hoping it will calm my racing heart. No such luck. I haven't realized how touch-starved I am until I touch Shiloh.

Until she touched me.

I open the door awkwardly and carry her in. The receptionist pulls off her glasses as we approach. Goddammit, it's my old buddy Eric's mom, Bonnie. Her eyes bug when she looks at me, her mouth agape.

I haven't seen her in years, and now I'm caught carrying another girl like I'm a third-rate prince. Perfect.

"Hey Bonnie, this is our employee, Shiloh Abbott. She got into an altercation with a raccoon. It bit her on the leg," I say, hoping the story would distract Bonnie enough.

"Oh dear, are you okay?"

"I'm fine," Shiloh says, smiling sweetly. "You should see the other guy."

A one-note *ha* leaves my mouth, and Bonnie zeroes in on me. "Jackson, it's just so nice to see you. It's been a long time."

What should I do? What should I say?

I settle on nothing.

Sweat percolates on my forehead and my gaze falls to the linoleum.

Shiloh's eyes bore into me before she looks at Bonnie.

"You must be new to town. I'm Bonnie Richter," Bonnie says, holding out her hand to Shiloh. They shake hands, ignoring the trickle of fresh blood down Shiloh's leg.

"Bonnie, Shiloh Is bleeding."

"It's fine," Shiloh says, and gives Bonnie a smile. "My grandpa is Earl Abbott. Do you know him?"

"Oh, of course. Is Stephanie your mother?"

"Yes," Shiloh says softly.

Bonnie looks at her with wide eyes, a look I know all too well. She pities her, like she pities me.

"I hope your mom is doing okay. She was friends with my little brother…"

"She's doing wonderful. I'll send your best wishes. It was nice meeting you," she says sweetly to Bonnie as I walk her to the chair to fill out her paperwork on a clipboard.

Maybe Shiloh is hiding something too.

As Shiloh reads each question carefully, I shove my hands in my pockets and pace. I haven't been in a medical facility in ten years, not even to see my own doctor. In here it smells like fake rainforest, the antiseptic smell masked well enough. Walking back and forth helps with the nerves.

"Shiloh Abbott," a nurse calls. I offer my forearm, and Shiloh takes it. Her fingertips feel like a balm on my skin as I walk her to the door.

"I'll be here," I say. All I get is a smile as the door closes behind her.

Bonnie still studies me like I'm a celebrity in the wild paying a parking ticket. I wish I could disappear, to avoid any questions she might ask. This town wants to see me break down, see me have emotions I can't control.

Joke is on them, though. I've shoved my emotions down so far, I'm not sure where they went.

Shiloh

A little white lie never hurt anybody.

There're things I've learned from being a woman. Tears sometimes get you what you want. A fake limp makes a handsome guy scoop you up like you're a damsel in distress.

He carried me like I was a pound of feathers, and his skin was warm under my fingers.

Being close to him was as exciting as I thought it would be.

He may hate me, but I felt comfort in his arms. I hate myself for wanting his touch, although he's given me every sign I'm the worst part of his day whenever he sees me.

Jackson's hands on me are all I think about as I wait for the doctor on the exam table, kicking my feet. As soon as I was inside the door, the nurse offered her arm, and I walked normally, although the scratch on my leg hurt a little.

Of course someone would know my mother.

In AA, they talk a lot about environment, and my mother feels like coming back to Goldheart could tempt her into sliding into her own ways. It's where she started drinking and doing drugs way too young, and where she would drop my sister and I off with my grandparents during the summers so she could follow around a new boyfriend. Goldheart reminds her of how she failed as a mother, even though Summer and I turned out okay.

When my mother decided to get sober four years ago, my sister and I decided to stop drinking with her in support and solidarity. Honestly, I never liked the taste of alcohol, and it always made me sick. Cutting it out was easy for me, especially knowing how addiction can be hereditary.

When Papa had his stroke, my mother was so close to moving back to help him, but I offered instead. My horrible breakup was even more reason to get out of Sacramento, to the town that held so many good memories for me.

This town has been friendly and welcoming, but I feel the pity reek off them, like a stench from moldy garbage. I can't stop thinking about Jackson and why he doesn't leave the brewery. I don't blame him. This town stares you down, and while most people haven't connected Stephanie Abbott with me since my mom hasn't been in town for so long, it's only a matter of time before everyone knows and looks at me with pursed lips, no matter how much my grandfather shuts it down.

Fidgeting, I wonder how much this will cost me. Doctors are expensive, and I don't have health insurance. Honestly, I can count on one hand the times I've been to the doctor. If this happened when I was a kid, my mom might've waited for me to foam at the mouth to take me, and even then, she might've not.

They administer the first shot of the rabies vaccine in my arm and advise me I have to come back three more times to finish the cycle. They clean the wound and dress it, and I now have a thick white bandage around my leg.

The doctor comes in and looks at the clipboard. "You work for the Finches' brewery, right?"

"Yes, sir."

"What is it with the Finches and raccoons?" He shakes his head. "We'll see you back in three days for the next dose of your rabies treatment. Schedule your follow-up with Bonnie up front."

"Thank you, doctor," I say, hopping off the exam table.

I forget my acting as I leave, walking normally. When Jackson sees me, there's a hint of a smile on his lips.

"Whoa, whatever they gave me, I can walk," I say. "It's the craziest thing."

He turns his head slightly, his eyelids narrowing to study me. *Inhale*, I tell myself, as he walks toward me, leaving me breathless.

"I'm glad you're feeling better. I don't have to carry you then."

"Nope." I flap my arms. "I'm out of the fainting danger zone. I do have to come back a few more times because of, you know, rabies."

"We don't want you to get that." Is that *genuine* concern?

No, we can't think like this. A man showing common courtesy is the bare minimum.

"How much do you think the bill will be?" I whisper.

"Don't worry about it, it's on us." He turns to Bonnie. "Bonnie, put it on our tab."

"We can do that. Take care. Shiloh, tell your mother I said hi and that I hope she's doing well."

I smile and wave, and I cannot wait to get out of here.

"You sure you don't need help?"

"I'm fine," I say. "Bonnie is nice."

"And nosy."

"I feel like that Goldheart's motto. Nice but nosy."

Jackson purses out his bottom lip. "You hit the nail on the head. Did your mother rob a bank or something?"

I shake my head. "It's a long story."

"Fair," he says, taking me to his truck and opening my door. "Can you get in?"

Technically, yes. However, it never hurts to ask for help. I believe in it with my whole heart.

It's not because I want to be in his arms again. Not that.

Jackson is rude and unfeeling. Not someone I should be attracted to, not someone I want to touch my skin. I shouldn't study his lips, wondering what they would feel like on mine.

"I need help," I say, holding the handle.

His hands grip my waist, lifting me so I can swivel to sit down. My breath lodges in my throat, and I don't release it until I'm in my seat. His hands rip away immediately and do not linger. He climbs in next to me, and I smile.

"Thank you for taking me," I say. "And carrying me. And waiting."

"Of course." He shoves his key in the ignition and freezes. "Interesting that you have a secret too."

I nod, biting my lip. More and more secrets are being added every day.

One being that no matter how mean he is, I still want to be near him.

9

JACKSON

"You seem weird. Weirder than usual," I say, popping a chip in my mouth as I study my brother. Reid has been hitting the alcohol harder than I have been. We're sitting on my back porch overlooking my parents' backyard with beers, and Reid's shoulders haven't dropped he's so tense. We ate dinner, and now we're just watching the fireflies.

"It's just...you know Annie's friend? Whitney? We saw each other at the market."

I lift my eyebrow as my brother takes another gulp. Reid attended college in San Diego and met Whitney in a creative writing class. According to Reid, he critiqued one of her stories, unintentionally started a war with her, and now she hates him forever.

I saw Whitney once at a distance when Annie brought her into the brewery. Beautiful woman, long dark hair, ample curves. Not really my type, but I know my brother and he wants her. Bad. I love when the universe taunts my even-keeled, uptight brother. It's hilarious.

"Did you flirt with her?"

"No, the opposite. She started arguing with me and I got

nervous, so I threw eggs at her. Got her shoes. They were expensive too." Reid stares off into space, taking a sip of his beer.

"You have quite the way with the ladies."

Reid takes an angry swig.

"Just avoid her."

"I try to, but she's *everywhere*. I saw her at the library, now the market. I know we live in a small town, but this is ridiculous."

I take a sip of my beer, and I know I can't say anything about Shiloh. If my family huffs one ounce of joy from me, their eyes get soft, and there it is again. The pity I hate.

They know about our trip to urgent care, but they don't know everything. How I picked her up, how light she was in my arms, how close her breath was to mingling to mine. How I thought about kissing her, multiple times.

I shouldn't feel like this. Shiloh is too happy, too positive. Too *young*. She's ten years younger than me, with an innocence I find refreshing, but she's still an employee. It's inappropriate.

Not to mention that I still haven't said I'm sorry. A normal person would've choked out an apology to the nicest person he's ever come across, but the words caught in my throat, even as she apologized for things she didn't need to feel sorry for. I should've laughed at the decorations like a normal person and let it go. I didn't, and now it's even more awkward.

"You should've come to the end-of-the-season party. It was fun," Reid says.

I shake my head. "My night of Scotch and British crime shows was far superior, thanks."

"You could've hung out with me," he adds.

"I was good right here. You should've ditched. I offered."

"I need something stronger," he says. "Can I get some Macallan?"

"Go for it." He disappears inside, and I inspect my beer bottle. I usually guzzle booze until the edges of my life blur and the thoughts halt. Tonight is different. I've drunk only half the bottle in an hour. I guess this is what "pacing yourself" looks like.

Reid reappears, handing me a glass with one ice cube. I inhale its rich oak and vanilla scent. Heaven.

We both take a sip, and Reid stares into the darkness. "Mom worries about you. I worry about you."

"Why is everyone so worried about me? I'm perfectly happy." I adjust in my seat, the wicker groaning.

"Mom wants the whole family together. You're in the family. She's not torturing you, Jackson."

I cross my legs and grab my ankle, desperate to hold something. Being in Goldheart is hard enough. If they could feel the way my skin crawls, the cold sweats, the clammy hands, they wouldn't force it as much.

"We are together. And people aren't my thing, Reid."

"They used to be your thing. In high school."

That was such a long time ago. The friends I had have faded away over the years, even though some of them are still living in Goldheart. After I saw his mom at the clinic with Shiloh, Eric called me and left a message. I want to call him back and see how he's doing, but the phone feels like a thousand-pound weight when I pick it up to try.

"I will kick you out if you say anything else about this." I take a swig, but the Scotch, usually smooth, burns all the way down my throat.

"Mom has been hinting that she wants the kids to get together and have a night off. Emily is campaigning for a Saturday night for us all to do something…"

"No, Reid. You know I can't go out into town."

"Fuck, Jackson. People know you're home. It's been nine months. Hiding just creates more questions, more mystery. You're the fucking enigma of our family."

I swirl my drink in my hand, my throat growing thick. My capacity for social interaction is so low that some days getting to the office and getting three things done feel like an effort. Being around people drains my energy to nothing, and I'm tired of stares. Talking with Bonnie at the urgent care was enough.

In this apartment, alone, is where I belong.

"At least participate in the Brewery Games."

"Fine. You sound like Shiloh," I say, taking another big gulp. I finally match my brother and pour more. This Scotch needs to work its magic and quick.

Reid looks at me with a blank stare and flubs. "Shiloh?"

"She keeps trying to get me to join things. She wanted me to go to the end-of-season party. She even decorated my office."

"I heard. You must've loved that."

"Oh, I did," I say sarcastically.

"Is she okay? I heard about the raccoon attack."

The feel of her breath on my cheek hits my memory and I cough in my hand.

"She'll be fine," I say. "It was our lovely niece who let the fucker in."

"Yeah, Emily needs to curb the raccoon enthusiast in Olive. It's getting out of hand. Jason Banning had it coming, but Shiloh…"

"Shiloh didn't deserve it." I balance my glass on the armrest. When I catch my brother staring at me, I flinch.

"Do you like Shiloh? Like *like* her?"

I scoff and laugh, muttering, "No, why would you say that? She annoys me."

"Why? Shiloh is the least annoying person I've ever met."

"Like…like, she eats peanut butter and jelly every day. With the crusts cut off, Reid."

"Peanut butter and jelly is phenomenal," Reid says.

"I know, but she eats it every day. No variation. She wraps it in wax paper. Who does that?"

"So?" Reid asks.

"Her sneakers? Why doesn't she replace them? They have a literal hole about the pinkie toe."

"Maybe those shoes are her favorite."

"There's always fur on her clothes."

"She dog-walks. She's always petting the dogs that come into the brewery," Reid says and narrows his eyes. He's onto me. "Those are stupid reasons to get annoyed, even for you."

My brother glares at me so I shrug. "She just does a lot of things that make no sense, that's all. Why is she happy all the time?"

"Um-hum," Reid says, staring at me.

"It's just, why does she care? Every other employee isn't up in my business, and *she* is."

"You should ask her." Reid is probably the sibling I'm closest to, but his deep exhale tells me he is frustrated beyond belief with me.

"She says it's sad. The way I live my life."

"Well, it is."

I glare at him, and he shrugs.

"Look, you go to work, you come back to this apartment. You don't see anyone, except for us when we force ourselves on you. You used to do stuff, man, that's all. You ran a fucking travel blog. You know what, forget it."

I swirl the Scotch in my glass.

The travel blog was a lifetime ago. I spent the better part of ten years in my loft in Seattle, leaving only to go to work and the gym. My co-workers were nice enough, but I socialized rarely, and dates were out of the question.

The whole time I socialized with anyone, all I thought about was her.

"The only thing I'll say is you can't hide forever," Reid says. "No matter what you think, people care about you. They want the best for you. Even if you don't want it for yourself."

"That's the thing. I already had the best." My throat closes as I think about her. It aches to think about her. That there were moments in Seattle I laid in bed, giving myself headaches because I wished I could bring her back.

I can't though. And that kills me.

"If you've been a dick, Shiloh deserves an apology. She doesn't deserve your bullshit."

"Do you think Whitney deserves an apology?" I ask.

"Absolutely not."

"Do you want to be the pot or the kettle?"

"Shut the fuck up and drink your Scotch."

10

SHILOH

I grab my messenger bag in the employee breakroom and close my locker, just to see Jackson leaning beside it. The breath leaves my body as I grab my chest.

"Holy cow, you scared me," I say with a chuckle.

I've thought long and hard about Jackson. He floods my thoughts at the most inconvenient times—during dog walks and hangouts with my grandpa. No matter how nasty he is toward me, I'm done letting Jackson crawl under my skin. Even if I thought I felt his hard shell softening at urgent care. His skin on mine felt like fire and consumed my wits, turning me into a lovesick schoolgirl. I say hi to be nice, but I've restrained myself from acts of kindness towards him. I channel it towards Ramon or my grandfather.

I've seen him more often at work lately. He does laps now through the taproom, and I swear he looks at me every time. He hasn't approached me, but when we catch eyes, I smile and wave.

This feels deliberate.

Is he trying to be handsome? He's leaning against the lockers, a classic move for a heartthrob. His shoulders fill out his Woody Finch polo shirt, the arm holes straining against his biceps. His piercing eyes study me behind his black frames, and I feel exposed. Good-looking men studying me always make me feel uncomfortable.

"How can I help you, Jackson?" I sound like a greeter at a theme park.

"What are you doing?" Jackson asks. "Now?"

"I'm picking up a dog for the Working Buddies' rescue. An owner surrender."

"Owner surrender?" He leans against the locker again, and I avert my gaze. If he cages me in, I'm a goner. *Don't look, don't look.*

I swallow hard. "Someone called the rescue, and they have a three-year-old German shepherd. They can't take care of the dog anymore, so we'll take ownership and find the dog his furever home."

"Forever?"

"Fur-ever," I say, bracing for the snark.

He purses his bottom lip out and nods once. "Cute."

I stare at him. Is this one of the other brothers in disguise?

Jackson pauses, his jaw churning. He looks up, and his green eyes hit me like a brick to the face. "Can I come?"

My jaw drops. The butterflies in my stomach fly in circles. "Really?"

"I would love to," he says. "Is that okay?"

No, aliens got him. This shell looks like him, with the long hair tied back and an overgrown beard. I've never seen him this...jazzed. Animated.

"We'll have to take my car because I have my dog stuff in it."

"Perfect," he says, following me. It's the second time I will be in a car with him, but I will be driving at least and not hurt. He looks down at my leg. It's healed nicely, but there's a hint of a white line. "How are you feeling?"

"Good! No fever or desire for human flesh," I joke. I expect crickets from him, but he chuckles.

Jackson is acting like he tolerates me. What's wrong with him?

I know what will make him break.

"Is pop music okay?" I ask as I turn on the ignition. Mandy Moore's sweet voice floats from my speakers. She is my comfort music, and I anticipate this surrender will be emotional for me, so I need her more than anything.

Jackson's forehead creases as he deciphers who it is. "Is this...Mandy Moore?"

I nod, bracing for slander against my favorite pop star's name. I can take hits when it's about me, but I will go to war over her.

"Aren't you a little *young* for Mandy Moore?"

"I heard her first on the classics station."

I keep my face deadpan while Jackson's head hits the headrest. "No, you didn't."

"Sure did." My smile breaks, and I bite my tongue between my teeth. "My mom liked her. We listened to her a lot growing up in the car."

Jackson presses the back of his head into the seat. "I almost had a heart attack. You're good."

"Like I said. I'm funny."

He pauses. "I haven't heard her music in over ten years. Is this from the movie about ballet?"

I'm shocked he knows that.

"Yes. My mom still owns the VHS. We used to watch it all the time, although it went whoosh." I sweep my hand over my head. "Like all the sex stuff. It was a big shock when sex wasn't just two naked people hugging on a bed."

Jackson drops his head back and lets out a howling laugh. I could cry. Getting a laugh like that from him feels like a gold medal at the Olympics.

"You are…"

His words trail off as he closes his eyes. Mandy sings about wanting to be with someone, even for a night, and invisible ants crawl between the hairs on my forearm.

I'm what….?

I would be lying if I hadn't thought about kissing this frustrating man's lips, see if his sourpuss attitude would melt. On the other hand, I should stop romanticizing horrible men and see them for who they are, not for their potential. Jackson is mean, grumpy, and has a chip on his shoulder against the whole world.

But I can't stop getting into a car with him.

"Do you rescue dogs often?"

Him asking questions is giving me hope that he doesn't hate me. I nod. "I volunteered for a rescue in Sacramento. They mostly fostered and re-homed senior dogs. Once in a while, we would save at-risk dogs. When I came to Gold-heart, I found Working Buddies and immediately volunteered. Ramon's aunt runs it." I choke back tears. No matter how many times I talk about rescues, it breaks my heart every time.

Jackson's brows crinkle more. "Why do people give up senior dogs?"

"I want to believe people have good reasons, but honestly, some people are assholes," I say. Jackson flinches at my cursing. Good to keep him on his toes. "They give them up for a bunch of reasons. They get a new puppy; they don't want to see the dog deteriorate and die. When I finally buy a house, I want some land so I can have as many senior dogs as possible. Big, small, I don't care. A dog should have a real home at the end of their lives."

I take a sharp inhale through my nose to keep the tears away.

"This means a lot to you."

I nod. "It will break my heart every day, but I have to do it. For Rory."

My shoulders hunch at my vulnerability, and I want to fold into myself.

"Who is Rory?"

"Rory was the best dog who ever lived," I say. "He was my soul dog. I hope every dog I save gets to the rainbow bridge and can give him an update. Tell him I'm doing okay. Rory would want to know I'm doing okay."

Jackson nods, and his Adam's apple bobs as he looks out the window.

I didn't cry mentioning Rory. I'm proud of myself.

I look at the piece of paper and pull over to the shoulder in front of a small home with gray shingles, nestled in an alcove, surrounded by tall trees.

"Do you have a picture? Of Rory?"

"Sure." I open my phone and scroll a little, finding the last photo I have of us. Rory is gray in the muzzle, but his mouth is open and the tongue dangles. I always thought he was smiling when he did that. Jackson takes the phone from my hand, and our thumbs brush. I swallow.

Jackson holds it close. "You look happy."

I nod, taking my phone back. "That dog made my whole world. We were together for three years, and it wasn't long enough."

"What happened?"

"Cancer. Two months ago. I loved him so much, I felt like my body would split open when he died."

Jackson's throat moves, a vein popping on the side. Moisture collects at his hairline.

"Are you okay?" I ask.

"Yes," he says. "I'm sorry. About your dog."

"I think I'm ready for some snuggles, aren't you?"

"Us?" he croaks. Breath catches in my throat.

"No, the furry kind. Come on." To avoid any awkward-ness, I bolt from the car to pop the trunk. After clipping a treat pouch to my shorts, I grab the leash and the slip collar. Jackson stands there with his hands in his pockets.

"Here we go." I grab the folder of paperwork. Glancing over the checklist, I breathe in and out, calming my nerves.

These never get easier for me, and while I can brace for heartache, I usually cry in the car afterwards. The dog usually snuggles me, which makes it better.

Now, I have a grumpy man with a ponytail who was repulsed when he thought I meant snuggling with him.

This has been a weird day.

He says nothing as we walk up to the house, his body inches from mine.

"Do you need me to hold anything?" he asks, his hand accidentally brushing against mine again. I stiffen, and he notices.

"Sorry," he says.

"It's okay."

It's really not. It's not normal to feel sparks, buzzes and flares when you touch a man there's no chance you will ever be romantic with. That doesn't happen.

We knock on the door, and a small woman in her mid-fifties opens the door. Her shoulders slump, and dark circles crest under her eyes. I hear high-pitched whining from inside, and while my stomach clenches at the sound, I step inside with the most comforting smile I can give.

"I'm Shiloh Abbott with Working Buddies' rescue. This is Jackson, he's shadowing me today."

He lingers outside, and I wave him in.

The woman crosses her arms as we step inside. The house is tidy and bare, with mountains of cardboard boxes in the corner.

"I'm Carrie, pleasure to meet you. Let me get Koda. I crated him since he tends to charge open doors."

"Not a problem," I say.

She walks to the other room, and we stand there. I try to focus, but Jackson's presence distracts me, jumbles my thoughts. It was a mistake to invite him, since dog rescue is my safe space, my comfort. The place I go to feel the most like me.

Jackson makes me squirm.

Nails scrape against the hardwood as a dog pulling on a leash like he's dragging a sled comes around the corner. Carrie lets the leash slip and the dog charges, putting its front two paws on my chest and toppling me over.

I grab Shiloh before she falls over, as a huge German shepherd licks her chin.

My arm still loops around her back as I lean in. "Are you okay?"

"I'm fine." Her giggle sounds like music as the dog makes playing noises, jumping from side to side, the tail beating vigorously. The shepherd has tan and black fur and vibrates with puppy energy, sensing Shiloh is someone he can trust.

She gazes at me with her lips parted, so I rip my arms away. My cock pushes against the zipper of my jeans. Did I get aroused just by holding her?

"I am so sorry," Carrie says, covering her mouth. "He has no manners. My dad never got him formal training. Hence this."

She points to a ragged, large hole in the wall. Koda looks at it and back at us with pride.

"It's okay," Shiloh says, giggling, rubbing the dog's ears. "He just needs some training."

"He doesn't bite or nothing. Jumps, obviously. Wants to smell every bush. Every. Bush."

"Every smell is just so powerful," Shiloh says in the dog's face with a baby voice, giving the dog one last rub.

No, I can't be jealous of a dog.

"It breaks my heart to give him up, but I have four dogs, and my mom can't take care of him. He deserves so much more than being cooped up in a house," she blurts, taking a hold of the leash.

"Where is your dad?"

"He...died. Pancreatic cancer. One day he was fine, and then one day, he *wasn't*."

The woman's shoulders slump even further, like the weight of her grief is a physical presence.

I know that feeling all too well.

Seeing her raw and fresh loss tightens my chest. My mouth dries, and the tingly sensation in my temples returns. Between Shiloh's dog and this woman's father, I've reached my cancer talk quota for the day.

"I need some air," I say, touching Shiloh's shoulder. She freezes with my contact. Why did I feel the need to touch her? Pulling my hand away, I whisper, "I'm sorry," and Shiloh gives a small nod.

"I need to evaluate the dog. So, maybe thirty minutes? Is that okay?"

"Sound good," I say, stepping outside. It's finally cooling in the evenings, and dusk is settling in. I shove my hands in my pockets, since they can't stop shaking. Deep breath in through the nose, out through the mouth. Panic builds in my chest, and breathing slows it, suppressing it to the pit of my belly, where it always lives.

I don't know Carrie or her dad. She didn't look at me like she had heard stories or recognized that I carry the same weight, even though mine has been years, and hers is still fresh. But I don't know what my body would do if I stayed longer, if she explained more why she couldn't keep the dog.

Shiloh looked at her with no judgment, no pity. Only compassion.

Watching Shiloh in her element and loving on a dog stirs something inside of me.

Sure, she's pretty, with her long blond hair and wide blue eyes. Her smile and laugh are contagious. It's her effervescence that draws me in.

When I caught her, sparks shot through me, and I had to test it further. Touching her shoulder felt like more of the same.

She's tiny compared to me.

Ten years my junior.

My family business's employee.

She doesn't know the saddest thing about me.

I pace the length of the dirt shoulder, kicking rocks, when Shiloh peeks her head out.

"Give me five minutes. I might need your muscle." She disappears back inside.

"Okay," I say, approaching the house. I walk onto the porch, noticing the bench. I wonder how often Carrie's dad sat there, spending his evening with the dog at their feet. My chest tightens again, and I take more deep breaths, in and out.

The door opens and the dog bolts out the door, nails scurrying against the wood, pulling Shiloh with him. She zooms past me and hands me the dog's leash, and I brace. The dog hits the end of the line, yelps, and springs back.

"Thank you," Shiloh says, turning toward the woman and hugging her. "Best of luck with everything."

"Thank you, Shiloh, you've been lovely. Nice to meet you," Carrie says as she crouches down to the dog's level. Koda comes right to her, licking her face and jumping on her. She cries into the dog's fur as the dog pants. "Be a good boy," Carrie says, standing up, wiping her eyes.

When the door closes and it's just Shiloh, me, and the dog, we start walking, but Koda goes between my legs, almost knocking me over and jamming his hard head right into my junk.

"Not the nuts," I say out loud, swinging my leg over the furry body wiggling under me.

Shiloh giggles as I teeter. "He's a handful."

"No kidding," I say as we step off the porch, but the dog pulls me. "I'm so bad at this."

"Let's switch," she says, swapping me the paperwork and toys for the dog. For how tiny Shiloh is, she handles the dog much better than I do, even though I have at least eighty pounds on her.

"This dog is a menace to society."

Shiloh laughs, more music to my ears. "He just needs training and exercise. Lots and lots of training. We'll find him a good home. He's got a good personality."

She opens the backseat and the dog jumps in and whines, tongue dangling and flicking with his pants.

Shiloh and I get in the car, and the dog instantly sticks its tongue in my ear.

"At least buy me dinner first," I say to the dog, and Shiloh giggles. It's quickly becoming my favorite sound. "You know, my parents had a shepherd."

"That's why I decided to work at Woody Finch. The German shepherd in the logo. The Dog Hall of Fame. I saw the dog, in your family photo."

"Woody. He was a great dog." Swallowing, I continue. "The dog...well, I was watching the dog the first week I moved back from Seattle. My parents went on this epic vacation to Europe for their anniversary, and the dog got sick. It went downhill quickly. I couldn't be in the room when they did it. My siblings went in so the dog wasn't alone, but I couldn't be there. I...."

"It's hard." She covers my hand with hers with a pat. We look at our hands and look away. Her hand leaves mine and goes back to the steering wheel. "At least your siblings could go in with him."

The look on Woody's face only comes to me when I'm soaked through with bourbon. Guilt has weaved its way through this year, but Shiloh's comfort soothes it. There's no judgment emanating from her, and it allows me to melt into my seat.

If my siblings hadn't come, I would've gone with Woody. No one should be alone when they're actively dying, especially a dog. My siblings knew I had already watched someone I loved drift off to sleep never to wake again. How it broke me and fucked me up.

I'm still fucked up. I could barely look at my siblings when they emerged, Emily's face streaked with tears and Cameron sniffling and turning his head. Reid made sure I was okay as we walked to my car and he drove me home. Even though a tear did not leave my eyes, I've thought about that day constantly since.

When faced with situations that may trigger me, I run. It's how I operate, how I function. I've accepted being a prisoner.

"Your dad must miss Woody so much. He and I race to the dogs every time we hear one is at the brewery. It's become a running joke."

My version of a laugh comes out as a huff. "Running, racing. Puns."

"Oh yeah. I'm funny. *And* I usually beat your dad."

"At least you didn't French a doodle the other day. It's because my dad eats lots of bacon."

"Who says I haven't kissed a dog on the mouth?" She flashes me those blue eyes, and I freeze. Is she flirting with me? "I'm a great kisser."

My cheeks grow red. Why do I wish I was a dog? Again?

Koda the German shepherd has settled in the backseat, looking cute as hell, chewing on the nylon bone Shiloh brought.

"Now that the dog has calmed down, I wanted to tell you I'm sorry for how I've acted. If you can't tell, I have a lot of anger, and I took it out on you. I'm very sorry."

Shiloh doesn't hesitate. "I accept your apology. I don't know what it is, but I can tell you have had a hard time."

"Oh?" I ask.

"Jackson Finch, I know you're all stuffing, no steel."

"Conspiracies," I say. "I do not accept that."

"The way you are with Koda? I'm onto you. Squishy, soft center."

I lean in, close enough to smell the vanilla on her skin. It jolts me, but I still move closer. Why am I whispering? "Don't tell anyone."

"I won't. Your secret is safe with me." Her smile drops, and she rubs her lips together. I must be staring because she blurts, "I'm not looking for a boyfriend."

My blood runs cold. I whip my head away, erect in my seat. "I wasn't flirting."

Saying that out loud feels like a lie. Shiloh accepts it, though. "Good."

I look back and the dog has settled, curling up like a black-and-tan croissant. "I think Koda finally calmed down."

Shiloh stops at a stop sign and looks back. Her bottom lip juts out. "I think so too. This part just guts me. We'll find you a good home, Koda, I promise."

The dog pops up, panting, sticking his head between us as we drive. The question rests on my tongue. No, don't ask it, it's not appropr—

"Why don't you want a boyfriend?" I ask.

Shiloh's gaze focuses on the passing trees. "I just got out

of a situation. It wasn't great, toxic, and I just want to focus on my job, dogs, and my grandpa for now. Not romance."

I chuckle to myself. The way she explains herself so adamantly, it's adorable.

"What?" she asks, her eyes alarmed.

"I didn't say anything." I did laugh. "I'm not laughing at you, I promise. It sounds like a good idea. Taking a break. Relationships are overrated."

"Really?" she asks. "What about you?"

"Just as single as you."

"That deserves a high-five." She holds up her hand, and I roll my eyes before I slap mine to hers.

She doesn't realize how off-limits I am, how the thought of another woman entering my life romantically makes my body seize and my arms break out into hives. There is no way I'm attaching myself the same way I did in the past. I flew so high, with nothing to prepare me for the trip down, crashing into a burning pile of ash.

There's no way I will risk that again. It hurt like fucking hell.

"You're safe with me," I say. "I'm not interested either."

"So, friends?" Shiloh asks.

"The most platonic of platonic friends," I say. I look back again, and the dog's eyes flutter asleep, subtle snores whistling through its nose. This dog looks like a smaller version of Woody, and it clenches my heart.

My phone buzzes in my pocket, and I pull it out, my brows concaving as I read it.

Emily: Finch siblings out on the town this Saturday night. You in?

My forehead tenses as I study the message.

"Why do you look like someone died?"

My lips part involuntarily, and I wipe my forehead. That

question, meant to be funny and endearing, is the opposite, but I swallow any response.

"My sister said my siblings and I are all free this Saturday. Suggested we go out. She must've talked Mom into a team-building Finch sibling thing."

"That sounds fun," Shiloh says, turning toward me, her smile falling. "Are you going to go?"

"I don't know. Public, people. Emily or Cameron will want to do something embarrassing."

"You should go. I believe in you. Get out of your closet cave and have fun."

"I'm very fond of my workspace," I say. "I don't get out much."

"I've noticed. Why is that?" she asks, focusing on the road.

"It's complicated." I grip my hands together between my legs so she doesn't see them shake.

"Well, it means a lot that you came with me today. Since you don't get out much," she says. "It was nice to have company. Thank you."

"You're welcome." It's my turn to blurt when I say, "I can come on your dog walks. If you want more company besides the dogs."

She smiles. "I would really like that."

"I promise I'm not coming onto you, though."

"Fine," she says. "I didn't expect you to."

"It would never work. Between us."

"I agree," she says with no hesitation.

"First off, you're way too good for me."

She says an "Um-hmm" as we drive.

"Second, you're my family business's employee."

"Also true."

"Plus, I'm just mean. Inside and out."

She shakes her head with indignation. "I disagree with

you there, Jackson. You have a gooey center. Like those fancy nut clusters you get at Christmas."

"Just call me Nutty," I joke. A laugh leaves my lips, and I can't remember the last time I laughed so much in one concentrated period.

"Like I said, I would crack you like a walnut," she says. "If we're going with nicknames, I like the nickname Wally more."

I chuckle again. "Okay, we're onto nicknames. You're Sunny from now on."

"Fair enough." She looks out the window. I've never met anyone like her. "Sunny and Wally, dog walking Extraordinaires. Sounds like a sitcom."

Am I smiling, joking? "We'll have ten seasons."

Shiloh shakes her head. "The best shows stop at six."

The dog pops up with its long tongue wagging. Shiloh rubs the dog's ear. "Do you like car rides? Are they your favorite?"

The dog tries to climb over the console into the front seat, and I block it with my arm. The dog whines in frustration.

"I think you should go out with your siblings. I think it would be fun. Would make a great episode."

The dog nudges against me, giving me another wet willie, and for a moment, I forget about everything. My existence centers around Shiloh, the dog, and Mandy Moore.

For the first time in years, a true smile crosses my lips.

Being home and drinking by myself was getting boring anyway. It won't be that bad. My siblings will protect me.

"Promise me you'll go," she says.

"I promise."

We smile at each other, and she pats my hand again, letting it rest on top of mine for a beat too long.

Friends, that's all we are. All we can be.

12

SHILOH

The sun is setting as I walk into my grandfather's house. I've been taking so many deep breaths to help with the sadness I feel for Carrie and her family. It must crush her she can't take care of Koda, her dad's beloved dog. We will find an amazing home for that animal.

I told her as such when I gave her a hug, and she put her hand on my cheek.

"Thank you," she said, pulling me in for another embrace.

Focusing on Koda and Carrie distracts me from thinking about Jackson.

He swore he was not flirting as he leaned in, touching me before he excused himself from Carrie's house. Jackson chooses his words carefully and judiciously, his touches rationed out. The Jackson in my car was a completely different person.

When I enter my grandfather's apartment, I'm so lost in my thoughts that I don't see him seated in his usual spot.

"Hey there, girlie," Papa says from his recliner. His glasses perch on his nose, as he turns the page in the new thriller I passed to him, about two sisters who have a tenuous relationship and then murder is introduced. A small plate full of crumbs and a glass with an inch of watered-down iced tea sits next to him.

"I hope you left some crackers for me."

"I promise, I restrained myself." His eyes do not leave the book. "Where were you at?"

"Picking up a dog," I say, dropping my bag on the side table. I stop when I see what's there.

"What is that?" I point. There's an arrangement of my favorite flowers set in a crystal vase—lilies and dahlias, in explosive colors of yellow, and orange, and pink. I love flowers to the core of my being, but my stomach drops because I know who they're from.

The flap of the card envelope stands erect.

"Did you read my card?" I ask.

"I wanted to make sure they weren't for me. I've been quite the ladies' man at Bingo."

I tilt my head down, peering at him. "Are you showing women your Air Force picture again?"

"Nooo," he says, closing the book and resting it on his lap. "They're for you."

My hand jitters as I open the card to the familiar black scrawl of Mark's handwriting.

Miss you more each day. I hope this break will send you back to me. I love you. xoxo, Mark

I roll my eyes. He refused to say "I love you" to my face but says it the moment I leave. The exact second I stand up for myself, and he deployed those three little words like an ace up his sleeve.

"That boy is gaga for you."

"Yeah," I say, throwing the card in the trash. I won't throw the flowers away; they didn't ask to be cut for that man.

This does not mean Mark wins. Not even close.

There's not much to tell, really. The further I get from

him, the more embarrassed I am that I got involved with him.

We met as servers at Tuscan Grove, a chain Italian restaurant. When we worked the same shift, we would make each other laugh and find quiet corners at after-work co-worker get-togethers. I fell hard for his sense of humor and general good nature.

I always hoped for a kiss in our private moments, and it felt like it was heading that direction. While Jackson rarely touches anyone, Mark loved to put his hand on my shoulder if I said something funny and he insisted on at least two hugs each shift we worked together.

After months of banter and shoulder touches, I told him I had a crush on him. He told me he had a girlfriend.

"I don't want to lose your friendship," he had said. "If things were different, maybe we could try."

Nothing changed.

He still found me on my shifts, ran out my orders before I could, asked for his daily two hugs. My other friends at Tuscan Grove started to notice, and everyone who didn't know about his girlfriend thought we were dating.

"I wouldn't be okay with you if I was his girlfriend," a co-worker told me after Mark touched my lower back and reached around me for the soda machine.

"Just ignore him. He's leading you on," Summer, my sister, had told me as she moved me into the house she rented. I took her advice. I went on blind dates; I adopted my dog Rory from the local shelter; I moved on. After weeks of avoiding his touches and his presence, Mark showed up on my doorstep with flowers, telling me he broke up with his girlfriend and wanted to try. That he missed me and didn't want to lose me.

It's why I have a beautiful bouquet on my grandfather's table. It worked so well last time.

As we dated, I fell harder, "I love you" on my tongue every time we hung out. It was a fairy tale for the first year. Then, it darkened and morphed, until I couldn't recognize it anymore.

After the first year, Mark began to lose interest in me. It first started as nights away with his friends, a couple times a week, to long stretches where Mark had plans every night, with no space for me. "You don't drink, Shiloh. There's nothing worse than being sober around a bunch of drunk people," he would say. I always told him I could come, get a soda or something, but he always found an excuse for me not to go.

"You don't know Colby. It would be weird."

"Your bedtime is nine-thirty, we'll be out until at least two."

"You won't have fun."

I never met his friends. I never met his parents. Summer did her own sleuthing, and he didn't have a good reason, like a girlfriend or a secret double life.

He just didn't want to incorporate me into his life.

There would be stretches of days he wouldn't call me, just to blow up my phone when I didn't answer him, the exact minute I made the decision to let him go. The affection and sex came and went with his moods. If he felt like he was losing me, he held my hand, put an arm around me, showed me the smallest bit of attention. Any crumbs he gave me, I licked them up and panted for more.

When we had sex, I always consented, but there were lots of nights I slept over that I cried myself to sleep because I felt used. I've always enjoyed sex, but it became mechanical and quick, with nothing in it for me.

That man stole my spark. My sister was so worried.

"I know we didn't find anything. Trust me, we *looked*," Summer said as we sat on the couch, watching *A Walk to*

Remember for the umpteenth time. "But you should dump him."

I didn't because I was hopelessly in love with him.

So, the nights he went out, I picked up extra shifts, saved my money. Rory and I would snuggle when Mark didn't touch me.

The night Rory died changed everything.

We had just gotten home from the vet, and I was hysterical, crying in my sister's arms as our roommates circled me. Kelsey and Peyton had just moved in, but were attached to Rory in the short time they knew him. They knew how much that dog meant to me.

Mark didn't. Or he didn't care.

Instead, he kept plans with a friend he hadn't seen since college, when I was obviously in pain and grieving.

It was the fatal wound to our bleeding-out relationship.

I believe that everything happens for a reason and that Rory left the world so I could finally gather the courage to break it off permanently.

When I ignored his calls for a week, he showed up and apologized profusely, smothered my face with kisses and dried my tears.

"Give me a chance," he asked, and I shook my head. He always did this, and I refused to fall for it this time. He knew I had put in my two weeks, that I was moving to Goldheart to take care of my grandfather.

"No, I can't," I said. "You don't love me. I'm moving anyway."

"I'm here because I love you."

He knew I would fall for that, and he was right.

"I will be in Goldheart for six months. We can discuss it when I get back."

"Okay," he had said, his face shining bright.

Mark now called and tried more than he ever did in the

time we were together.

I hoped he would lose interest after I moved, that he would finally let me go.

He never loved me. He loved my attention. But he still did things like this. What I wouldn't have given for a bouquet of flowers right after Rory died. I would still be driving to Sacramento every chance I got.

I would still be in love with him.

I've been touching the blossoms for minutes when my grandfather turned his head.

"Are you going to throw the flowers away too?" Papa asks.

"No," I say, touching the soft petals. "They're too pretty. We'll just pretend it was one of your friends from bingo. Who is your favorite?"

"Gloria," Papa says immediately.

"Who is Gloria?"

"A lady. A very nice lady."

"Ooh, do you have a girlfriend, Papa?"

"I'm too old to have a girlfriend," he says, taking his glasses off to rub the bridge of his nose. My grandmother died five years ago, and I know he misses her. I miss her. She burnt popcorn in the microwave every time we visited. We used to watch *E.T.* constantly and play Rummy tiles. Sometimes, I think about the fact she never saw her daughter finally get sober. How proud she would be of us.

Still, I could cry seeing my grandpa getting butterflies about someone new.

I had them today when Jackson looked at me.

"Papa, what do you know about Jackson Finch?"

He blows out a whistling breath. "That's a doozy, girlie."

"Is he a good guy? He came on the owner-surrender with me."

"He did?" Papa's bushy eyebrows knit together in confusion.

"We're getting to know each other. We're friends," I say.

"You are? Are we talking about the same Jackson Finch?"

I shake my head. "It was Jackson. Ponytail, glasses."

Papa shakes his head. "Stay away from him, girlie."

"Is he a bad man?"

"No, I don't think so. He's just an uphill battle. Pastor Williams and his wife, Marla, have been trying to reach out. Nicest people you'd ever meet. He won't talk to them."

I want to ask why, but I feel like it will crack open all the gossip about Jackson.

As curious as I am, I want to hear it from him.

My phone buzzes. Before I dropped Jackson off at the brewery, we exchanged phone numbers.

Jackson: I'm going out with my siblings. We're doing karaoke. This is your fault :puke smiley face:

I hold up my phone. "Jackson is going out with his siblings. To karaoke. He's getting better."

Papa's eyebrows raise. "That's interesting."

I shoot him a text back, a GIF response of an enthusiastic thumbs-up.

"He's trying to change. To be better," I say.

"I hope so. Just don't want you to get your hopes up. He's not all there," Papa says.

"I won't. There's not a chance of anything romantic happening between us."

"Good. What are we doing for dinner? How about we go out?" That's the great thing about my grandpa. He lets things go quickly.

I bite my lip. I've been making grilled cheese every night, and he grumbled last time. I'm so exhausted I could crumble to the floor in a ball, and I know he would love takeout, not the healthy meals he eats. Still, childhood habits die hard. Parting with money makes my breath quicken, my heart race.

We agreed I would pay for food if I stayed here to make

myself feel useful. Still, my hands shake as I pull out the takeout menus. I hold up a fan of three of them. "Chinese, Italian, or pizza?"

"Pizza. Please don't order pineapple again. Fruit doesn't belong on pizza."

I chuckle. "Sure thing, Papa. Pepperoni with mushrooms and olives?" Papa sticks his thumb up and purses his lips in agreement.

My phone buzzes again as my thumb hovers over the hyperlinked phone number on Booker's Pizza's webpage.

Jackson: It was nice hanging out with you today, my most platonic of platonic friends.

My heart switches from thumps about spending money to his text. I can hear the timbre of his voice in my head, saying these words. In my imagination, he jokes, gives me a look that makes my legs shaky.

No, that text means nothing. Just because the grump says one nice thing doesn't mean he likes me like that. Hopes will not reach sky-high proportions. Just gratitude, not flirting.

We also made it clear we weren't looking for romance, but tell my ovaries that.

When the pizza arrives, I hand over the cash with shaky hands. Papa and I eat our weight in pizza, and I drink two root beers as we watch *Blue Bloods*, shouting at the TV and giggling when the other yells something with passion. I say goodnight, get into my PJs, and get into bed.

My grandpa is the love of my life. He has to be.

However, when I sleep that night, I have the same dream I did the night before my first day, but it's different. We're still at the lake. It's still golden hour, with the warm glow casting a blanket of light.

The same woman pulls me by the hand to the man, who now has a face, when he didn't before.

The man in my dreams wears glasses that constantly fall

down his nose, with hair a little too long and an overgrown beard, like an unruly bush in someone's backyard. The woman leads me again by the arm, and I resist her. The dream woman continues to coax me, but I fight and dig my heels in.

I wake up in a cold sweat, because now I realize the man in my dreams is Jackson.

13

JACKSON

When we walk into the Swift, I know instantly I should've stayed home. There're way too many people here. My palms sweat and my mouth dries as I walk through the crowd, finding a table. This place is muggy because of body sweat. Gross.

I located all exits in case things become too overwhelming. I need to obtain lots of alcohol to make this night bearable.

The night promised loads of cringe, and it delivered in the form of my dorky, younger brother.

I'm not proud of this, but we bullied Reid into singing "A Whole New World" with Whitney.

My brother Reid has loved *Aladdin* since he could barely walk, and when Whitney and Annie showed up, I thought he would clam up and be his usual stiff-as-a-board self.

Instead, he accepted the challenge with no shame. I was immediately glad Shiloh talked me into coming. I laughed so hard I flopped in my chair, and Emily, Cam, and Annie looked at me like they might need to sedate me.

The alcohol helped. My shoulders have lowered, and I'm not scanning the room for social landmines. Because there are so many people, I've blended in, especially as I've stayed seated. Reid and Whitney have disappeared to the bar, Cameron and Annie are talking and cuddling, while Emily and I sit, sipping our cocktails and feeling very, very single.

"It's just you and me, Jackson," Emily says. We touch glasses and sip.

"Do you think Reid can land Whitney?"

"If he steps up his game." We both look around, but we don't see them.

"Did you talk to Olive about the raccoons?"

"Oh yes, we discussed it thoroughly. I tried to remove the cat food for Thelma and Louise, and Olive threw a fit. But it's for the best. We can't have any more raccoon attacks, and they come in threes. I'm terrified for what comes next."

"No shit."

"No shit is right." Emily drops her hand on my forearm. "Thank you for coming out with us. It's nice to have the gang together." Her hand on my forearm feels awkward, but I don't move.

"No problem." I set my drink down. "I don't need an 'I-told-you-so', but getting out of the house is nice. Might need to do it more."

"Getting out is fun. It's also nice to see you."

I cough behind a closed mouth.

"I heard you went to a dog thing."

"Who told you?"

"Shiloh."

Her name sends shivers through my limbs. Sometimes, I take a spin around the taproom to look at her. Seeing her smile is the best part of my day. My dad taking Koda would make her burst confetti. The wheels in my mind turn.

"We picked up a very energetic German shepherd. Same coloring as Woody. Maybe we can see if Dad wants him."

"I don't think Dad is ready for another dog. He cried over the Fosters' twelve-year-old Shepherd the other day."

"Really? I think Dad will like this dog."

As soon as the words leave my mouth, my sister's head swivels. "Huh. Is Shiloh getting to you, Jackson?"

"No," I say. My blood pressure rises. Maybe it was a mistake to come out. I breathe in and out. This is fine. I am fine. "Dad likes dogs. There's one that might be a good fit for him and needs a home. That's all."

Emily's eyes narrow on me. I spent one pleasant afternoon with a beautiful-inside-and-out employee. That's it. "Stop looking at me like that."

"I'm not looking at you like anything." Emily swirls her straw in her drink. "We can mention it to Dad, but we shouldn't push anything."

"We can see if the dog gets adopted in the next few months, and if not…"

"Yeah, that's a good plan."

I brush my hair away from my face, although it's tied back in a ponytail.

"You can have a professional cut it, you know. Wouldn't accidentally give you bangs."

Last time I tried to cut it, I cut the front pieces too short and now they don't reach the elastic my hair ends up in, most of the time. No matter how big of a pain in the ass, I refuse to cut it. The last time it was short was when I was happy.

"It might be time for a change, Jackson," Emily says.

It's my turn to swivel my head. "You've been single almost as long as me."

"I have an excuse. She's eight years old and loves raccoons."

"You deserve love."

"So do you." I chug the rest of my drink and let out a sigh. "I just got out of the house. Baby steps."

"And I just told my very opinionated daughter to cool it with the raccoons. To baby steps." Our glasses come together, and Emily drains the rest of hers.

"I'll get you another."

"Thanks, Jackson. Gin and tonic, please."

I head to the bar. Carl, the owner, is a good man, and the folks at the bar care more about bullshitting than what I'm doing.

My shoulders relax, and I take a deep breath. No one stares at me or asks questions. This is a nice time. I'm glad I came.

Out of the corner of my eye I notice my siblings watching me. I smile and hold up my hand. They wave back, and I see the care in their eyes. If it means so much to them, I can get out of the house once and a while. I can go over to my parents' for dinner.

It's all about baby steps.

14

SHILOH

I love the fall.

It's officially October in Goldheart, and chilly mornings have arrived, my favorite. The trees around Woody Finch Brewery are changing colors to vibrant oranges and red. On my meal breaks I like to go outside and stare at the colors dancing with the breeze. Sometimes I read, but mostly I eat my peanut butter and jelly sandwich at my favorite picnic table and marvel at the scenery.

Today, Emily relieved me for an early meal break around four, before the after-work crowd floods the brewery, folks who wander in weary and tired from a long day. I'm not complaining; today is especially lovely. I grab my lunch bag and sweater and walk outside, admiring the red barn the Finches refurbished and thinking about how lucky I am to be here.

This was the right decision for me.

Sacramento will always be my home. I miss my sister; I miss my mom. However, I got my hope back, being here. My life is curated to what I want, without the influence of a boy who only decides he wants me when I don't chase him.

Before I sit down, I pet a Rottweiler after asking permission from the owners and let the dog smell me before rubbing her ears. The dog groans and leans into my hand, licking my palm.

Thanking the owner, I walk to my favorite table, elated it's free.

My butt barely hits the bench before Jackson appears.

"Hi," he says, holding his own bag.

"Hi." I saw him for a brief moment at the Goldheart Market when I was shopping for Papa. It was in the middle of the afternoon, and he didn't look stressed or anxious. We said hi, but he left abruptly when Bea, the owner, came down the aisle towards us.

He's joined me for a walk with the local shelter's longest resident Bubba, and we were quiet, even when the dog stopped to smell a bush.

Other than that, he hasn't texted me since that "platonic of platonic friends" text, and I had to start turning my phone off at night so I didn't constantly check it.

No matter how much I see him around, I still bust wide open with happiness when he finds me. The butterflies in my stomach flap manically.

"I was wondering if I can join you. I have my own sandwich." He holds up the bag like he's displaying a fish he caught.

"Sure." I shouldn't want to hang out with him, I shouldn't want to talk to him, but I do. I know it's best we should avoid each other, but I feel an invisible magnet between us when we're in each other's proximity.

I need to avoid him. I could be pulled under again, wishing for a man who doesn't have the capacity to want me. Papa is right.

He takes the opposite bench, facing me, diagonal so our knees won't touch. I open the wax paper around my sandwich and stare down at it. Boring peanut butter and jelly.

Today, I just made it quickly since I was running late, but sometimes I use cookie cutters or cut it fun ways to jazz it up. I unpack a bag of chips as I watch Jackson unwrap his exquisite sandwich. It looks like there's chicken and red peppers and green lettuce. Saliva pools in my mouth as I watch him take a good bite and drop his sandwich.

"Do I have pesto on my cheek?" he asks after he swallows.

I shake my head with a smile. "Your sandwich looks good, is all."

He picks up half and thrusts it across the table. "Do you want some?"

"No, I can't," I say, waving off the offer, although drool collects at the corner of my mouth. I point to my sandwich. "I have my own."

"You know, it's been a while since I've had peanut butter and jelly. You want to swap halves?" Jackson holds out the half closer. "Like we're eleven?"

I chuckle as I stare at the half. It is not a fair trade—my cheap, homemade sandwich to his gourmet, store-bought one. But I still take it, because I need to know if it's as good as it looks. He takes the half I offer and bites into it, scrunching his eyebrows. I bite into the chicken pesto sandwich, and flavor hits me. My eyes roll back embarrassingly far as he chuckles, his mouth full of peanut butter and bread.

"It's good, right?" he asks.

"Oh my goodness." I wipe my mouth with a napkin he gives me, and I devour the rest of it. The plump chicken, the cherry tomatoes drizzled with olive oil. The roasted pepper pesto. It's the most delicious thing I've eaten.

"It's been twenty years since I've had peanut butter and jelly. It's tasty," he says.

"It's been twenty-four hours since I've eaten it," I joke as I take the rest of my original sandwich and find the will to eat it. How does one go back to monotony when you've had something that good?

"Why do you eat it every day?" he asks. "I'm just curious."

"A trauma response to poverty," I admit. I choke down the sandwich and wash it down with a can of generic root beer I bought that's fine, but not amazing.

Jackson's forehead creases around his eyebrows.

"You don't like to spend money?"

I shake my head. "It gives me anxiety. Like a lot." I don't mention that handing over my card at the grocery store always feels like agony.

"You bought me coffee, though."

I nod. "I like to spend my money on other people. I hoped it would make you feel good, so I did it." I open my chips and offer him one.

He stares at my chips. "Are you sure?"

"It's the least I can do because my peanut butter and jelly does not equal your delicious masterpiece."

He plucks a chip and crunches down. His eyes expand in delight. "Damn. It's also been a little bit since I've had a salt and vinegar chip."

"They're the best," I say.

"Far superior to any other chip."

My hand freezes in the bag. "Thank you for sharing your sandwich."

"Thank you for sharing yours."

He bites into his remaining half, chewing and avoiding my eye contact. I study him, instead of studying my favorite tree.

"Why did you join me?" I ask, propping my elbow onto the table. "I'm definitely not complaining."

A slight smile crosses his lips. "Wanted company."

I look down so he doesn't see my goofy smile. "Did you have a good time at karaoke?"

"It was nice." He gives a rigid finger point. "I did not sing. Still, I had a good time. It was long overdue to get out with my siblings. It had been a while."

"I miss my sister so much."

"Where does she live?"

"Sacramento. Near McKinley Park."

"The homes are nice around there."

"Definitely," I say. "I lived with her for a little bit."

"Why did you move here?"

"My grandfather. He had the stroke, and my mom works a lot, so I offered to go." *And to get away from Mark.*

I study Jackson. He looks happier, lighter. His eyes aren't as red, and his skin is pink instead of tinged gray when I first met him. His smile used to look like it hurt; now it breaks naturally. His beard is slightly trimmed back.

"You look good," I say.

"Yeah, I'm going on walks now. With dogs. It's been good for me."

I smile at the ground. "I'm going to walk Bubba tomorrow if you want to come."

"Sure," he says. I'm smiling until my phone lights up and I look at it.

"Why don't you give up?" I ask my phone. I cover my mouth. Oh no, I said it out loud.

"Was that one of the reasons you needed a change?"

I nod. "It's a long story."

"I got time. I also got…" Jackson pulls out a little baggie. Is that a chocolate chip cookie? It looks like the good kind from Gold Roast that Tara orders from a fancy bakery in Auburn and gets shipped in. It looks like it's made with a stick of butter each and the paper wrapper is soaked through with oil, but I don't care.

He drops the cookie to the table. "Have you ever had one of these?"

I shake my head. "They always look so good, though."

"It would be rude not to share." The cookie is massive, with lots of chocolate chunks and a glistening coat. He breaks the cookie in half slowly, like it's for a commercial. The chocolate is melty and drips onto his fingers. I let out a squeak as he licks them.

I wish he would lick me like that.

He hands me half, so I'll have to settle for that.

"Cheers," he says, holding his half up, and I touch my side to his in a salute.

The first bite is crispy on the outside and gooey in the middle. I prefer my chocolate chip cookies a little under-cooked, and these are perfect.

"Oh my God." Covering my mouth, I stifle a tiny groan. This cookie coats my mouth with rich sweetness, and I want to cry. "This is better than sex."

Jackson coughs violently on a bite. I'm going to be as red as a stop sign.

"Well, I'll get you more then."

"Okay," I say as I take the last bite, closing my eyes to center my experience. I hold up a finger as I chew. This was the best meal break I've ever had. Maybe I need to treat myself to a good sandwich once in a while, instead of suffering through the same thing over and over.

"Now, that I've shared my cookie with you, I want to hear about who won't give up."

"Mark, my ex-boyfriend. Actually, I'm not sure if we were boyfriend-girlfriend." My cheeks heat. It's embarrassing I was in a situationship for over two years after two years of pining, falling deeply in love with a man who just saw me as convenient sex. A desperate girl hanging on his every word. He might've been dating multiple people besides me; I don't know.

"How do you not know if you're boyfriend-girlfriend?" Jackson takes a swig of a bottle of water.

I run my tongue over my teeth looking for leftover crumbs. "We never had the talk. He didn't treat me like a girlfriend. We didn't really hang out that much when we dated. Mark liked to go out but said I couldn't come because I didn't drink and I'm not fun."

"I've always wondered why you don't drink."

"My mom is a recovering alcoholic," I say. I watch him, waiting for his expression to change, but it doesn't. His eyes are expressive. Open. So, I continue.

"She drank my entire childhood. There were times she forgot to pick my sister and me up because she was so wasted. When I rode the school bus home, I would find her asleep on the couch, surrounded by cheap wine bottles. Sometimes she forgot to grocery shop. Money was always tight because she was a single mother with no help. One time my sister and I ate pads of butter for dinner. There were months we lived off government assistance and I shopped with an EBT card. I still grab for things I know are covered, even though I'm paying for myself."

Jackson shudders, and I hold my reaction. I've seen his family and how they were raised. They own multiple homes in a tourist destination, and his dad had enough money to fund a business. The resources to find an investor when he needed help.

Mark came from a similar background and said off-handed comments about my history. I know Jackson wouldn't.

"Alcohol had such a hold on her that she couldn't see anything else. I know she loved us, and when Summer and I confronted her to get her to stop, it finally worked. She got sober four years ago. I never really liked alcohol, so Summer and I decided to support her and be a sober family. Summer has a handful of drinks, but never around Mom."

"Where's your dad?"

My throat closes, but I croak out. "Gone."

"You've never met him?"

"No," I say. *Do not cry. That man did not want you.* "My mother got pregnant by her boyfriend in high school with me. My mom went to Quartz High School, right here. I've looked for him, although I've heard he's long gone."

"Is he the father of your sister too?"

I nod. "He came back once when I was barely a year. Long enough to get my mom pregnant again. He's never met Summer."

A tear rolls down my cheek and I wipe it away. "I'm sorry. I don't know why I'm crying. He doesn't deserve it."

Jackson covers my hand with his, his thumb rubbing the back of my hand. I look up at him, wondering if he feels the sparks that I do. How I think about him often. That the subject of my dream was him.

He looks down, and all I see is the top of his head. His hand clasps mine as he watches his lap. His whole body takes a breath and lets it go.

"Do you want to hear something sad?"

My heart stops. Is this it? The reason Jackson is the way he is?

I'm not sure if I want to hear it. This was just supposed to be a simple lunch where I look at the changing colors of the trees. Instead, we're baring our souls. I told him why I don't drink and why I eat the same cheap lunch every day. He now knows about Mark.

Now, he might tell me why he doesn't leave his house. Why he just exists and drifts through life.

"Is this...the big thing?" My heart is in my throat.

He looks up, his eyes rimmed with red, making his eyes look even greener.

"I was married. To the love of my life."

"Okay," I say.

"She died."

I try not to react, but I want to cry more. *Breathe in, breathe out.* My stomach still drops to the floor.

"What was her name?" I ask.

"Amy. Amy Louise Finch."

My middle name. That's why he walked away at the barbecue.

"I'm so sorry. That's awful."

I reach across the table, covering his hand with mine. He flinches, and his jaw clamps. Then he clasps my fingers in his. He shakes our hands together and looks up at me. I see the sadness in the corners of his eyes.

"It's a great middle name." I smile. "Of course, I'm biased."

"It is." He looks at me one last time before he pulls his hand away.

I*'m so sorry. That's awful.*

No "how did she die" or "how long were you guys married?" All she needed to know was that my wife died, and I loved her. That was enough to earn her sympathy.

Of course, Shiloh would know the right way to respond. She would eat peanut butter and jelly every day for lunch to buy her boss's asshole son a coffee and Danish to make him like her. She would grab my hand, knowing a hug would be too much. She would save countless dogs, although she cries in the car afterwards.

I feel so stupid for spending so many months being annoyed by her. Avoiding her.

Life is a series of coincidences that folks try to make sense of. Nothing is meant to be, nothing is destiny. When Amy died, people tried to say comforting things like "everything happens for a reason" and "it was God's will," and I wanted to scream "bullshit" at the top of my lungs.

But if I *did* believe in destiny, Shiloh was meant to find me at this moment.

It's like I'm really seeing her for who she is. The wind

takes some loose curls from her braids, making a halo around her, like she's an angel. I was so wrong about her.

"So, now you know why this town feels sorry for me."

"They don't feel sorry for you. They care about you."

I nod, looking down at my lap again.

"I care about you," she says. My head snaps up. She waves her hand. "I'm keeping my promise. I have not fallen for you so don't worry."

I say nothing. Friends is all we can be. Dating her is impossible. She needs a whole man. I'm just a shell of a person who spent the last ten years walking through waist-deep mud. It doesn't stop me from wanting her, wondering if she tastes like vanilla too.

Her sex comment earlier came from nowhere, and it made me cough. I can't let the mention of it affect me, because I will think about Shiloh naked and on top of me constantly if I let myself.

"I want to hear more about Amy. When you're ready. She must be special if you picked her."

"She was." Suddenly, my throat grows scratchy and my eyes stress. I cough into my hand. "Give me some time, and I'll tell you everything."

"Promise?"

"Promise," I say.

"I think you like me, Jackson Finch."

"A little bit." I hold my fingers apart an inch.

"I'll take it!" she says. "I feel like the newspaper needs to know. *Man who likes no one likes Shiloh Abbott a little bit.*"

A laugh leaves my throat.

"You know what will make front-page news?" she continues. "I get you out and about."

"Only if you're my bodyguard."

She looks at herself and giggles. She's a full foot shorter

than I am and probably weighs less than a hundred pounds. "Sure. I'll start working on my bicep curls."

"I'll pay you in sandwiches."

"Oh no, I hate those. Don't do it." The hint of a smile on her lips develops to a smirk.

"I see that little smirk." I point at her mouth. "You're excited for the pesto."

"I am," she laughs. "Do you want to join me on my dog walk tonight too? We can be each other's bodyguards. I was kind of nervous because it's dark, but you can go with me."

"When?"

"I'm walking the dog at eight."

"Sure." I fiddle with my hair since some pieces escaped my rubber band. I tuck them behind my ears.

"Is your hair bothering you?" she asks.

"A little. I cut the front pieces too short."

"You cut your own hair?" Her whole face stretches.

I confirm, and she covers her face. "Jackson, Jackson, you just became friends with the right lady. I know how to cut men's hair. I'm not a professional or anything, but I used to cut hair and get paid in Caramel Apple Spices from Starbucks."

"You want to get paid in sandwiches *and* overpriced drinks?"

"Absolutely. I'm good. You should let me."

I touch my stub of a ponytail. We just started talking about going out in public, but cutting my hair seems like a huge step.

"I'm not talking about a bowl cut. I could just trim it and even it out. Or we can take all of it off, so you don't even *need* a ponytail. You would look even more handsome, I think."

"You think I'm handsome?" Our eyes lock, but she looks away first.

Shiloh gives a sharp head bob. "Absolutely. Imagine what

the single ladies will do when you have a fresh cut, courtesy of me."

Single ladies. Getting back out there. Grumbling under my breath, I look at this ball of energy in front of me. To be honest, the only person I would want to be remotely interested in is her.

It can't happen, though. I'm bound to destroy her heart.

"Well, think about the haircut. I'm glad you're going to walk with me. The owners live a little off Main. I'll text you the address."

"I'll drive you," I offer.

"Thank you. It's a date." Her eyes close slowly. "It's a friend date. Not a date date."

I laugh at her insistence. She wants me to be aware that we are never going to date. It makes my life easier. If she gave me a glimmer of interest, a nugget of intrigue, I might kiss her and see what happens. And what will happen is a shit show.

Shiloh deserves so much more than that.

16

SHILOH

"I think I'm ready for you to cut my hair," Jackson says, as a French bulldog sniffs a patch of daisies, his little snorts so darn cute. Jacques, the French bulldog, is a regular client and likes Jackson more than me, even though I've bribed him with treats and belly scratches.

Jacques and his owners, Glinda and Richard Holmstrom, live in a blue Victorian off Main, surrounded by a white picket fence and vibrant hydrangeas. Jackson meets me outside the fence when I walk the dog every Monday, Wednesday, and Friday. I suit up Jacques, and Jackson waits with his hands in his pockets.

It's been a month of dog walks together, and he hasn't missed one walk with Jacques. He even goes with me to the shelter to walk Bubba, who mostly sniffs the weeds growing between the cement cracks around the shelter.

Sometimes we walk and say nothing. Sometimes, we talk about the brewery or his siblings or the dogs in the neighborhood. He lets me talk about the dogs I'm obsessed with at the local animal shelter or the latest episode of *This is Us*. He teases me for being an old lady stuck in a youngster's body, and I call him a curmudgeon.

One walk I prattled on, and I asked him if my monologue was bugging him.

"No," he had said. "I like hearing you talk."

To me, that's more romantic than ten thousand roses.

Our walks make me feel close to him, and I look forward to seeing him on the other side of the fence, every time.

This week, I've been better about shooing away the urges to grab his face, see if there is a spark between us. When I feel like this, I usually make an awkward joke about being friends, how I don't want to date him, how broken I am from Mark.

I'm such a liar. If he expressed a hint of interest, my clothes would fall off.

We are quite the sight when we walk Jacques. I'm five-one barefoot, and with my uniform of overalls and braids, I look like I'm seconds from being trafficked. Jackson is more than a foot taller than me. The irony since I asked him to join me so I wouldn't be kidnapped.

We haven't talked about Amy again.

He doesn't mention her in passing conversation, or reference what their time together was like. He just lets me talk and sometimes adds words to our conversation, and we enjoy each other's company. That's good enough for now.

Now, he's ready for me to cut his hair. I could bounce, I'm so giddy. While I think he's handsome with the ponytail, I don't know how I'll react to him with shorter hair. I've imagined it, though.

I'll have to contain myself.

"I'm tired of my hair in my face," he says, pushing his front pieces behind his ears.

"How short were you thinking?"

"I trust you."

"How about a mohawk?"

"As long as it's green," Jackson jokes. "Just make it look good. I have every faith in you."

"I'll make you so good-looking."

"Because I'm a hag right now."

"You look like a hermit mountain man."

"Just the look I was going for." That day he asked me to cut his hair, he put his hand on my shoulder, and waves of sensation flared in my torso.

That's how I ended up knocking on his door on the Wednesday before Thanksgiving.

That morning, I straightened my hair so I could wear it down. I decided on a big sweater that reaches my knees, black leggings that have faded to a dull gray, and my favorite sneakers with a hole that has gotten larger so I can see my sock. I really need a new pair and have almost bought new ones twice, but my heart beats too fast thinking about replacing them.

I bet the first woman Jackson dates will be sleek and elegant, with naturally bone-straight hair and high cheekbones. In my mind, she is tall and slender, but still has boobs and a butt. A woman with poise and a college education.

Whoever he chooses with be the opposite of me.

I parked at the side of the garage to avoid detection, but Jackson promised me his mother would be preparing for Thanksgiving so she wouldn't notice. I climb the stairs to Jackson's studio and knock.

I shiver as he opens the door, the warmth enveloping me like a hoodie fresh from the dryer. We've reached the time of year where I'm always cold—my hands and feet like ice blocks, and I wear multiple layers so I don't shiver. I'm wearing a long-sleeved shirt and a tank top underneath the sweater.

"Cold out there?"

I let out a "brrr" as I walk in. He barely looks at me as I

walk into his living room. His hair is down, reaching his shoulders and his beard is trimmed, cut close to his jaw.

"Did you...trim your beard?"

He rubs it and smiles, the gleam of his teeth bright. "I did. Does it look good?"

"Better than good." I meant it. This will be harder than I thought. "You're going to look like a whole new person."

"The bum look is out."

"You look great now. You'll just have shorter hair."

I walk in, smelling leather and coffee. There's bottles of bourbon and whiskey on a silver cart next to his cabinets and a large TV in the corner of the room. His living room is small but decorated. There's a Woody Finch Brewery poster I've never seen before and black-and-white photography on the walls of different places in Goldheart, including the mine.

My eyes trace the dark grooves of the mine's outline as I feel him walk up behind me, close enough to feel his body heat.

"Mom invited you and your grandpa over for Thanksgiving, right?"

"Yes," I say. "I can't wait. I was stressed on what we were going to do. I don't know the first thing about Thanksgiving food. I hope we won't be a burden."

"There's more than enough. My mom loves inviting people over. It'll be great."

"Will you be there?" I ask.

Jackson grimaces. "My mom might murder me if I don't go. I don't know. Maybe if there's lots of bourbon."

Jackson has been making great strides toward participating in life, but there's moments he retreats and backslides. It's hard to know when it will happen. The only consistency I have noticed are our walks with Jacques. He always goes to those. Other things are hit or miss.

"Where do you want to do it?" he asks.

My heart thumps as I look around the space. I notice his bed, pushed into the corner, and my mind flashes to a daydream I've had too often. Him over me, kissing me, kissing my neck. Being in the same room with Jackson and a bed is more than I can handle. I focus on the table, where he's placed two towels.

"Let's do it here," I say, spinning a chair out.

Jackson sits down, and I put my hands in his hair. It's greasy and unkempt, the ends dry and the scalp oily. It's probably been a week or more since he has washed it. No point in shaming him. We'll work on getting him on a more regular schedule.

"Let's wash your hair, and I'll cut it wet," I suggest.

"Of course, let's go to the bathroom." He walks with the towel around his shoulders. When we get into the bathroom and he turns on the faucet that goes into the white porcelain tub, he puts his hands on his hips, contemplates the situation, and pulls his shirt off before I can cover my eyes.

"This will be easier," he says, tossing his shirt on the counter.

"Oh my God," I say, creating a visor with my palm.

He grins. "I should've asked if you were okay seeing my naked torso."

"It's fine!" My "fine" squeaks, and I want to run away. "You look very, very nice."

He chuckles. I can't help it; my eyes drag down his tufts of chest hair, the definition in his abs. When I look up, I'm caught, and I swallow.

"Do you want me to wash my hair, or do you want to?"

Should I? I try not to touch Jackson. I shouldn't touch him. *He doesn't have a shirt on.* However, I'm not certain he can get his hair as clean as I can, and I know touching him is a necessary evil.

"I'll do it," I say. "Kneel."

"Yes, ma'am," he says, dropping to his knees.

I must be flushing bright red, because Jackson lowers his face level to my pelvis and another fantasy flashes through my mind. His hands pulling down my jeans, pulling my underwear to the side. His lips covering my center, taking one long suck. The thought is so intoxicating I have to brace myself to the wall.

Why are you thinking this? Wash the man's hair! His hair is gross, full of dust and motor oil and bacteria.

That calms me down enough that I can function as Jackson bends over the tub.

His behind looks so cute.

No! Motor oil and dust!

He turns and leans over, setting his glasses on the counter. I notice the corded muscle in his back, the light freckles dusting his shoulders. His hair flops over into the tub as I turn the water on. He dunks his head under and makes a guttural noise.

"It's so cold!" he says.

"You're a big, tough guy. You can handle it," I tease as I squirt a dollop of his shampoo into my hand. I rub my hands together and push the product into his hair. Working it to a lather, I avoid looking at his muscles. How they create grooves in his skin, lines I want to trace. He's not meaning to, but he's flexing, since he's holding himself up by the lip of the tub.

He groans as I massage his head. I'm just trying to get all the buildup and gunk out from his scalp, that's all. I'm not trying to elicit any reactions that will make me think about that bed more. However, his groans transport me to another fantasy, of him above me, thrusting in and out.

No, I can't think like this. We're just friends. He's a widower, who said his late wife is the love of his life. I bet she was amazing. I bet if you compared her to me, there would be no contest. Amy would win every time.

So, I evict the thoughts from my mind and focus on the task at hand. Lather, rinse, repeat.

"Do you condition?" I ask.

"No, is that something I need to do?"

"Yes," I say, as I work the conditioner I brought into his clean hair. He groans again as I work his scalp and lower his head under the faucet, rinsing the suds down the drain. I avert my gaze, so I don't focus on his long neck or the two divots that peek out from his pants.

"Okay, you can stand up," I say. Jackson pops up, and I don't look away fast enough. There's his torso again, his abs as shredded as his back, with a light dusting of hair along his chest. I'm not quick enough because I'm still looking when he puts his glasses back on.

"I'm sorry," I say, shielding my eyes.

"It's fine, Shiloh. We're friends, right?"

"Right," I say, turning quickly, inches from the edge of the open door. Jackson turns me into a klutz, and there's no way he thinks anything about me is attractive.

"Watch it, I'm not taking you to the urgent care again," he says. I glare at him, and he says, "Okay, I would, but I would make fun of you."

"Fair enough," I say, as we walk to the kitchen. He sits down with the towel over his shoulders. At least I won't be distracted by his shoulders anymore.

I comb out his hair, flicks of water touching my arms. Nerves make my hands shake. Between the closeness to his naked torso and the pressure to cut this man's hair well, I'm a mess.

"I trust you, Shiloh," he says. He must sense my anxiety.

"Okay." I brought my clippers since I do Papa's hair now and splurged on a set, so I open my kit, with my scissors, clippers, and all the different blade extensions. I first take a comb to separate out the top, which I want to be longer and take a hair tie so he looks like a genie. He's directly in front of a mirror, and I can't help but giggle.

"What?" he asks as he looks in the mirror, and he immediately busts up in laughter. "Did I always look this ridiculous with long hair?"

"No, just right now."

"It's definitely for the best it's coming off."

"I agree." I take my scissors and wonder how to troubleshoot. I've only given haircuts to men who need a clean-up, not a whole different haircut, so I decide I'll just get the lower bits shorter first so I can use the clippers.

"I'm going to remove some of the length first, so it will look goofy." I take huge chunks and cut them with my scissors, five or so inches of hair fluttering to the ground.

"I can do goofy, as long as you fix it."

"I will. This is so fun. It's like a hair jungle," I say as I continue to bushwhack all his hair, going around the crown of his head, making it shorter. It's choppy and uneven, and it's a "trust the process" moment.

Jackson looks down. "That's so much hair."

"How are you doing?"

"Great. I feel lighter already."

I press my hands onto his shoulders, and my laughter won't stop. Jackson is a sight, with his choppy lower hair and his top ponytail. He laughs too, full and bright. His hand lands on mine and stays. My throat closes and the laughter goes with it. I pull my hand away and turn to the table.

Catching my breath, I chose the two-inch attachment and attach it to the clippers, turning them on. I buzz the sides first, and once that is sheared, I go around the back of the head. He keeps his head still as I take more and more hair off, until all that's left is some stubble where his longer hair used to be. Our hand touch is in the past, a fleeting moment.

"Looks like you have some gray coming in, Wally," I say, touching his sideburns with my finger.

"You gave some to me," he jokes. Our jokes sound like an old married couple's, and I love it. This time, I don't respond. I just keep going, until the entire back is even, and I switch the attachment to a more generous length, making sure the shaved part faded into the longer hair I want on the crown of the head.

Instead of picking a different clipper, I think a more old-fashioned style would work, the type of haircut my grandfather likes. Jackson has a classic, handsome face—strong jaw, defined nose, soulful green eyes. I comb his hair out and take strand after strand, cutting it straight over his head until it's all even. Then, I comb it a different way to check. When I shear it sideways to take some of the volume out, Jackson lets out a sound of surprise.

"Okay," I say when I'm all done, brushing some rogue hairs off his shoulders.

Jackson stands up and walks to the mirror. He runs his hand through his hair and turns his head to the side. A long strand of hair falls over his brow, and I curse myself.

The haircut is good. A little too good. I just made this situation a thousand percent harder for me.

"I do have gray coming in. What business did I have to have such long hair?"

"You're not balding, so at least there's that."

"No kidding. It's so weird." He turns and points to his neck that's three shades paler than the rest of his body because his hair covered it. "I have to work on my tan. I didn't know it was this bad."

I laugh as I start to clean up. After he puts a shirt on, he basically pries the broom out of my hands so he can sweep up his own hair.

"Let me," he says. Our fingers brush. and I swallow.

"You had a lot of hair," I say, walking to the table and zipping up my kit. Once we're cleaned up, Jackson inspects his haircut one last time. I catch a hint of a smile.

"You did a great job. Thank you." He opens his arms, and I'm taken back. We haven't hugged before, ever, and now he's asking for one.

I don't turn down hugs. Especially from handsome men.

Walking into his embrace, I'm swallowed by him. My cheek presses against his broad chest as he sways side-to-side with me in his arms. My arms sit on his waist as he kisses the top of my head, and I almost crumble in a pile.

He's hugging me because we're friends. Nothing more.

This is exactly what happened with Mark. I saw things that weren't there. Jackson still loves his wife. He hasn't spoken about her since that day in October, but I know she is still in his heart and his thoughts.

Jackson holds me so tightly, I can't pull away. This is a hug of close friends. Nothing more.

I don't want to pull away, but I do.

His fingertips trail down my arm, and I hold my breath.

"Thanks again," he says, and he finally takes his hand away. "I love it."

"I'm glad," I say. Crossing my arms, I try to create a mental barrier as well, but it doesn't work.

"I'll see you tomorrow," he says. "For Thanksgiving."

Oh good, he's going. That means he's doing better. "I'll see you tomorrow."

"Don't tell anyone that you were the one to do my hair. Just pretend like you're seeing it for the first time. I'm not in the mood for... speculation."

"You got it," I say, pointing a finger gun. Why am I such a nerd?

"Bye, Shiloh," he says. I half-expect him to go for a goodbye hug, but he doesn't. He just stands at the top of the stairs as I leave.

Once I'm in my car, I wipe my forehead.

"Oh my God," I say, shaking my hands.

17

JACKSON

I hear a knock in the middle of my morning coffee and reading time. Shiloh mentioned once on one of our walks that she always starts her day with thirty minutes of reading her current book with coffee and I thought it would be a good habit, so I started doing it. It's now something to look forward to and I've been getting up earlier than usual to get it in.

Tucking my bookmark into my spot, I stand up and walk to my door, opening it to find my mother.

"Happy Thanksgiving!" she says brightly, walking past me without an invitation. I don't say anything because she does own the place. She covers her mouth in shock. "Oh my God, Jackson, you cut your hair!"

"Do you like it?" I shake it, and it feels odd. Light.

She touches the short part and I let her, turning around so she can see the full look. Shiloh did an amazing job. For someone with no formal training, I'm impressed.

"The long hair was bugging me."

She covers her mouth again, and I see her nose scrunch. Tears are imminent. I roll my eyes.

"What, Mom?"

"The last time your hair was that short was right when Amy..."

"I know," I say. "That was a long time ago. It's just hair."

"This feels like a big deal." She wipes her eyes, and without thinking, I take her in for a hug.

"I can't remember the last time you initiated a hug." She just holds me, putting pressure on my ribs, like she'll lose me. I feel a little uncomfortable, but I stay. This means a lot to her, and whatever I feel is insignificant.

When she pulls away, she touches my cheeks, and my gaze darts to the floor.

"Thanksgiving is today. Are you coming to dinner?"

"Yes," I agree without a fight.

Shock covers her face, then a smile. "Good. Five o'clock."

"Okay." I cross my arms. My mom looks down at my T-shirt and jeans, my tidied beard, my clean apartment. She notices the steaming cup of coffee and my book. Checking her watch, she looks up.

"Wait, you're awake."

"I am." It's eight o'clock and I got to bed last night at ten, the earliest I've turned in since I moved home. Last night, I drank one glass of bourbon and slept *hard*. The sleep was so good, I forgot about the haircut and scared the shit out of myself when I looked in the mirror.

My mother still watches me. I shrug. "What?"

"It's just, you've been different these last few weeks. What's the change?"

Shiloh Louise Abbott. I don't utter those words; I just shrug.

When she came over yesterday with her hair down around her shoulders, wearing that oversized sweater, I had to catch my breath. My haircut and the hug fucked me up. I opened my arms, and she walked in without hesitation. She was so tiny in my arms, I thought I would break her with how tight I held her.

I'm worried I may give away what I feel when I see her at Thanksgiving. I may look at her too often, try to get her to smile with one of our jokes. What Shiloh and I have is just ours, no one else's to dissect or analyze. It's more than friendship, but it can't reach romance.

I watch the guests arrive from my window.

First, Annie and Whitney arrive. Something is going on with Reid and Whitney, for sure. First, karaoke, now she's showing up to family events. It'll be interesting to watch, at least.

Shiloh and I have the potential to be interesting to watch too, but I can't add any fuel to the rumors. There've been plenty.

People have noticed how much I join her for lunch, how often I sneak into the employee breakroom to place a cookie in her locker. I now frequently buy her sandwiches from Subtown, and she mentioned once she wanted to try everything on the menu, so every time I go, I pick a new one. The hits so far have been the pesto chicken and the meatball sub.

As far as cookies go, she's a chocolate-chip girl so I don't get her anything else.

Chatter from my parents' house drifts up to my studio, so it's time I make an appearance. That morning, I dressed in a new long-sleeved shirt and clean jeans. Shiloh left some styling product, and I run it through my hair so it will behave. Since it's a holiday, I grabbed some cologne from my medicine cabinet, just because.

Spying on our guests is my way of stalling.

There's a nip in the air when I exit my apartment, and I skip down the stairs to the back of the main building, opening the sliding glass door. There's no one in the living room; most of the sound is coming from the foyer.

I wasn't nervous, but I am now.

Time to load up on some bourbon. Reid greets me, trying to hug me, but I squirm out of his grasp. All I care about is whiskey.

He asks me when I got my hair cut, and I grumble out a response. My family closes in on me, staring at me, commenting on the new look. I didn't think this all the way through, but it's fine, I just need whiskey now more than ever.

My parents don't have quite the excellent selection I do, so I pick a new bottle of Four Roses and look for a tool to cut the seal.

"Jackson, let's wait to eat before you open the whiskey."

Breathe in, breathe out.

Mom doesn't realize how much I need this, just to stay.

I cut it anyway. I pour a healthy amount into a short glass and take a sip. It burns my throat, creating a trail of fire. The caramel and malty flavor calms my nerves.

"You know what, I'll join you," Reid says, finding his own glass. He doesn't pour as much as me. We clink our glasses together. This glass of bourbon will make the evening bearable. Maybe future dinners I can cut back, but I need this tonight.

Holidays are always hard, especially this one.

As I take another sip, I hear the sweet voice that trumps bourbon in things I need.

"Thank you so much for having us, Mrs. Finch," Shiloh says, hugging my mother tightly. She walks into the foyer more, and we lock eyes.

"Hi, Jackson. I like your hair."

She looks so beautiful. Her blond hair cascades down her front, in straight ribbons, making her look like a doll. Her blue sweater brings out her eyes and I want to hug her so badly, but I can't. Too many eyes.

Everyone is already watching Shiloh and wondering why she's saying hi to me first, the Finch sibling that interacts with employees the least.

My family will pick apart our friendship like vultures.

"Hi. Thank you for coming," is all I can muster.

What I really want to do is pull her by her hand and leave. Find a spot where we can be us, without all these eyes staring. Her lips turn down, and she nods, understanding where we are. Why I must act like this.

She saves the interaction, by lacing her words with honey. "Thanks for inviting me. This is wonderful!"

Shiloh offers to help, and I sip my whiskey, my glass almost empty. When I look up, I see Earl staring at me. I nod once and hold up my glass.

"Can I get you one?"

"No," he grumbles. He still stares, and I didn't expect to feel more uncomfortable, but I do.

I want to tell him that I would never hurt Shiloh. That we're friends. Good friends. Too many eyes in this room, too much studying. I want to talk to her, but I can't.

She passes me on the way to the bathroom and grabs my hand. It's quick, a brush of the hand, but it calms me.

We go around the table, saying what we're thankful for. My brother and Annie say they're thankful for each other, and then it comes to me.

I want to follow their lead. *Shiloh. Shiloh is who I'm grateful for,* is the truth.

It's not something I want to say. What I have with her is mine. No one should be able to claim it.

"Pass," I say.

"You have to say something," Shiloh whispers across the

table. Her blue eyes plead with me. She doesn't know she's the reason I'm here.

I grumble. "I'm grateful for my family, I guess. And whiskey."

The table notices. No matter how much we tried to hide it, Shiloh has a pull on me. She's my life preserver when I'm drowning and the only thing keeping me afloat.

No matter how much I try to hide it, everyone at that table can sense I would do anything for her.

What they don't know is how it eats away at me, the guilt so strong, only whiskey can numb it.

18

SHILOH

J ackson warned me he wouldn't out me as his hairstylist.

I didn't expect the arctic front. I've thought about it every which way, anything to avoid bruising my fragile feelings. I grabbed his hand, and he held it briefly, the only reason I didn't burst into tears in the bathroom.

His family watched his every move, so the haircut meant something to them. Jackson may be pulling out of a multi-year-grief period. He looks better, he interacts more.

I notice how he's coping, though.

The several glasses of bourbon. The avoidance. Drifting through his loved ones' conversations like a ghost.

I refused to let Jackson's behavior ruin my night. I talked with Whitney and Papa; I talked to Tara, the owner of Gold Roast, and her friend, Owen, who have a similarly complicated friendship like Jackson and I have.

At least Owen is willing to admit he's friends with her, ready to face the inquiries. I know Tara wants to, but Owen is hesitant. He'll come around; I just know it.

Jackson, on the other hand...

It would be my ex all over again. At the end of the day, I

want a man who wholeheartedly charges toward me without hesitation. It took Mark years of friendship to give me a chance after his ex-girlfriend dumped him. I can't wait for another man to be ready, to decide I'm the one. The one would know immediately, and Jackson and I have been friends for a few months now. Besides one nice hug, there's no hint I could be it.

That crushes me.

The least he could do is act like my friend, no matter what people we know say.

The day after Thanksgiving, I open the fence to leave the Holmstroms' property with Jacques's leash in hand to find Jackson standing there, ready to be my bodyguard. Like nothing happened.

"Hi." He looks so handsome, with the gray in his temples and his glasses, and his Henley that hugs his chest. His hands are shoved in his pockets, and he teeters on his heels.

Don't get distracted, don't let him off too easy.

"Hi," I say curtly as I walk past him, the French bulldog thrilled and then immediately confused he can't jump on him. Usually, Jackson gets in at least two hundred pets before we start walking with the squirming, grunting Jacques, but today, we ignore him.

I ignore him. Jacques keeps looking back, hoping for pets.

"Shiloh, wait," Jackson says, taking two steps to catch up to me. Dang my little legs.

I try to smile, but I want to cry.

"What's wrong?" His voice is sincere, and I want to crumble.

"Nothing's wrong."

"Shiloh, I was married, and I know that is a load of horseshit."

I huff out a breath. "Why did you ignore me at Thanksgiving?"

"I got nervous. My whole family was there, and I didn't want everyone to ask questions. You saw how everyone asked Owen a thousand times why he's not dating Tara. I didn't want the same thing for us."

"We're just friends. There's nothing to report or to be embarrassed about. Are you embarrassed about me?"

"No," he says. "It's broad daylight, and I'm walking with you. Anyone can see that we're friendly."

"Then, why is it a big deal with your family? I just felt...ignored."

He stops and turns me by the arm. The dog sits on its rump and looks up with us, the tongue flicking at rapid speed. He looks down at me. "It is a big deal."

"Why?"

Jackson clams up and we start walking again, letting Jacques smell bushes. He lifts his leg every other foot and we do not talk.

"Am I your only friend?"

"I think so," he answers.

"Oh." Deep sadness blooms in my chest. We pass neighbors out on their porch or folks watering their plants. They all greet us, and Jackson holds up his hand in acknowledgment. We keep walking.

"I had friends. But when Amy died, I isolated myself. I let lots of good friendships go. Some didn't know how to deal with my grief. Most people don't know what to do when it's been eighteen months and I still couldn't get out of bed some days because I missed her so much. In some ways, I feel like I'm finally moving on in ten years and that's terrifying."

I feel this in my soul. I've stopped thinking about Rory every morning when I wake up. The other day, I realized I hadn't thought about him at all, and it caused me to break down.

He was really gone.

I can't imagine what it must be like to lose a spouse. I've never had a romantic love that strong, and whatever I feel for Jackson is a small crush, nothing more. It's not like I'm falling in love with him or anything.

He touches my arm and I turn. "I'm sorry that I ignored you. Forgive me. And can I please pet the dog now?"

"You're forgiven," I say, stopping. Jackson kneels, and the dog beelines toward him, jumping and outstretching his paws on his knees.

"Hi, buddy, what's up? Did you get any turkey on Turkey Day? Oh, you're my little buddy."

I cover a laugh as I watch them together. Jackson sits down on the pavement and allows the twenty-five-pound dog jump all over him, bathing his face with kisses. Ever since he started joining me on walks, Jackson says he liked this dog because their names were similar. I laughed out loud when he said that.

"What do you say, Sunny? Do you forgive me?"

"Yes, I do," I say. A car rolls by slowly, watching the town recluse lose his mind over a French bulldog. "The townsfolk are seeing you."

"Let them. I'm on a walk with a great person and a great dog."

That makes me melt.

He stands and we continue walking, making a right onto Turner, encountering our first baby hill to tire out this pooch.

"It's cold today," I say, shivering.

"You're always cold," he says. "Here."

He opens his jacket. Because of his size I could probably tuck myself under his armpit and hide like candy you take into the movies. Snuggling into him is not the best idea.

He just called me his best friend. Mentioned Amy.

There's nothing more than friendship for us, and that

must be enough. I'm cold and his body is so warm. My heart beats faster.

"I'm okay. We should speed up and get back."

"Do you think the short legs can handle it?"

"Hey!" I say.

"I meant the dog."

"Oh," I say with a laugh and look down at the pooch. We do have to watch French bulldogs on walks because of their flat faces and how small their nostrils are for them to breathe. Jacques is doing great, even though I'm speeding back to his house. My teeth chatter. "I think he'll be fine."

We hang a right on Grant.

"What's going on with the German shepherd we picked up? Koda?"

"As good as can be expected. The fosters are working on manners with him, working on reactivity. We've had a few people express interest, but I think the foster mom is being particular. She has four so she can't necessarily keep him, but she really wants him to go to a good home."

He nods. "My dad should really meet that dog."

"I think he should. The rescue owner loves Woody Finch and knows the story. It might work out. Let your dad know, and I can set up a meet-and-greet."

"If we get my dad in the same room as that dog, he will adopt him. One hundred percent."

"Bring it up to him. All he can say is no." I sigh. "I really want a dog."

"Why can't you have one?"

"My grandpa's apartment is too small. And I don't know where I'll be in a few months." I pause before I look up at him. "If I could, I would adopt Bubba in an instant."

"You love that dog."

"So much," I agree. "I'm going to walk him tomorrow. Want to come?"

"Sure, what time?"

We discuss as Jackson studies the ground. After we hang a right onto Goodwin, we head back toward Main. The dog's pants grow louder, especially in the silence emitting from him. I try not to shiver. I couldn't resist another snuggle offer.

"When are you planning to leave Goldheart?"

"I don't know," I say. "Papa tells me every day he doesn't need me, but I think he likes having me around. It's a great place for now. I like what I'm doing—working at the brewery and walking dogs like Jacques. I just really don't know what I want to do. I'm twenty-six, and I don't have my life together. At all."

"I'm thirty-six, and I don't have my life together," he jokes. "I live over my parents' garage. I work at my family's business. Widowed. *Very* single. *I* don't know what I want to do with my life. My younger brothers are falling in love, and I just feel *left*."

"Is Reid finally dating Whitney?" I ask, animated.

He turns to me and narrows his eyes. "I don't know."

"Well, I hope they're falling in love. That would be wonderful."

Jackson nods. "He's a knucklehead, but he deserves it."

What about you? I want to ask. Even if it's not me, Jackson deserves to find love again. Even if he lost it once, there's always more to find. If he decides to date someone that is not me, I will be so jealous, I won't be able to function.

"What about you?" he asks. "Thinking of dating anyone?"

I can't because all I think about is you. I shake my head. "I'm like you. Very, very single."

"Look at us. Two single folks."

"The most single of singles this town has ever seen," I say. We reach the Holmstroms' residence, and I turn toward him.

"I have to get Jacques inside. I forgot his sweater. Mine too."

"Okay, I better get going."

He opens his arms again and like a dummy, I walk into them, inhaling the leather-whiskey smell ingrained in his clothes. His arms are strong around my shoulders as he kisses my head and I melt. I can't help but press my body into his and he pulls me tighter.

"Ask your dad about the dog and let me know?" I ask.

"Will do. And Shiloh?"

I turn back toward him. "Yeah?"

"Any guy would be lucky to be with you," he says.

The words tumble from me before I can think. "You too. You deserve to find love again. Even if the first time was enough."

His face reveals nothing, his cheeks still as stone. My lips press together in a closed mouth smile as I wave goodbye and walk into the house with Jacques.

As I take the dog out of its harness and hang up the leash, I let out a whistle of breath.

19

JACKSON

Y*ou deserve to find love again. Even if the first time was enough.*

Shiloh said that to me, like I haven't been thinking about her constantly. I look for her when I go into the taproom; I've memorized her schedule. I know exactly what sandwich I've gotten her last and which one I will get her next.

I've started a note in my phone all about her. Her likes, her dislikes. Her mom's name, her sister's name.

There's a whole section on Rory.

I can't stop hugging her. I can't stop thinking about lifting her so her legs wrap around my waist, pushing her hair away, so I can taste those strawberry-stained lips. Every second I'm not with her, I want to be with her.

I'm addicted to making her smile.

It all makes me feel very, very guilty.

My wife has been gone for ten years, and I no longer feel her presence. I'm too pragmatic to believe in spirits or signs. She really is gone. When people insist that a dead loved one is with them, I just roll my eyes.

However.

A force pulls me to Shiloh, like moth to a flame. She dragged me in, against my will, without me knowing. A force taps me on the shoulder, pointing to her, telling me she needs to be in my life.

It's not Amy, but if it was, it would make sense.

Amy thought of everyone before she thought of herself. The only thing that really made her sad about dying was all the people who were left.

There was one good day toward the end, when we watched *Home Alone*, and her weak laughter made my heart hurt. She grabbed my hand while we sat on the couch during a scene of Kevin walking in the snow, and she told me, "I want you to be happy. Please be happy without me."

It drove an iron spike through my stomach and twisted.

I never kept that promise.

That morning ten years ago is on my mind, going into our weekly family meeting.

Our investor, Dan Price, isn't coming to this one, thank God. I emailed the November numbers, and he sent me a selfie of himself shirtless on a beach in Hawaii with his wife, Makenna, her sunglass frames bigger than her bikini top. It came with this message: *Don't bother me, I'm on vacation. Just don't spend all the money this month and use your best judgment.*

My family has taken this as an opportunity to drop bombs.

Annie and Cameron announce they're pregnant. Soon after, Reid announces he is seeing Whitney, which is more shocking to my mother than the fact that my goofy brother Cam is going to be a father. Annie cries. Mom freaks out.

Whitney is adamantly childfree, and my mother is fixated on the idea that Reid won't be a father if he stays with her, even though Cam is literally giving her another grandchild to spoil. Usually, I'm quiet at these things.

Not today. I stand up to make my point.

"Enough, Mom. Reid is a grown man, and he can decide

what he wants. He doesn't need you badgering him."

It's like I'm finally speaking up for myself.

Reid thanks me, but they keep discussing having kids or not having kids.

Reid, always the peacemaker, tries to smooth it over and ropes me into this.

"Even if Jackson and I never have kids, that's fine..."

Like all hope is lost for me.

There was a time that kids felt inevitable, with Amy. Now, I'm the lost cause of this family.

We discuss company business, but Reid's comment haunts me.

Do I want to be a dad? Is that something still in the cards for me?

I didn't really think about it until now.

Frankly, since I started spending time with Shiloh.

When we discuss Christmas gifts, Reid and I tell our family that we have Shiloh's present taken care of. Reid confirms, since we've discussed it.

My entire family's heads snap to me. Reid nods at me, and we steer the conversation away, far away, that I have an idea for one employee only.

Reid and I discussed it last week over some Macallan. Since then, Reid's been deep in research mode, his favorite mode. I found money in the budget, and we're doing it. Shiloh hasn't been clear on how long she's staying; however, I'm hoping to change the brewery in honor of her.

My mother makes an off-handed comment later in the meeting, when Shiloh's name comes up and I smile at the mention of her name.

"You're smiling. Is there something going on?" she asks, and the corners of my mouth drop.

I love my mother, but her memory is as short as a goldfish's.

"Is this meeting over?" I ask.

"I think so." They all look at me as I nod once and leave the table.

Storming off, I clench my fists, walking inside the brewery. The brewery is empty; it's hours until we open. My first instinct is to grab a beer to calm my nerves, but that won't fix anything. All I need is a couple breaths, and I will be fine.

I walk to my office, my sanctuary, and close the door. I look at the Post-it note Shiloh left yesterday.

Thank you so much for the cookie, Wally! You're the best. Sunny

She wrote the words in black ink and drew a tiny heart by her nickname in red. It's adorable, and I put it on my shelf without thinking, even securing it with tape.

I stick the note back where I put it, smoothing it against the shelf so it will stick. My pinkie touches the heart and I study it before I take out my to-do list for the day to start pounding out today's tasks.

I lose myself in work, typing away. Eleven, our opening time, passes, and I know Shiloh is here for her shift. Usually, I would wander out and say hello, say a joke to get a smile. Maybe secure a hug if no one is watching.

Today, I stay put.

I can stay away from her. Friends can go a full day without seeing each other. However, if she comes by my office, I will turn around and talk if she wants to. If she texts me about her lunch break, I will one hundred percent go.

I'm on my last to-do list item for the day when Emily walks in around one-thirty. My stomach growls and my throat is dry, but I'm so focused that my sister has to punch me in the shoulder.

"What?" I say, turning around.

"You might want to come out to the taproom."

"Why?" I ask.

"There's this guy here for Shiloh. I think he's an ex. He

won't leave. I think she needs you."

I gnash my teeth together. "Is his name Mark?"

"I think so," Emily says. I push my sleeves up and explode out of my chair.

That motherfucker is going to get a piece of my mind.

She follows me. "Is he bad news?"

"We'll find out," I say.

20

SHILOH

Mark stands in front of me, and I cannot believe this is happening.

His phone calls had petered off, finally, and there've been no more flowers, no more texts. I thought he'd finally moved on.

Until he showed up here, at my place of employment, about an hour's drive from his home.

"Shiloh, baby, can we go somewhere to talk?"

"No." I cross my arms.

"Come on, don't be like that."

"Be like what?"

"Cold. This isn't you."

He should've been grateful for my warmth if he wanted to keep it.

Leaning forward, I press my hands into the bar, my shoulders hunched to my ears. When Mark walked in, Ramon looked at me with wide eyes and an "oh shit" on his lips and asked if it was him. Ramon's about to fall over, he's listening so intently. He's been wiping the same spot for three minutes.

I lower my voice to a whisper. "What are you doing here?"

The taproom's collective attention is on us. Mark still looks devastatingly handsome with dark eyes and dark features, wearing a sleek black bomber jacket. He's shorter than Jackson and leaner, and now that he's in front of me, I feel nothing. He waltzed into the taproom like it would be easy to crook his finger at me and I would leave Goldheart in a heartbeat.

He doesn't know I've changed. I'm not the same girl who left Sacramento. Even though we're just friends, Jackson has shown me how I should be treated. A man who has no interest in being out in public accompanies me on walks, buys me sandwiches, and loves to listen to me ramble. Mark never did that.

Before a word leaves my mouth, the shape of Jackson Finch hulks toward him, with Emily trailing behind. Steam is practically billowing out of his ears when he looks at Mark.

"Mark, how about we go outside?" Jackson asks calmly.

"Who are you?" Mark asks.

I don't condone violence, but Jackson looking at Mark like he's about to avenge for me makes my core clench.

Ramon gives me a nod when I say, "Mark, let's all go outside."

"Okay, but who is this motherfucker?" he asks, pointing to Jackson. I take Mark's arm to pull him, although I don't know what good it will do.

I regret not grabbing a cardigan upon leaving the heated taproom, because it's bitter cold today. There's reports we may get a dusting of snow tonight. I shiver, and then I feel warm material cover my shoulders as I stand outside the brewery. Jackson's eyes catch mine as he finishes putting his hoodie around my shoulders. Mark's mouth is agape.

"Shiloh, who the fuck is this?" Mark points his finger at Jackson, like he's my new boyfriend. Let him think that.

Jackson rubs his hands together, his biceps constricting under the sleeves of his long-sleeved shirt. "Did she ask you to come here?"

"No, but she wasn't answering my texts or phone calls."

Texts and phone calls that ended over a month ago. I wonder if Mark started dating someone else, and she wouldn't put up with his bullshit so he's crawling back to me.

"What made you think her not returning your texts or calls means 'come see me', buddy?"

Calling Mark "buddy" infuriates him. Mark's ears are red as the Woody Finch building, and his hands ball into fists at his side. He's not a fighting man, but I wonder if Jackson will push him enough that he takes a swing.

Turning around, I see a few people lingering in the doorway.

"Let me talk to my girlfriend," Mark says. "This has nothing to do with you."

I laugh out loud. He's never called me that, ever. I was his friend the one time I met his sister by accident at the mall.

"I can see you're a historical revisionist, because that's not what Shiloh told me," Jackson tells him.

He turns to me. "Are you letting this guy speak for you?"

I wrap Jackson's warm sweatshirt around me, letting the sleeves swallow my hands. "Sure."

"Are you fucking each other?" Mark asks, his voice growing louder.

There's a collective gasp behind me. People watch us like Jackson is an endangered species at the zoo. This is the most they've probably seen from Jackson, and it's all because of me. It's sick how much satisfaction I'm getting from this.

"Are you fucking her? It's a simple question."

"No, I'm not," Jackson says. That admittance, although true, saddens me. "But if I was, everyone would know she was my girl. She would go everywhere with me. I wouldn't leave her at home because I was so immature I couldn't drink around my sober girlfriend. You fucked up, buddy. That woman—" He points to me, and our eyes lock. My mouth parts as he turns back and points to him. "Is the best thing you've never had."

"Did he just quote Beyonce?" Emily mutters next to me.

Mark's lips part, and he's vibrating with anger.

"She's in love with me! Not some country hick who drives a truck and drinks Coors Light."

That does it. You can insult Jackson's hometown, but he draws the line at assuming he drinks light beer.

"Leave my family's property. Now."

"Or what? Are you going to hit me?" Mark walks right up to Jackson, who has at least thirty pounds and three inches on him. Jackson could break him like a twig. My hand is still over my heart for what Jackson said to Mark. How he stuck up for me.

"Back up, buddy," Jackson warns. I cover my eyes with my hands but create a break in them so I can see what's about to happen.

Embarrassment creeps through my chest. Whatever did I see in Mark? Jackson has been more of a friend to me than Mark ever was. I want to fold into myself for ever thinking Mark was fantastic, that he was sexy.

He's nothing compared to Jackson.

While everything about this is problematic, my core clenches watching Jackson stand up for me and insinuate he could please me in bed better than Mark could.

"Is this okay?" I whisper to Emily. "Like the business won't get in trouble?"

"Please. The PR we'll get if this guy tries to hit Jackson.

Goldheart folks hate guys like Mark. Look at everyone just staring. This is epic."

"I'm going to ask you again. Please leave," Jackson says.

"Not until I talk to Shiloh." Mark touches his chest to Jackson's. Jackson's jaw grinds and his nostrils flare, but he's keeping his cool impeccably.

"Back up, buddy. This is your last warning."

Woody Finch's customers are watching like Romans at the Coliseum.

"Or what?" Mark bumps Jackson's chest again.

Jackson pulls out his cell phone. "I'm calling the police."

Jackson turns and walks away, and I've never been prouder.

It all happens in a flash. Mark follows him and pulls his arm to spin him and lands a fist right in Jackson's cheek. His glasses go flying and he stumbles a couple steps, but he stands up, cracks his neck, and winds up, delivering a much stronger right hook to Mark's jaw. Mark lays flat on the ground as Jackson shakes out his hand.

Mark deserved that.

"Get that piece of shit out of here," Jackson says, pointing, as he rubs his cheek, red from the impact of my loser ex's fist.

Three men descend onto Mark, picking him up by the arms.

I rush over to Jackson and touch his arm. He tried to turn his head away from me, but his cheek is puffing up by the second.

"Are you okay?" I ask.

"Fine. He didn't hit me that hard. He probably wishes he hadn't."

The guys park Mark on a picnic bench, his elbows on his knees and his head hung low. I find Jackson's glasses and hand them to him. Miraculously, they didn't break.

"I'm so sorry I brought this drama. I thought he was done, honestly," I say.

Jackson touches my arm. "Don't be sorry. He needs to learn he can't throw away a person like you."

"Let's get you some ice, Jackson," Emily says. She jerks her head toward Mark. "Do you want to talk to him?"

I shake my head. "No. I don't want to talk to him ever again."

"Do you want me to call the police? Put hands on him?" Emily asks, pushing her sleeves up and tightening her ponytail.

"Please don't punch him, Emily," I say.

"Let me at him. I had a horrible customer leave a one-star review, so I have some anger I need to unleash."

"You can yell at him. I'll take care of Jackson."

"I can do that," Emily says as she storms toward Mark, surrounded by the same three men who carted him away like a corpse.

I take Jackson by the arm, although he can walk fine by himself. Our customers pat his arm, telling him he did a good job and they're proud of him. We walk to the employee breakroom where there's ice and a first aid kit.

Sitting him down, I turn to the cabinet and find the white box and a cup to fill ice with. I pull a plastic bag out of our stash and fill it with ice. We don't talk as I rummage for what he needs.

"Okay, let's see what we have," I say, after the items I need are spread on the table.

My fingertips touch Jackson's cheek so I can tilt his head to the light. There's a small cut, about an inch long above a swelling, reddening bump. It could develop into a shiner, and I will do everything possible to mitigate the damage.

"Do you need to go to the ER? I can drive you. Pay you back."

"No, it's fine." Jackson contorts his face, opening his eye wide and moving his jaw. "Man, it's been a long time since I've been punched. It wasn't very hard, but still." He winces as I dab a cotton ball drenched with hydrogen peroxide on it.

"You took it like a champ."

"I tried," Jackson says. He looks up at me. "I'm sorry I spoke for you."

"It's okay."

It's more than okay. It was the sexiest thing a man has ever done for me.

I can't say that to him. Our friendship confuses me, but it's my favorite thing about my life in Goldheart. I don't want to mess it up.

"You deserve the very best, Sunny. The very, very best."

Swallowing is hard as I wipe away the residue and pat it dry with a clean cotton ball. He touches my wrist, briefly, and drops his hand back in his lap. My heart thumps at his touch, and I hold my breath, so I don't inhale his scent.

It's becoming harder and harder to be around him and my stomach not to do a full gymnastics floor routine. Right now, it's going for the gold medal.

"Did you learn first aid at the same place you got haircuts?"

I laugh. "My sister Summer used to get in fights when we were kids. She was called 'Stinky Summer' one too many times by Tamra Watson. I learned how to do laundry at seven because of that. And how to dress wounds so Mom wouldn't notice. She still did, but I got better at it. We also covered a black eye once with makeup."

"Summer sounds like a riot."

"She is. Let's just say she would've hit Mark first and asked questions later. You have a lot more restraint than her." I press the bandage down to make sure it sticks, and my fingertips drift to the swelling around the gauze. His skin is puffy, but soft. He takes my hand and drops it, holding it. He intertwines his fingers with mine, and I cannot breathe.

Time stops. I do not know what is about to happen. I'm standing in front of him, and Jackson is at my chest, staring up at me.

This feels romantic, but it's not. It can't be. No way.

"Thank you, Shiloh."

"You're welcome" comes out breathier than I expected.

Jackson lifts out of his seat and towers over me. I swallow, hard, as his hands rest on my arms. His stare sears me. My eyes close, and I lift my chin slightly. The air moves, and I wonder if he's lowering his head or if he's lifting the ice to his chin. The door opens and I jump, stepping back, out of Jackson's grip. Jackson spins away, creating distance between us.

"Mark's gone," Emily says. "Lance is outside. He wants to talk to you."

Lance is the chief of police in Goldheart. I've met him a couple times when he's come in for a beer on the weekends with his wife.

"I'll be out soon," Jackson says.

If this was a moment, it's now over.

Jackson holds the ice to his face as he walks out, lingering in the doorframe. "Thanks for your help, Sunny." Emily follows him out and I'm left in this breakroom, shell-shocked.

I scrunch my nose and shake my face. A cold sweat overcomes me. Was he lowering his head to kiss me? My eyes were closed so I can't be sure. He could've pitied me, laughed in a way you don't make sound.

She thinks I'm going to kiss her, she's so silly. That's absolutely what he was thinking.

21

JACKSON

I almost kissed Shiloh.

She looked up at me with lips parted and temptation was too great. Because of the height difference, I had to bridge the space between us, and my neck was mid-bend when my sister interrupted. Shiloh jumped back when she saw Emily, and I spun away.

"Do you think this is right?" Emily asks as we park at Goldheart Community Park. I wait for my sister to mention it, but she doesn't bring it up, even as we're on the way to bamboozle our dad. We hatched the plan last week. Our dad is the hardest person to shop for. He always says he doesn't want anything, he has everything he needs. The man will wear his favorite T-shirt until it has holes in it and reads all his books from the library. He loves beer, but he would be insulted if you gifted him anything but Woody Finch, and it makes no sense to give him his own product.

However, this is the one present we can get him, but we can't show up with the dog. There's too much at risk. I want to make sure my dad wants the dog. That's why we're orchestrating a blind date that my dad doesn't know about with Koda.

"This could be a disaster, but this is a really good idea," Emily had said when I brought it up.

"I figured since the last one died on my watch," I say with a chuckle, but Emily looks at me with a straight face.

"Don't joke about it. That wasn't your fault," Emily says. "It was just a freak accident. You had nothing to do with it."

"Kinda feels like it was," I say as we walk to the park. Patches of melted snow adorn the ground, but the dog still looks alert, the tail standing straight up and flowing back and forth as we approach. He's not barking; that's good.

The director of the rescue, Priscilla Veracruz, waves, her dark hair hidden by a soft grey beanie.

"Hi Jackson, nice to see you again," Priscilla says, shaking my hand and then shaking my sister's hand. I kneel and the dog puts his paws on my knees, licking my face like it's made of chicken breast.

"So, you remember me," I say. I rub the dog's head, and he opens his mouth, panting. "How has he been?"

"Rambunctious, but he's a happy-go-lucky dog. Loves people. The prior owner did a great job. So, your dad? We're surprising him?"

My sister and I nod and let out a dual sibling breath. "We're not sure he's ready yet. His previous dog died at the beginning of the year."

"I know. We were so sad when Woody passed."

I tilt my head. "You knew Woody?"

"He got Woody from the rescue. He's been donating to Working Buddies for years."

"Did you know?" I ask Emily. She shakes her head. "Do you think he knows about the dog? Is this not a surprise?"

"No, he doesn't look at the pictures. Says he'd take them all home if he did," Emily says.

"Do you know if Randy is ready for another dog?" Priscilla asks.

"We don't know. We just think he needs to meet him."

"I get it. He's great."

Gravel crunches a few feet away, and we turn to see our dad's black Suburban pulling up. He hops out, with a confused crinkle of the eyebrows.

He wears his uniform—distressed jeans and a forest green polo shirt with the Woody Finch logo on it. He's a guy who always smiles, is always in a good mood, but he melts when he sees the dog.

"Priscilla, it's nice to see you again." He takes her in a half hug before he goes for what he really wants. The dog.

He kneels, and Koda approaches him slowly, then goes for his face, tongue first. He wiggles under his hands as he pets him. "Who is this?"

"This is Koda. Isn't he sweet?"

"Is this why you wanted me here?" he asks, looking back at us. He still pets the dog, without a hint of anger, rubbing his erect ears so effectively, the dog leans into his hand and groans.

"This is the dog Shiloh and I picked up a while ago, and I thought he might be a good fit. For you," I say. "He has similar coloring to Woody."

"Good personality too," Priscilla says. "He needs some training, but nothing you can't handle."

"You're just a puppy," my dad says, rubbing the dog's neck. Koda's tongue flops over the side, long and goofy. Dad gets close, and the dog nips at his nose lovingly.

I wasn't home when he first got Woody; I had already escaped to Seattle to get as far away from this town as possible. Emily told me about shredded flip-flops and the time Woody stole a whole package of tortillas from the counter and ate them all. Eventually, the dog calmed down once he realized he was safe and home. My dad took Woody everywhere. When he opened the brewery, he designed the office with a dog enclave, a carved-out space for a dog bed, dog bowls, and a hidden compartment for treats and toys. He still brings out the toys once in a while for the dogs that visit the brewery.

Without a dog to love, my dad smiles, but it's not the same.

He still rubs the dog's ears, and I can see the wheels in my dad's brain turning. He's thinking about how it will work. If he can love a dog as much as Woody.

"Did you two seriously set me up?" Randy asks. His hands haven't left this dog's fur, and the dog is living for it.

"Maybe," Emily says.

"It's time. Woody has been gone for almost a year," I say. As that comes out of my mouth, I shudder at my own hypocrisy.

A year did not even put a dent in my grief, and now, I'm telling my dad to get over a dog I'm sure he loved more than me.

Dad stands up, looking at the dog and Priscilla. His smile is sad, his eyes glassy. I know he misses his buddy, and seeing a German shepherd always gets him sentimental. He finally says, "Priscilla, excuse us. I'd like to talk to my children privately."

"Of course," she says. The dog is already distracted by a squirrel running up a tree.

Dad guides us closer to the jungle gym, his hands still on our mid-backs.

"We just thought you might want to meet the dog," Emily sputters.

"I appreciate it, sweetheart. I really do." He looks back at the dog wistfully. My dad does not hold in his emotions. He cries at movies, hugs us for no reason, and showers dogs with scratches and pets. His way of living gives me vicarious anxiety. I spent the eight years I was with Amy masking every emotion I had, bottling it, pushing it down.

Making sure no one, including Amy, saw the hurt and fear I had inside.

It must be so freeing, just to feel out loud.

My dad rubs the bridge of his nose. "That dog is really nice. I just...I don't think I'm ready. It's too much."

"It's okay, Dad," I say, as I slap his back and put my arm around him. "If it's not this dog, it might be another one."

"Thanks for arranging me to meet him, though," he says. Tears fill his eyes. "I just...I can't. I know that dog needs a good home, and I know I can give it..."

"I get it," Emily says, walking into Dad's arms. He wraps his arms around her, whimpering, as he breaks down. It makes me uncomfortable to see my dad cry. I know it's my thing, why I can't see it. I know Woody's passing wasn't my fault. I know Amy's passing wasn't my fault.

However, I witnessed both.

Guilt follows me like a stray dog, looking for chicken.

How could I love someone with my whole soul and turn around, years later, and feel for a woman who came out of nowhere?

I didn't expect Shiloh. Maybe that was the whole point.

22

SHILOH

"I'm not coming out," Jackson says from behind the bathroom.

"Come on out," I say into his door, cupping my voice so it travels. "I bet you look great in it."

"This is absolutely ridiculous, Sunny."

"Everyone will be jealous. Come on out."

I hear him coming before he opens the door. His sweater has bells and everything.

When he opens it, I gasp. "Oh my goodness, it's better than I expected."

"Please tell me other people will have ones this ridiculous as well."

"Absolutely. However, yours is the best."

Ugly Christmas sweaters is in my top five of favorite Christmas things.

The sweater I got Jackson is possibly the best ugly sweater I've ever seen.

His sweater is knit, showing a set of washboard abs that insinuate Santa has a six-pack and nipples pierced with bells. The ripped torso is against a mound of snow with a

Christmas tree and a mountain of presents. The abs disappear into red pants with a white fur trim.

"I look so goofy."

"Have you seen mine?" I put my cardigan on that comes complete with a battery pack because tree lights are woven within it and there's tinsel draping off it. Switching it on, it flickers and makes my face glow.

"Ugly sweaters are getting out of control." He looks down at it. "I can't believe I'm going to a party. In this. You're a bad influence."

"More like a *fun* influence!" I flick one of his bells. Jackson pretends to be aroused, his eyes closing blissfully. His eye is healing nicely, although there's a faint greenish-yellow hue to his cheek, instead of the pronounced bruise that was there right after it happened.

When we almost kissed in the breakroom.

I must've imagined it since he hasn't tried anything since. The hugs are platonic, nothing too long or too close. No more head tilts into mine. All I want for Christmas is Jackson, and I don't think I'll get him wrapped up in a present anytime soon.

It's just a crush. It will go away once I move back to Sacramento, once I let this go. It's a friendship that's convenient because of proximity. Once I'm gone, Jackson will retreat to his apartment and office, going back to ignoring folks who care about him.

I'll enjoy this version of Jackson while I can.

"Are you ready to go, my ripped Santa?"

"That's Mr. Santa to you," he says, turning to the hall mirror. He swings his hips back and forth to ring his bells, and I giggle. I grab my keys, getting one more bell flick in.

I offered to pick up Jackson so I could be his designated driver. My end of the bargain was the ugly Christmas sweater, and he gave me a death stare when he saw the sweater in all its glory.

I laughed for three minutes.

There's no hand touching or even singing on the way to the party. Everything is chill and casual between us.

You have been friend zoned, I think to myself, and I could cry it's so depressing.

We have so much fun together, and he told me I'm his best friend. Maybe that's all he has in him, to be someone's best friend right now. Although I would love to be promoted to lover. My mind races to inappropriate places all the time now.

His broad shoulders in that sweater are not helping.

"What are you thinking about?" Jackson asks.

Your tongue on my skin. "Pizza," I blurt out.

"Honestly, same. Not your kind, though."

"Pineapple on pizza is a delicacy," I say.

"My mom only orders that for you. No one else touches it. Fruit on pizza is gross, Sunny."

"People eat it! I've been to more of your family's parties, and I can confirm Emily eats it too. There's not a single chunk of pineapple left."

"Traitor. We should turn her out of the family," Jackson says.

"You can't," I say. "She's my favorite Finch."

His mouth drops like I just accused him of liking Fireball. "I thought I was your favorite."

"I bet Emily would appreciate a sweater like that and wear it proudly."

"This sweater is amazing. I love it. It's so fancy." He shimmies again to make the bells ring.

"That's better."

"Am I back on top?" he asks with a wink.

Don't think about sex. Do not think about him over you, I repeat to myself, holding my steering wheel as a death grip. The night is peaceful as we drive. With the right soundtrack, it could be either the scene for a horror or a romantic comedy. It rained earlier so the roads have a sheen, and the moon is full in the sky. Jackson and I are nowhere near romance, but I like to think that we're more than friends in this moment.

Even if it's just pretend.

"You're so quiet. Very unlike you."

I laugh, because my mind speeds through thoughts, all about him. Still, I deny it. "Just watching the road."

We arrive at the brewery and park in front. Jackson's face grows paler, as he inhales and exhales dramatically.

"You'll be fine. Everyone will be so happy to see you. I promise."

"I hope so. At least this amazing sweater my beautiful friend got me will be distracting enough."

Beautiful friend. I smile hard, to avoid any tears slipping free. This is a holiday party. No one should be sad at a holiday party.

Still, here I am, longing for something I can't have.

We walk into the space, decorated in gold and green, Michael Bublé's version of "Have Yourself a Merry Little Christmas" playing from the speakers up front. The sweaters are tacky and exquisite, but Jackson has the best one. He's been coming to more events, so people greet him with smiles and happiness, rather than curiosity or pity. He shakes the hands of everyone who approaches us. He told me a few weeks ago that I started a hug epidemic with him—people saw him hugging me with zero hesitation, so others started following suit. Cameron attacks him with a bear hug. Emily fits in his arms. Reid takes him in for a side hug.

I did that. It's because of me.

"Did Shiloh drive?" Cameron asks, handing Jackson a

beer. "That sweater is fantastic." He flicks one of Jackson's nipple bells.

"Yes, Shiloh drove, and yes, this is all Shiloh's fault," Jackson says, wrapping his arm around me. I analyze everything—the placement of his hand, how close his arm is to my back, whether he pulls me in or keeps me with enough space between us. My mind races so quickly that it's over before I've clocked it.

"It's a Christmas miracle," Emily says. She's the one to get misty as she smiles, wiping away her tear with a flick of the finger. "I'm just so happy we're all here together."

"Emily, do you think it's time for Shiloh's surprise?"

My face drops. A surprise? For me?

"What? You didn't need to get me anything," I say.

"It's not for you, per se," Jackson says, bumping into me. There he is, touching me again. "You inspired something."

Emily brings a glass bottle, full of a dark brown liquid. I squint in confusion.

"Turn it over," Jackson says into my ear. I try not to shiver.

I spin it, and I see the Woody Finch logo. Then I read the writing, and my mouth stretches in shock.

Rory's Root Beer. Non-alcoholic.

Made in Goldheart, CA

"This is just a prototype," Reid says. "We're still working on the recipe. Plus, our investor doesn't necessarily know we're testing it."

"I think Dan will say yes, but we need an official taste-tester," Jackson says. "A lot of sober folks might want to come and hang out with their friends, and now they have an option."

I can't help it. Big tears explode from my eyeballs.

He brewed me root beer. He named it after my soul dog. It might as well have been a diamond ring.

Jumping into Jackson's arms, I'm still crying, hiccuping with the tears.

"I guess she likes it. We'll wait until she tries it," Reid says.

"This is the sweetest thing anyone has done for me," I whisper. He rubs my back, and my legs wrap around his waist, anchoring me there. Mark never did anything like this. This is bigger than all the flowers and love notes I've ever received.

This is a gift on my behalf to folks like me who don't drink. It's a gift to my mother, who has an option when she comes to visit and wants to see where I work. The present is bigger than me; it does good.

It's my favorite kind of present.

When I detach myself from Jackson, Reid pries off the top and hands me the bottle. "Now, this is just the rough draft. Let me know what your thoughts are, since you are a connoisseur."

I wipe my tears away to tip the bottle back, letting the icy drink hit my lips. Once it hits the back of my throat, I cough. Violently.

It is not very good. It needs more flavor. Right now, it's a root-beer-flavored water.

"I don't like that face," Reid says, pointing at me. "Is it that bad?"

"It's fine, um…"

"Shiloh translation: it sucks, Reid," Jackson says. I let out a sigh of relief because I won't be the one to say it.

Reid rubs his beard. "Listen, I brew extremely hoppy beers for a living. I've never done this before."

"You'll figure it out. I'll help you. You have a good start. Thank you." I take Reid in for a hug, and he pats my back rapidly.

Once I pull away from Reid, Cameron slaps him so hard

on the back he lurches. "You better get your act together, Reid. You have a smoking hot girlfriend now, and I have a smoking hot pregnant girlfriend who demands a tasty non-alcoholic beverage."

"Shiloh, I promise I'll work on it," Reid says. "You will be my official taste-tester."

"Of course," I say. "It was a great first try!"

"You're too nice," Reid says.

Jackson leans in, and my eyelashes flutter at his proximity. "Be brutal. Reid needs to hear the feedback."

I stifle a laugh. Looking around the circle as they argue about root beer, my insides feel so warm, and it's just not my cardigan. The Finches carry a shared wonderful childhood, and for this moment, I pretend like I belong. Like I am a Finch, not an Abbott. I love my family, but any person would be so lucky to be a part of the Finch family.

Cameron looks up and then down. He points to a spot three or so feet to my left.

"Shiloh, will you stand there?"

"Sure." I take my spot like an actor in a rehearsal.

"And Jackson, stand next to Shiloh."

Jackson is more skeptical than I am. His eyes narrow. "Why?"

"Just do it."

He does, and then Cameron smacks his hands together and points. Emily covers her mouth. Reid waves his hands and says, "I want no part of this."

There, hanging next to the disco ball, is a bunch of green. Blood drains from my face. No.

Mistletoe.

Redness sprouts on Jackson's cheeks. I wonder what it means. Is it good? Embarrassed? Is he about to murder his brother?

All could be possible.

"It's tradition," Emily says. "You have to kiss her."

"That's not real mistletoe. You tricked us." Jackson's protests sink my heart like the Titanic. He doesn't want an excuse to kiss me.

"It's okay, Jackson. It's tradition." I turn toward him, and Jackson's lips quiver in silent protest. His wide eyes are startled, like he would rather kiss a rabid raccoon.

Will he go for the lips or a cheek? A platonic forehead kiss?

I try not to, but I'm hoping for a brush on the lips.

"Okay, fine," he says as he centers himself directly in front of me. My eyelids stay open, since I'm not going to be the person who closes her eyes, expecting a fairy-tale kiss, just to get a kiss fit for a relative. He leans in, and I swallow so hard it must be audible.

His lips land on my cheekbone, and my eyelashes flutter. Our contact sends a jolt through my torso, through my limbs. His hands stay at his side and when he pulls back, his eyes flick back and forth, searching my eyes for an answer. I smile widely; my entire jaw must be visible.

Jackson chuckles under his breath to no one in particular. "That was awkward."

"So awkward." I went from the highest high, to the lowest low. Maybe I wished too hard to be a little sister to the Finches, and now that's all he sees me as.

23

JACKSON

My sister shows up at my door at noon on New Year's Eve.

While the brewery is open, my parents tried to give the family today and tomorrow off for some semblance of work-life balance. We pay double-time so it's not difficult to find employees who need extra cash. I didn't spend my night wisely. I poured glass after glass of Scotch, chasing away my dread.

Every one of my family members has checked in on me, starting at nine this morning.

First, my mom knocked on my door, delivering a thermos of hot coffee, straight from her French press ("it's the best way to drink coffee, Jackson. I should've gotten you one for Christmas") and my beloved Danish from Gold Roast. I took it and invited her in, which resulted in her staring at me for ten minutes as I ate. She asked me if I was doing okay no less than eight times and finally left after getting a three-minute-long hug.

Reid called, while Cameron texted. Cameron is currently my favorite sibling.

Emily has always been confrontational, so an in-person

visit it is. I can ignore phone calls, but she figured out I will always open my door.

"Where's Olive?"

"With Mom." Emily walks in without an invitation. She crosses her arms and turns, looking me up and down. "So."

"So," I say, my head pounding. I sip some water to get rid of this hangover, but it's not helping. Yet.

"Do you have plans for tonight?" Emily asks.

"I don't know," I say, although I know what I'm planning. It's been ten years, today, and I hope going back to the spot where I lost her would help. Maybe the lake can tell me something, what to do about Shiloh.

I can't stop thinking about her. I also can't stop feeling guilty about it.

When I kissed her cheek at the Christmas party, I downplayed it, pretending like it didn't faze me. I wanted to kiss her for real. Take her in my arms and lift her to my lips, sink my fingers into her hair.

As Shiloh and I've gotten closer over the last few months, my feelings have only intensified. Fantasies of taking her to bed, spreading her out on my comforter and devouring her body—her lips, in between her legs, her breasts. Since Amy died, I have had zero desire to be with another woman.

Until a sober, sunny pixie who loves dogs came into my life. Forced me to be her friend.

Now I can't imagine life without her.

The way I'm feeling today reaffirms why it was a good idea not to pursue something. Shiloh is a beautiful and pure woman. I will fuck her up. After everything that has happened to me, I can't drag her down with me.

"I don't want you alone tonight. I don't think it would be healthy. I think you should call Shiloh."

"It's been ten years. I'm fine."

My sister tilts her head. She's always been able to see through my bullshit.

"Honest question: have you dated? Since Amy?"

I shake my head no. I rub my beard and run my fingers through my hair.

"Follow-up question," Emily says, and I tense. "Have you kissed anyone since Amy?"

I swallow and avert my gaze, shaking my head.

Emily covers her mouth. "I'm so sorry. We made you do that…"

"Shiloh is a good friend. I've kissed her on the head before."

My sister glares at me, and I don't know why. "Have you talked about Amy with her?"

"She only knows that I was married and that my wife passed away." No matter how many times I utter that phrase out loud, it still feels like a twist to the heart.

"Why don't you talk about her?"

"It's hard." My voice cracks and I grumble.

"You can't move on if you don't process it, Jackson." My sister means well, but my shoulders still hunch, and I can feel my rational mind shutting down. Emily continues, although I'm fighting my anger like a fire-breathing demon in my chest.

"I think Shiloh likes you. Like really likes you."

That can't be right. We're just friends. I run my fingers through my hair again. "I care about her."

"Do you think she's pretty?"

Of course, I do. I think about her hair and how it's so soft when it brushes my skin. How her blue eyes connect to mine, reach into my soul, and we recognize each other. When she walks into my arms for a hug, how I feel lighter, better. It's more than her beauty for me. I would be lying if I said I never got aroused around her. Quite the opposite. Every time I see her, I'm fighting it.

Emily rests her hand on my shoulder. "Maybe see what happens? You could be happy. With her."

"I don't know if I ever have it in me again. To be in love again."

"I think you do." Her hair falls in her face, and I see the pity. This is rich, coming from a woman who got pregnant in college and dropped out. She has not been on one date since she's had Olive. Or really talked about Olive's dad.

"Don't act like you didn't do the exact same thing when Olive came along." My words crack like a whip.

Emily's face scrunches into anger. She steps within feet of me, and while she's several inches shorter than me, she scares me.

"I *stayed*. I showed up for my responsibilities. People gossiped about me, but I still lived my life. I didn't get the *luxury* of running away. You forget I loved Amy too. She would be so hurt to see you living like this. She wouldn't have wanted this for you. You claim you loved her, but you pretend like she didn't exist."

I want to scream. I want to throw things and shatter it against a wall. Instead, I cross my arms, breathing in and out.

"You should really talk about her. I think it should be Shiloh. She's the best friend you've got, and she's a better person than me because I would've stopped being your friend a long time ago if I weren't related to you."

Emily walks to my door and her hand rests on the doorknob as she turns around. "I still love you. I want what is best for you. You just make me so fucking frustrated sometimes."

She rips the door open and leaves. Her face after I fired back imprints on my brain. Out of all my siblings, she's the strongest. Emily is the type of person who you think is okay because she puts on such a convincingly stoic front.

Then one day she crumbles.

I'm not sure how long I stand in the middle of my studio, letting her face and words cycle. When I come back to myself, I'm seated at my couch, my fingers drumming the couch armrest.

This is the worst day of my year. I just made this the worst anniversary of them all.

24

SHILOH

"What are you doing tonight?" I ask my sister on speaker phone. I swipe the nail polish brush across my big toe, getting some skin. "Papa is already in his pajamas with his nightcap."

"Papa is drinking?" Summer asks, alarmed. I caught her while she prepared to go out with her group of friends for New Year's. Summer still drinks once in a while, only on special occasions. She told me she's planning on one glass of champagne at midnight.

"No. Ben and Jerry's."

"Ooh, what flavor?"

"Cherry Garcia."

"Nice choice, Papa. I need to get up there to visit."

"We would love to have you. We're currently watching *Lost* from the beginning. We watched four episodes tonight. It's really addicting." I yawn. "I think I'll go to bed soon."

"Raging New Year's."

"Absolutely. You know me." My phone buzzes in my hand, and I pull it away from my ear, confused.

"Jackson is calling, I have to go."

"Maybe he's finally cashing in on that booty call." I've

told Summer about Jackson a little bit, how he punched Mark when he started it. "I like him already," Summer had said. "I can't tell you how many fantasies I've had of punching Mark."

She also made fun of me constantly because my crush is obvious. I hope she can hear my rolling eyes.

"Have fun tonight. Love you. Make good choices."

"Make some bad ones."

"Bye, Summer." I end the phone call and pick up his.

"Hey, what are you doing?" I ask.

"I'm at the lake." No happiness or light in his voice.

"Oh. Isn't it cold there?" There was a slight dusting of snow the day before last and it didn't last long. However, I have to imagine the wind is icy and unrelenting.

"Can you meet me here?"

I look at my phone. It's ten-ten. It will be dark and cold, but Jackson is asking me and whenever he asks me to do something, I jump at the chance. Always. No matter how cold I will be.

"Give me twenty minutes. Where are you?"

"Right off of the southwest access."

"Okay. I'll be there."

After taking my nail polish off (I was doing a terrible job anyway) and dressing in multiple layers, I drive to the southwest access and turn off the engine. I pull out my phone to dial Jackson's number, but I see a small beacon of light and get out.

I can make out the lake, a strip of dark blue ink against the black sky. The stars are so bright, glimmering like twinkles in a child's eye. Lights from houses frame the lake, and it's so peaceful in this spot. It's cold, but I understand why Jackson is out here.

Shivering, I walk toward the light and see the seated outline of a person. They are hunched over on a blanket, holding a block. The lantern sits next to them, lodged into the sand.

"Jackson?" I ask, my voice small.

"Hi Sunny," his strong voice says. He pats the blanket next to me, and I sit down, my big jacket touching the material of his sweater.

"Why are you out here?" I ask, my teeth chattering. "It's so late. And it's New Year's Eve."

"Are you cold? I have an extra blanket."

"Sure," I say. He wraps me in one. I wait for him to explain why he's sitting alone in the dark, with only the wind whipping the lake waters into baby waves on the shore.

After a few minutes, he says, "Today is the anniversary of Amy's death."

"Wow," I say. "Really?"

"Ten years. She's been gone longer than we were together."

Darkness covers his face, so I can't search his features. Am I on the verge of hearing everything? I'm ready and unprepared, all at once.

"She loved this lake. She wanted to see it one last time. I tried to talk her out of it, but she was so stubborn. I put as many layers on her as I could, and we drove out here."

Jackson wipes his face, his face pointed to the dark ink of the water. "She always loved New Year's. Said it was your annual chance to start over. She made resolutions every year, and she's still the only person I've ever known who stuck to them. On New Year's Eve, she would always tell me what hers were, and ask me if I had any. I never did. The night she died, she didn't tell me any. I know now she was trying make it to one more new year. When the clock struck midnight, I turned to kiss her, and she was gone."

I wrap my arm around him, pulling him close. He sniffles

as our foreheads touch. If there was a way to take his pain, I would.

"How did you meet?" I ask.

"High school." He laughs from deep within him. "Amy and I were in the same classes growing up, and she was always nice to me, but we didn't really know each other. She was quiet, kept to herself, didn't really have friends.

"I was in my junior year, and I had no extracurricular activities for college. So I decided to join band. My friends made fun of me for weeks, but I loved it. I played the snare."

I point to myself. "Clarinet."

"No kidding."

I nod, although it so dark he can't see me. "Played it all four years. Got first chair and everything."

"Look at you, Miss Fancy Pants."

I grab Jackson's hand and interlace my fingers with his. "Tell me more about her."

He squeezes my hand. "Amy made me feel welcome immediately. She played the flute. Band was surprisingly fun. We went on these band trips together, and I would sit next to her every time. The more time I spent with her, the more I wanted to be around her. I kissed her at the Homecoming game, and that was it. We went to the dance together, and she wore this pink dress. I will never forget the way I felt when I saw her. I felt so *alive*. I think I fell in love with her then."

This breaks my heart since I know the ending of the story.

Jackson inhales. "We had been dating for three months when she was diagnosed with leukemia."

"Oh, Jackson."

He takes another ragged breath, and I forget about the cold or the wind. All that matters is this man I care about deeply telling me about the most pivotal person of his life.

"She tried to break up with me. Said she didn't want me

to see her like this. I was already in love with her so there was no way I was letting her go through it alone. I refused, and she nodded once. She grabbed my hand, and I saw a tear in her eye.

"When we were killing time at chemotherapy, we made a New Life List. She loved New Year's resolutions, so we made one for when she went into remission. There were so many. See a Broadway musical in New York. Take one perfect picture. Amy was really into photography. Try sushi. See the town in Ireland her grandparents were from. Go to college. One day, she asked me to pull out the list, and she said she wanted "marry Jackson Finch" on it. I started planning the proposal immediately. The day she rang the bell that the cancer was gone and she was officially in remission, I took her to this spot and dropped down to one knee and proposed. She said yes. We were twenty.

"We got married in a small ceremony in her parents' church and had brunch after. We went to Ireland that next week for our honeymoon. We started knocking out the list, bit by bit. I had been taking classes while she was in treatment, but Amy got to experience college for the first time. She wanted to be an oncology nurse. The night she graduated she spiked a high fever, and we took her to the ER. We found out the night we marked off the last item on the New Life List that the cancer was back.

"I kept insisting we make a new list for when she beat cancer again, but she was hesitant. She knew it was different that time. Treatment didn't work. She just got sicker. We tried everything. We did a stem cell transplant, and that didn't work, and it became clear we were going to lose her. She was put on hospice around Thanksgiving."

He's quiet, but I hear his breath quake, silently crying out years of unexpressed emotion.

"Is that why Thanksgiving is hard?"

He nods. Jackson grabs my hand, encased in a huge mitten, and pulls me close.

"Her dad's insurance couldn't afford an at-home nurse, so my dad stepped in, no questions asked, and arranged it. We moved into my parents' house, and Amy had a full set-up and a full-time nurse. I can never repay my parents for what they did."

Jackson wipes his face, but a tear drops on my cheek. I'm glad he's getting this out. My gut tells me he hasn't told this story in full to anyone, and I'm the first person he's telling it to.

"I'm honored you're telling me about her."

The tears flow freely from my face; I don't bother to wipe them away. My heart breaks for Amy, a woman I've never met, and how much Jackson loved her.

My tears must've given silent permission to Jackson because I hear his tiny sobs with his tears, and we hold each other.

When the tears stop, we sit there in silence. I check my phone and we're inching closer to midnight.

"I wanted to drink today. I wanted to, so bad. I usually get so hammered, pass out, and don't make it to midnight. I picked a hell of a year to be sober for this. That's how I ended up out here, crying my eyes out, to you."

"You shouldn't feel ashamed for crying. You loved her."

"I did. Very much."

"She sounds amazing. Like I would've been friends with her."

"I think you would've been good friends. You remind me of her a lot. She was always helpful. Always giving. Thought about others more than herself. She was a much better person than me. I still can't believe that she chose me. Me."

My bones ache with his words. She would've liked me.

The woman who Jackson has held a candle for, all this time, had some of my qualities. It's flattering and breaks my heart.

"I know why she chose you" comes out as a whisper and he turns his head.

"What did you say?"

"Nothing! Do you have a picture of her?" I ask, changing the subject. "I didn't see any in your house."

"Sure," he says, pulling out his phone. He sniffs as he scrolls through. "I keep a good one of us on my phone, although most of them are on my hard drive."

His fingers stop and he freezes, staring at his screen before he turns it to me.

My heart drops, seeing it.

It's their wedding picture. Amy is freakin' gorgeous.

She stands next to Jackson in a lacy, long-sleeved gown, holding a bouquet of white flowers, the most elegant bride I've ever seen. She's tall and slender, with dark hair curled around her shoulders. Her skin is clear, and her makeup minimal. I see a hint of a gold ring on her left hand, and my stomach clenches.

His ring on her finger.

My eyes drift to young Jackson next. He's clean-shaven with a big smile, bigger than I've ever seen on him. His hair is shorter than it is now, even with my haircut, and he looks so handsome in a brown suit with an off-white tie. They are both so young and happy, and the way Jackson holds her in the photo gives me goosebumps. I'm getting a glimpse of how he was before.

When he was happy.

He tucks the phone away and sniffles, staring out to the lake. The wind has died down, and now it's calm and the surface looks like glass.

I glance at my phone. Twelve-oh-one.

"Happy New Year," I say.

"Happy New Year," he repeats, looking out to the lake. He still holds me, and I'm warm in his arms. I cannot get used to this. I am just a stand-in for the woman he wants with him on this day. That woman who made him so happy in the picture.

"Why did you come?" Jackson asks.

"You asked me to," I say. "I care about you."

"You care about me?" he repeats.

"Yes, very much." *I think I love you. No matter how messed up you are, every time you touch me, I go weak. However, I don't think you care about me in the same way and rightfully so. You've already had one love of your life, and there's only room for one of those.*

My words hang in the stillness of the night, the gravity of his story and words. I know I should pull back, that I should save my heart from inevitable heartbreak.

I can't.

"Thank you so much. For being here," he says, bringing my hand to his lips, laying a kiss on my knuckle. "That's your New Year's kiss."

I want to jump out of my skin, but I keep it cool. "Thank you. Wasn't sure I would get one this year."

"I'm sure you didn't expect to ring in the new year with a crying grown-ass man either."

"That too."

"If things were different…" he says and trails off. My spine shoots straight as I try to decipher his facial expression in the darkness. "If *I* were different…"

My breath catches in my throat, but I press my palm into his forearm. "Don't say it."

"Don't say what?"

"Whatever you're going to say. About us."

"Okay." His head turning back to the lake. He grabs my other hand and pulls it in, tucked into the warmth of his body.

"We're great friends," I say out loud, hoping I will believe that's all we are. That my hopes cannot raise higher than a good companionship. Jackson Finch is off-limits, not because he's the boss's son or because my time in Goldheart is temporary. I've been down this road with an unavailable man before, and my heart knows better. I've heard *If things were different* before.

Jackson is not remotely available, and although I'm desperately in love with him, I can't let myself be broken again.

After a few moments, he says, "I don't think I'm going to drink for a little while."

"Oh?"

"Yes. I think I need a break. I didn't drink today. Or yesterday, I guess."

"It's always a good idea to take a break. Do Dry January."

"Dry January?" He pulls me closer, and I resist my thoughts going anywhere but finding warmth.

"People take January off from drinking as a new year reset."

"That's my New Year's resolution, then. Don't drink in January," he says. "What's yours? Do you have a New Year's resolution?"

"No." *Fall out of love with you. Stop dreaming about you. Stop thinking about you every second of every day.*

We sit for a few more minutes, the temperature plummeting. Jackson no longer keeps my shivers at bay; I'm vibrating in his arms, the only sound we hear is teeth chattering.

"I think it's time to go home," he says. "Do you want to come back to my place?"

I freeze under his arm. I know he doesn't mean anything sinister, and I ache to go. It's not a good idea, even if it's to hang out. He has limited places to sit, and sitting on his bed would break me.

"It's probably best I go home," I say, standing as he stands as well. He wraps his arms around me in a hug, his chin resting on my head.

"Thank you for coming," he says. His lips brush against my temple, and a fresh shiver goes through my body. "Text me when you make it home safely."

"You're welcome," I say. "I'll text you. Call me later if you're having a hard time today, okay?"

"I will." He walks me to my car, and before I can get in, he takes me in for another hug. This one lingers, and I could melt, even though it's thirty degrees out.

When I drive away, I start sobbing, my vision so blurry, I consider pulling over, but I want to get home. Tears drip from my chin as I pull into my grandfather's apartment complex. I lean my forehead against the steering wheel and cry.

I cry for Amy. I cry for Jackson. Although it would mean Jackson and I wouldn't be close like we were, I wish she were alive to ring in the New Year with him.

In honor of her, I will try my best to fall out of love with her husband. That's my New Year's Resolution.

I fucked up.

First, I said out loud that I want to take a break from drinking, and now I haven't had a drink in five days. It's torture. I almost accidentally drank twice, bottle of Scotch in hand before I remembered my promise to Shiloh. Telling her of all people I don't want to drink was an even worse mistake because I can't backpedal. I will not be drinking until February first, and it sucks.

The embarrassment of New Year's plays in my head constantly, because I can't numb it with alcohol.

That's not the worst of my mistakes from New Year's.

The biggest one: I cried in front of Shiloh. I unloaded everything about Amy to a woman I have non-platonic feelings for and then asked her to come back to my place. As soon as the words left my mouth, I wanted to take them back. I didn't expect sex or any physical intimacy, but I hoped she would say yes. I'm not sure how she took it, if she saw it as completely friendly or saw the unintentional sexual overtone.

I've tried to run into her at work, but it hasn't worked. I've texted her a couple times, receiving short responses.

Since I'm not drinking, my mind ping-pongs from one speculation to another.

I'm so lost in my own thoughts at our Wednesday meeting that Reid slams my favorite beer, the Prospector IPA, in front of me, before I can decline. Our investor, Dan Price, is back from his vacation, and he likes to drink, no matter what time it is, so we usually partake as well. We used to do coffee and pastries, but Dan just drank beer and was happy with crackers so we don't swing by Gold Roast anymore.

The man has millions of dollars, but throw together a small charcuterie and serve him beer at nine o'clock in the morning, and he's completely satisfied.

"How was your vacation?" I ask Dan, touching the beer but not drinking it.

"Beautiful. Enthralling. Rejuvenating. Highly recommend."

"Did Makenna have a good time as well?" Emily asks.

"The best. She's been working so much that it was good to get away." Dan studies the phone and sighs before putting it away. "Did everyone hold down the fort?"

Reid nods to me and takes over.

"We had an idea while you were gone, Dan, and we're working on it. As you know we have an employee who doesn't drink…"

"Shiloh Abbott. Lovely girl. Does anyone know if she's single? My lawyer needs to meet someone, ASAP."

"She's single." I cough afterwards, my throat scratchy. My entire family glares at me. "Anyway, we came up with an idea for our sober folks who come in. Shiloh loves root beer, so we've been considering adding one to the menu. We can roll out some of our lower-performing beers to free up the funds…"

"Say less, I love that idea. Have you come up with a recipe?"

I look at Reid, and he nods. "We're working on it. We've made a couple batches. It's still a work in progress."

"Great, I love it. Let's do it," Dan says, smiling. He looks at me, and his smile drops. "Your face got three shades of red when I mentioned Shiloh. What's going on with that?"

My family leans in.

"Nothing," I say.

"Thumper saw you out at the lake with her on New Year's Eve. Him and Izzie snuck out there," Cameron says. Thumper is Cameron's best friend. He started dating his girl-friend, Izzie, a few months after they got stuck in a bank vault together when an ex of Thumper's robbed the bank wearing a chicken costume.

My family's chests are practically flat to the table to listen. Man, that beer looks delicious. I squirm in my seat.

"Are you interested in Shiloh? My lawyer saw her and was interested in asking her out. She was nice to him for five seconds."

"Um," I say, "I'll ask her. We're doing inventory tonight."

"Great. You let me know, then." Dan looks down at my beer. "Are you taking medication or something? Usually you're on your second one by now."

"I'm not drinking for the month of January," I say. The crowd whips back, their backs board straight, flabbergasted. I don't think they've seen me sober for a single meeting since I came home to help with the brewery's finances.

"Good for you," Emily says. "Truly."

"That's great, Jackson," my mom says, her voice quivering with emotion.

Cameron moves the beer to Reid. "Here. You need it."

Whitney broke up with Reid at Christmas. He's been moping around the brewery ever since. Reid takes a big gulp and winces. The Prospector is extremely hoppy, even for us, and you can't drink it quickly unless you want to crawl out of your skin.

We discuss a few more business matters, and I provide Dan with December's numbers. He nods and looks at them, but mostly he drinks and eats salami.

"If there's nothing else, I need to get going. I have my personal trainer in an hour, and if I show up intoxicated, he'll make me do burpees until I throw up." He stands and shakes everyone's hand.

When he gets to me, he pulls me in. I'm almost a foot taller than him, but I'm generally intimidated by him.

"Talk to Shiloh."

I'm not sure what this means.

Thinking about Dan's lawyer dating Shiloh gnaws my stomach. I've met him once, and while he's a nice guy, he's not right for her. He doesn't know what she likes or what gets her going. He hasn't heard stories about Rory and doesn't know what her childhood was like. He doesn't know how her laugh gets higher the funnier she thinks something is. That she's obsessed with Mandy Moore and chicken pesto sandwiches.

How she feels in my arms.

"You'll be okay, just the two of you, with inventory?" my dad asks. The rest of my family studies me.

"Absolutely. I don't think it will take too long." My dad is closing the brewery early tonight; usually Wednesdays are the deadest days of the week. When we discussed who in the family was going to do it, most of them came up with excuses. Cameron had an ultrasound with Annie, Emily had to pack orders for her jewelry business, Reid mumbled something and my parents dismissed him because he's sad.

Cameron nudges me on the way back to our offices. "There are no cameras."

"What?"

Cameron's voice grows louder. "I said, there are no cameras back there. It's on the honor system."

"What are you talking about?"

"Dad didn't like the idea of spying on our employees or the staff. No matter how much Reid suggests it, he refuses to do it. So, if you were to try something with Shiloh…"

"I'm not going to try anything with Shiloh." She refused my invitation to my house, so I doubt she'll want to do anything in a semi-public place. I walk past Cam, and he follows me like a golden retriever.

"You and Shiloh will be alone in the brewery. Not a soul in sight. Mom and Dad have that dinner…"

"Did you all conspire to make this happen?" I hate that I'm the center of my family's schemes right now.

"No, we didn't. However, Shiloh is a great choice, to you know. To get back out there."

"She's an employee! She's my friend! And she's twenty-six. I'm not just going to use her to break some seal." My fists clench at my sides.

"The eldest son doth protest too much, methinks."

My brother quoting Shakespeare? What is happening?

"Okay, Queen Gertrude," I say, walking into my office. Sitting down in my chair, I spin to my computer, but my oafish brother follows me.

"I see the way you look at her. It's different. I just…" Cameron trails off as I turn around. My glare causes him to back away with his hands raised. "Just remember, no cameras, and no one outside can see in."

He finally leaves my office. I prop my elbow on the desk and rest my chin on the heel of my hand. The numbers swim on our master spreadsheet, and without thinking, I pull out my phone and open my text thread with Shiloh.

Me: *I'll see you tonight at seven-thirty*

I lay my phone screen down and rub the length of my face.

The phone buzzes, and I turn it over.

Shiloh: *Can't wait. See you then.*

I can't wait either.

26

SHILOH

Taking a deep breath, I stand in front of the employee entrance door. I've raised my fist to knock three times but chickened out because I know who is on the other side.

Seeing Jackson is easy. He's my friend. Sure, he cried in front of me and opened up, and I have so many hormones charging through me every time I see him, but I can keep that under wraps. Right?

"You're being silly," I say to myself as I knock on the door.

Jackson opens the door, seconds later, and he smiles bigger than I've ever seen from him.

"Sunny, hi," he says. His body language tells me he wants to hug me, but I don't lean in. It's best we keep this professional. Purely platonic. I will keep my New Year's resolution.

"Hi, Jackson. Are you ready to do inventory?" I ask, using his name instead of Wally. His eyebrows collapse into each other, and his smile is unsure as I pass him. After I shed my jacket, I push the sleeves of my long-sleeved shirt up. I wanted to look cute but not too cute today. My hair is down, and the only makeup on my face is a quick slick of mascara. I tell myself I wanted to feel pretty for me, but I'm a liar.

Jackson's hair looks nice, completely combed back, and his beard is trimmed, light years better than when I first met him. I gave him a trim around Christmas, and he's taking my styling advice. He smells so good, like manly cedar and amber, and I can't get too close to him because I will smell him like a vampire in *Twilight*.

He offers to take my jacket, and I hand it over. I cross my arms, my nipples perked from the cold air. It's not from Jackson, no, it's not.

A low warm glow from behind the bar is the only light source. The brewery looks so different empty against the pitch black of nightfall.

I look at my reflection in the window, wondering what I'm doing here. Why I willingly put myself in a situation to be disappointed by another man, a man who doesn't want me as much as I want him. This will be a battle of wills. I can be just friends with a devastatingly handsome, broken man who has the heart of a marshmallow. A man who platonically created a whole new menu item for me because I don't drink.

"We'll count the cans first and then move to the items in the storage room," Jackson says, going to our beverage cooler behind the bar. "I'll give you the amount, and you can write it down."

"Sounds good." He hands me a clipboard with a printed spreadsheet to add in the numbers. I drop it on the bar so I can hop up, but I'm not strong enough or it's too tall for how small I am.

"Do you need help?" Jackson asks. There's levity in his voice. "I can lift you."

"I'm good," I say, although I'm sweating. Two more failed attempts, and I feel a hand on my waist I wasn't prepared for. He plops me on the shiny surface and the space between my legs clenches.

Just a friendly friend helping you out. There's nothing sexual about this.

How I wish that was true, that he would plop me on a surface and devour me.

Adjusting on the hard bar top, I grab the clipboard and place it in my lap.

Jackson opens the refrigerator door, and he begins counting the beers, shouting the type and the numbers to me. His smile is always present nowadays, and it's so handsome I have to look away sometimes.

"Dan came to our meeting today," Jackson mentions. "Twelve of the Prospector IPA."

I mark twelve on my sheet. I really like the Finches' investor Dan. He's a hoot. "Oh? How was his trip?"

"It seems like it was great," Jackson says. "Do you know his attorney? Andrew?"

I remember a thin man with glasses who I chatted with for ten minutes one day when Dan brought him in. "I met him once. Seems nice enough."

Jackson stops, raising his chin. "Dan asked if you were single. Supposedly, Andrew mentioned something."

"Really?" I ask. My conversation with Andrew didn't have a breath of flirt in it, but it flatters me that he's interested.

"Yeah." Jackson pauses, his hand on top of a can. "Are you?"

I cover my chest with the clipboard and bite my lip. I don't know how to answer that.

The truth is too raw, too real. *No matter how I fight it, I can't be interested in anyone but you.*

"Andrew's nice. Maybe."

Is that a hint of a smile on his lips? Did his body just relax? "Maybe?"

My heart thumps in my chest, and the heat in my cheeks flare.

I have to do something to get over you.

He turns his head, and our eyes catch. My gaze drops down to my clipboard, and a string of curses cross my mind. Our eye contact gave me away, and now it'll be awkward, I just know it.

"Gold Dust IPA, eight," he says, letting the cooler door close on its own. He turns toward me fully, and his stare brands my skin. I mark down the number with a shaky hand and deep breaths.

"Sunny," he says. He inches toward me, one hand pressed to the bar. His nearness is driving me wild, and I need to keep my wits about me.

When I look up, his green eyes study me. I stand strong, meeting his gaze. If I can hold it, I can keep my secret.

"You're acting strangely. For you," he says.

"I am?" I ask, too quick to be convincing.

"You're being weird."

"*You're* being weird." I hop off the bar, accidentally brushing against him as I walk toward the cooler to count the next row.

"What are you doing?" Jackson asks.

"Our job."

"Shiloh," he says, his hand gripping my bicep. His hands hover on my arms, barely touching. I can't look up at him. Thank goodness I'm short, or I might grab the back of his neck and kiss him. My eyes focus on the wood grain on the floor.

"Look at me," he says. I resist until he takes one finger and lifts my chin. The earth slows down; I cannot breathe. My eyelids flutter as I finally look at him. His pupils flick back and forth, considering me.

I squeeze past him and let out the fakest laugh of my life. "Jackson, I'm fine. Completely fine. You're the one being weird."

"You just called me Jackson. Again."

"So?" I open the cooler and my fingertips dance on the can tops, pretending to count.

"Fine. I'll go out with Andrew. He seems nice enough."

"You'll go out on a date with him. *Him.*"

"Sure. Maybe it's time I get back out there. It's been enough time since Mark."

Jackson's eyebrows scrunch together, and his eyes narrow in on me.

"Now, who's being weird?" I ask. "You're my friend. Be happy for me."

"No."

My breath catches in my lungs. I stand up, inching close to him. "Why?"

For seconds, he does nothing, just shoves his hands in his pockets. "I want you for myself."

Did I hear him correctly? "What?"

He takes one step towards me, our bodies inches from one another's.

"I should've done this under the mistletoe."

Jackson leans down and takes my mouth with his.

His lips are frozen on mine at first. He doesn't move, just holds my arms in his hands. My body goes rigid; I'm thunderstruck. Is this really happening right now? Heat radiates through my cheeks as our lips fuse together, unmoving, testing.

My hands cup his jaw when he pulls back, his eyes dart back and forth. I rub my lips together and commit to be bold.

"It's about time," I say. Jackson scoops me up, in a tizzy of lips and tongues.

His mouth melts into mine, and my body is an inferno as our faces tilt back and forth, our lips moving together. The way his pelvis presses into me, I can feel the outline of his cock hard against my belly. We could make love if we wanted to, but this moment is too precious to rush. It's been months of buildup. I want to enjoy this.

We explore each other's mouths, and I sink into his embrace further. A tiny moan leaves my mouth, and he growls, his mouth leaving my lips to trail down my throat. My head bends, letting him take what he wants, my core screaming.

His hands drift to my backside, squeezing my ass, and my feet leave the ground as he sets my butt onto the bar top. He pushes my legs apart so he can fit between them; I'm taller than him now as we kiss.

I expected him to be rusty, but everything about this is perfection.

Kissing Jackson exceeds my wildest dreams.

We lose track of time as we kiss. I'm gasping for air, but I go back under.

I pull away and jerk when I see the clock. "Wally, it's nine o'clock."

"What?" He turns with puffy lips, his skin flush. "Oh shit."

"We need to finish." I scramble off the bar. I point to the hall. "I need to go to the bathroom."

Way to kill the mood, I tell myself.

"Sure, of course." He steps back and rubs his beard. The bathroom is unlocked and smells faintly of bleach, a last task for the closer to give the bathrooms a quick cleanse so they're ready for the next day.

When I look in the mirror, my chin is red from Jackson's beard and my flyways create a ring of blond around my head. I look like a mad woman, so I cackle. That really happened.

I made out with my best friend. He grabbed my ass. I felt his *cock*. I giggle like I'm in high school.

"What does this mean?" I whisper out loud to myself,

staring in the mirror. I mean, it means something. Am I the first person he's kissed since her?

All I can do is take deep breaths, pee, and wash my hands and rub some water on my lips. My chest tightens and I brace my palms on the sink.

Jackson is marking down a number on the clipboard as I come back. He says nothing as he hands it back to me and I hop back on the bar.

"Okay, back to business!"

"Shiloh?"

"What?" My smile stays when I look up to find his gaze searing through me.

"We should talk about this."

"What do you want to talk about?"

"That was nice."

More than nice. Electric. A moment I will relive for some time to come. "Yes."

"I don't want this to change us, what we are."

"I agree."

"Good. You're still my best friend," he says. He paces toward the merchandise and back. There's sweat at his hairline, and he rakes his hair with his fingers.

"Are you okay?" I ask, after he stares at the next row for well over a minute.

"It's just…" He turns his back to me. "…I haven't kissed anyone since Amy."

I smile wide and then press my lips together. "Really?"

"Yeah." He rubs his mouth and turns around. "I think I need a moment."

"Okay. Do you want to knock out the rest of inventory?"

His voice cracks when he agrees. I giggle as I walk by him to count the rest, and we finish by ten o'clock. When he hugs me to say goodbye, our embrace is longer, and his beard grazes my cheek when he pulls away.

"I'll see you tomorrow."

"See you tomorrow."

"Save me a seat at lunch."

"Of course." I raise to my tippy toes and lay a quick peck on his lips. He grabs my face, and we kiss again, laughing against each other's lips as we kiss in the doorway.

27

SHILOH

"I didn't think you could get more cheerful." Emily studies me like a lab rat.

Shrugging, I contain my smile. "Today is a great day."

"How was inventory last night?"

"Great. It took longer than I expected." *Only because we spent an hour making out.*

"Huh." She looks me up and down.

"Mom, look." Olive holds up her drawing, a raccoon and Mike Wazowski from *Monsters, Inc.* holding hands.

"She's obsessed with that monster now," Emily whispers. She raises her voice to Olive. "Great job, honey. That's so cute."

"Thanks, I know. Shiloh, did you see?"

"Of course, Martini. It's so good."

"I thought so." Olive studies the picture.

"Not you too. Calling my child by an alcoholic beverage."

I shrug. "I can't help it. It's so cute."

"I love that nickname, Mother," Olive chimes in.

"'Mother'? Who taught you that?" Emily reels back. "What happened to 'Mom'?"

"I call you Mother, because...comedy." Olive walks away, back to her designated table, covered in markers and paper.

"I can't with that child."

"Olive is literally the best." My phone buzzes in my back pocket. There's no customers in line, so I pull it out, my lips immediately curving.

Jackson: Come to my office. I have something to show you.

"Jackson wants me in his office."

"What?" Emily asks. Her chin tilts down, her eyes staring at me under her lashes.

"It has to be a question about inventory." *Or does he want to kiss me again? Or more?*

"Must be. I'll watch the front."

"Thanks." I sprint to the hallway. Running fingers through my hair, I take a deep breath. *Please don't let my face be bright red.*

"Hi." I knock on Jackson's open door, and he swivels around, grabs my hand to pull me in, and slams the door behind me. He stands to hover over me, and my breath catches as I look up at him.

"Hey," he whispers, leaning down to brush his lips against mine. "I couldn't stop thinking about doing this again."

"Me either." I'm caged in by his arms as he leans in, this time more urgent. Our breath entangles as he pins me against the wall, devouring me. It escalates as his hand cups my backside and his mouth travels down my throat. His fingertips flirt with my shirt's hem, leaving fingerprints of fire on my back. I reach to turn the lock and swallow, staring at him.

He pulls away and I nod, raising my arms. He lifts my shirt, slowly. I'm wearing my most-boring bra, a white one with a tiny flower between the cups, but Jackson looks at me like I'm remarkable.

I shiver with anticipation as his lips drift down the column of my neck to my collarbone, his tongue trailing my freckles and moles. He leaves wetness on my skin, my hairs stand on end, and my back arches with his touch.

"Are you okay?" he asks, concerned.

"Yes," I say, my throat dry as I pant, his hand drifting to between my legs. I gasp as his pointer finger rubs against the seam of my jeans, applying pressure to the most delicate part of me. I feel feral, unhinged, as my mouth searches for his.

I pull his shirt off and rub my hands down his torso, my fingers tangling with his tuft of chest hair.

"I don't want our first time to be in this office," he says.

"I agree," I say, sputtering out words between breaths. The area between my legs aches, screaming at me for having self-control. "Maybe we can do *something,* though."

I can barely breathe as he slips a strap off my shoulder and my back arches as his tongue flicks my nipple. He travels back to my lips, his hand cradling me. I'm a woman possessed as I undo his belt and slip my hand into his jeans to feel his hard length.

"You first," he says as he unbuttons my pants and I wiggle out of them with his help. As he pulls one pant length off, one at a time, I get a glimpse at his hard, broad chest, his defined abs, the hint of black boxer briefs.

My panties are just as boring as my bra, white and cotton and now damp from his mouth all over my skin.

He notices, and his fingers touch the wet spot and rub me. I can't breathe as his lips wrap around my breast. I can't believe it's been ten years for him, because it feels like he's been studying the female body like a scholar. He knows where to touch, and how hard, the cadence and rhythm. When his hand slips past the material to my entrance, slick with desire and ready for him, I can't form a coherent thought.

"Is this okay?" he asks.

"I trust you."

His hands grip the side of my panties, pulling them off. My thoughts spiral as he pushes my legs apart again, taking my mouth in one last kiss, then trailing his lips along my torso, until he's on his knees, in front of me.

He drags his tongue down from my entrance to my swollen bud, and it feels so good to be taken by him. I lean back on the wall, as he continues to flick his tongue against my clit, lifting me higher and higher, faster and faster. I moan, and he looks up, pressing a finger to his lips.

"You have to be quiet," he says. He lowers his lips to my clit again, and I buck against his mouth.

I run my fingers through his hair, reaching a breaking point as my mouth outstretches with no sound. I'm on a rollercoaster of pleasure, feeling the highest crest, just to fall. My walls clench and release, delivering the strongest orgasm of my whole life. It just keeps rolling and evolving until it settles, my body relaxing against his mouth.

When he looks up at me, his lips glisten.

"Do I still got it?" he asks with a laugh. I cover my mouth with my arm, laughing against it.

"Give me a minute." I can't even open my eyes that I'm so blissed out.

"Let me take a look at you." Jackson grabs my wrist delicately. His eyes catalog me from the top of my head to my toes. "I didn't think you could get more beautiful, then I saw you come undone from my tongue."

I tsk at him with my finger. "Ooh, you're good."

"Am I?" His eyes are half-mast with lust as I grip the back of his neck, pulling him to me. I kiss him deeply, tasting my desire on his lips. Now that I have my wits about me, I run my hands down his stomach, pulling him into me by his belt holes. My hand drifts lower and he freezes.

"You don't have to."

"I want to," I say, unzipping his pants and dipping my hand into the waistband of his boxer briefs again. When I grip him, he huffs out a breath.

"If you keep doing that, I'll make a mess."

"I know how to keep it contained," I say as I lower to my knees.

"Shiloh, you don't have to," he chokes out, his hands tangled in my hair. "This might be very quick since it's been a while."

I don't say a word, all I do is pull out his cock from his pants, pushing his jeans and boxer briefs down to under his butt. His erection springs forward and I take it into my hand.

"Oh fuck."

I spit on his cock, dragging the saliva down it to coat it for my fist. When I take him, I let it hit the back of my throat, gagging slightly as his hands smooth down my hair. I bob my head, in and out, as he leans against the wall, enjoying my mouth on him. His hands on my head thrill me as I continue, fisting him as I go in and out. He holds my head still and fucks my mouth.

"Shiloh, I'm going to come," he says, as he tries to pull out. Instead, I hold him there, taking every drop of him. When he settles, I sit back on my heels and wipe my mouth.

"You are spectacular," he says, kissing me again, not caring where my mouth had been, at all. In the past, blow jobs have felt degrading, expected with no reciprocation. This is completely different. I feel cherished and safe, and it's confirmed by the way he holds me and kisses my hair part.

"Very unexpected," I say, as I look around our area, locating my clothes. He hands me my bra, and I smile as I thread my arms through the holes. I finish dressing quickly and when I turn around, Jackson is tucking his shirt into his pants.

"I want to cook for you at my place. Give you a break from the all the PB&J."

"I would love that."

"Do you eat pork? I make a great pork chop."

I nod. My mouth is already watering.

"My parents are going out of town this weekend. We won't have inquisitive minds within spitting distance."

I swallow. Should I ask? No, I won't. Oral sex doesn't mean I'm immediately invited for a sleepover or that it's a date. That I'm a girlfriend. I learned that from Mark.

So, I nod and smile. "That sounds great."

"Great," he says. He shakes his head and leans in, giving me a quick kiss on the lips. "I can't promise I won't pull you into an office or closet again before then, though."

I shift the flowers in the vase, my fingers shivering with my nerves.

Shiloh is due any moment, and everything must be perfect.

I deep cleaned my apartment, cleaning corners I've neglected since I moved in. That morning, I went to the Goldheart Neighborhood Market, at the height of weekend crowds and picked up the food for our dinner tonight. Folks didn't look at me as much as I expected, and I enjoyed myself, bumping along to Richard Marx playing over the loudspeakers.

Bea, one of the owners, looked at my food and the flowers I grabbed by impulse by the front door. "Having a special someone over?"

While I didn't think it was any of her business, I said, "Yeah. I'm cooking."

"That's adorable. I'm sure she's special."

"She is," I said, collecting my bags and leaving, enjoying the milder January weather, the air was fresh from the rain the night before. All I needed was a light fleece this morning.

I don't mind if all the Bad Biddies know I bought flowers.

Shiloh is worth all the inquisitive glances, the murmured gossip. Whatever is happening with Shiloh is too good to hide.

My cock swells thinking about Shiloh naked in my office. She tasted like honey, and the image of her squirming and her back arching because of my tongue plays over and over in my head. If I think about her sinking to her knees in front of me, letting me come in her mouth, I can't handle it. It's more that I'm finally with a woman after all this time. It's that it's *her*.

It could only be her.

We kept our distance when we were both at the brewery, but yesterday I couldn't handle seeing her, with her braids and her tight jeans. Whenever a man talked to her, even if it was just to order, my pulse rose. She would smile at me like she always did, but I lost all my resolve. I caught her in the all-gender bathroom, cupping her face with my hands and laying a kiss on her lips, her arms wrapping around my neck.

"What was that for?" she asked.

"I wanted to." I leaned down and kissed her again.

The kisses just keep getting sweeter.

Breathless, she pulled away. "We should stop finding each other here. We'll get caught."

I pressed my forehead to hers. "I can't wait to get you alone."

She kissed my forehead, and hesitated before she pulled away from me. "Me either."

That's why I'm buzzing around my apartment, so anxious my hands are shaking.

I got pork chops as promised and planned to do seasoned potatoes and crisp green beans. It was a meal I made a lot for myself In Seattle when I had a free weekend. The potatoes were roasting already in various spices and olive oil, the pork chops were prepped, and the green beans cleaned and cut. I made sure to pick up Shiloh's favorite cookies from Gold Roast and her favorite root beer.

Dry January has been a struggle, but I've found my groove and settled into a rhythm. After a horrid string of non-alcoholic beers, I settled on sparkling waters. I have five different flavors in my fridge. My mind is clearer, I'm less sad, and I've never performed better in my workouts at my home gym in the garage. I've finished two books I've had bookmarks in for months.

All because of Shiloh.

I asked her to come over at five-thirty, even arranging shifts so she could have Saturday night and Sunday off. It required a lot of favors. The clock moves to a snail's pace as it inches closer to her arrival time, and when I hear a gentle knock at the door, I smile so wide I almost sprain my cheek.

When I open the door, I'm blown away.

Her hair is down and sleek, resting on a cream sweater. She's wearing light makeup, more than she usually does, but I can still see the freckles I love. She's a little taller as she walks in, and her boots click against the hardwood of my apartment.

"Hi," I say, taking her in a hug. I breathe her in, feral for her scent, how she smells like the most divine bakery.

I can't wait to clear that bakery out later.

"Hi," she says, breaking away, putting her purse down and seeing the flowers. "Oh, those are so sweet." She smells the petals, closing her eyes, and I shove my hands in my pockets, watching her enjoying the moment. "Thank you for inviting me."

She doesn't look nervous at all, but I'm sweating. This is my first date since my wife died, and it feels monumental.

Shiloh makes me feel at ease as she touches my arm as she walks by, looking into the kitchen. "Wow, this is a production."

"It's one of my favorite meals," I say, opening the refrigerator to get the pork chops out. "Do you want a root beer?"

Her face lights up. "You have root beer?"

"Of course," I say, pulling out the dark brown bottle. "Don't worry, it's not ours."

She giggles as she takes it. "I have every confidence that you'll figure it out and it will be delicious."

"We're getting close to not getting an immediate spit-take of the product. Emily said the last batch wasn't bad and she would consider giving it to Olive."

"Progress," Shiloh says. I pry off the top to the bottle and hand it to her. She takes a sip and closes her eyes again. "This is wonderful. Thank you for having me."

"You're welcome."

Why is she so pretty?

"I didn't get a chance to look around the last time I was here. May I?"

"Of course. Please."

I'm glad I cleaned the apartment.

Shiloh holds her bottle close to her body, walking around. My apartment is bare, except for some prints on the wall, photos Amy took on our travels that we printed and mounted. Shiloh studies each one like she's in an art gallery, smiling at the one Amy took of a street dog in Italy. "She did beautiful work."

Shiloh stops at our family photo, a picture my mother insisted on taking annually for promos as well as the Christmas card. We took it a week after I had been home when Woody was still alive. We all wore blue and went out to the lake, during golden hour. Shiloh looks at it closely, studying it.

"I've seen this at the brewery, but I never looked at you, per se. You look so sad in that picture," Shiloh says.

I join her, standing side-by-side. She loops her arm

around my waist, and I pull her in. We were affectionate as friends, so this progression feels so natural. She rests her head on my shoulder.

"I was," I say. You can see it in my stoic expression, how my hand rests on Cam's shoulder, how his smile juxtaposed to my grimace shows how much I didn't want to be there. The time of day was Amy's favorite, and according to her, the best time to shoot. During the whole shoot, I could only think about Amy, how every pocket of Goldheart carried a memory of her. Now that I have Shiloh, that I've been back, the town no longer hurts me just by existing.

"You have such a beautiful family," she says. "You all look alike."

"We do. The genes mixed perfectly." The joke was that my mother's genes took over, since we all have her dark brown hair and we're all tall, like her. Our smiles and green eyes are my dad.

Olive stands in front of Emily, holding each other's hands, a family within a family. Olive's hair is a lighter brown than our standard dark chocolate brown, and her eyes are a bright blue. Emily doesn't talk about Olive's dad much. Cam met him once, by accident, and said he was cool. We don't know the full story on why he's not involved, but we all want to have a discussion with him. Our sister and our niece didn't deserve this.

"To think, you'll be adding more to the next one," she says. I know she means Annie and the baby, but I can't help but picture Shiloh next to me, the golden hour bouncing off her blond hair, her bright smile lighting up the portrait.

"Come hang out with me in the kitchen." I lead her by the hand. We flirt with our touch—my hand going to her waist, her hand sliding across my backside. When I catch her, she gives me a devilish grin.

I prep while she talks, bouncing from topic to topic. She

tells me about the latest thriller she read, how Jacques the French bulldog barked at a golden retriever and almost started a fight he couldn't finish.

"I've never seen a golden retriever want to throw hands like that," Shiloh says. "I was so stressed out in the moment, but looking back, it's hilarious."

Shiloh covers her mouth as she giggles and I laugh too, imagining the dogs beefing with each other, barking from across the street.

"I'm glad I have this dinner to distract me. It's Bubba's two-hundredth day in the shelter, and Koda got returned today. I'm just sad for my two best boys."

"Oh no," I say, turning a pork chop over in the pan. "Why?"

"It happens. Working Buddies tries their best to vet all potential adoptees, but sometimes we can't predict what a potential adoptee would do. Koda needs lots of patience. I think the dog is grieving and therefore acting out."

"Can dogs grieve?" I ask.

"Absolutely. It breaks my heart." Shiloh sighs, taking a sip of her root beer. "I just want this dog to find his forever home so badly."

"We tried," I say. "I don't think Dad is ready yet."

"Losing a pet is hard." She swallows, and I know she's thinking about Rory.

"Are you going to get another dog?"

Shiloh shakes her head. "The apartment wouldn't be fair to the dog. Though I would take Bubba in a second."

I stop cooking to turn to her. "You love that dog so much. Do you know his backstory?"

She shakes her head. "We don't know much about him, but he's so cuddly. I feel like we recognized each other."

"I hope he finds a good home then."

"Me too."

I crisp the green beans, adding some olive oil and salt and pepper, covering them to keep them warm. I steal a kiss, long and slow from her, her breath rapid when I pull away.

"It's so nice that I get to do that."

She leans forward to grab another kiss as we hear something sizzling at a rate it should not sizzle.

"Shit," I say, rushing to the stove. Steam billows from the pan. I look in, to find the green beans a perfect green, soft, but crisp to the touch. I drain the water and set it back down on the stovetop. The pork chops are perfectly glazed, and I remove them from heat. The potatoes are a golden brown. "We're almost ready."

"I'll set the table," Shiloh says, walking past me, brushing against me, rubbing her ass against my front. I keep the groan in my mouth, thinking of all the possibilities later. She collects two plates and silverware, walking to my tiny bistro table against the wall. She sets it down and arranges it, tucking a napkin into each plate. I serve her, placing the food as perfectly as I can.

"This all looks so good," Shiloh says. "Maybe you can teach me how to cook."

"I could do that. I don't know how to do much, but I've perfected pork chops."

She cuts into the meat and takes her first bite. I hold my breath as she chews, and I expel it when her eyes widen in delight. "I've never had a pork chop this tender and...sorry to say, moist."

I cringe at that word, and Shiloh covers her mouth to laugh.

She takes bites of the green beans and potatoes, humming in satisfaction. I could watch her eat for hours. She takes such pleasure in life, big and small. Making her happy or delighted makes me feel incredible.

We eat and talk about everything and nothing. I half-expected it to be awkward, since we were friends for so long before we became more. It's the opposite—it feels like it was meant to evolve this way.

When she leans back, resting her arm on her stomach, I know I did my job properly.

"So," she says.

"So." I rest my own elbows on the table, my chin on my fists.

"We're all alone."

"That is correct."

"And your parents aren't home."

"They're gone until tomorrow afternoon."

"What ever should we do?" she asks, leaning back. Her expression is innocent, but I'm not that dense.

I want this woman on every surface of this apartment. I have lots of time to make up for, and I know it was the right decision. Shiloh is the reason I waited.

"Come here," I say, crooking my finger at her. Her eyebrow flicks as she stands up, dropping her napkin onto the plate. I swing out, my knees facing out. She stands in front of me, waiting. I pull her onto my lap. Shiloh straddles me, sinks down, her arms resting on my shoulders. She can feel how hard I am for her. That I want her so badly.

She leans in, hesitantly, as her soft lips greet mine. It's a sweet kiss at first. I push her hair away from her face, my thumbs brushing against her jaw as we kiss languidly, deepening our connection as our faces move side to side. I'm the first to breach her lips with my tongue, taking her deeper.

We kiss like this night is infinite. Anticipation has always been a thing for us, so we might as well drag it out as deliciously as we have been. She rips her lips away to take a deep breath and then I pull her in again. She rolls into me, and my hands reach inside her shirt, my thumbs feeling the edge of her jeans. Her skin is soft, and my mind needs to focus on something else, before I make a mess in my jeans.

I stand up and her legs wrap around my waist as I walk us to the bed in the corner. Sitting down, she settles on me as we kiss, my hands in her hair, her arms wrapped around my neck.

That morning, I drove to Auburn, a larger town twenty miles away, to buy condoms at a non-descript drugstore. The cashier didn't flinch, but the corner of my mouth turned. Even if nothing happened, buying those felt like the first step of an exciting adventure.

She pulls my shirt off me; my skin is blazing hot. I pull her shirt off as well, tracing my fingertips up her spine. She's wearing a black bra, lacy, that cuts across her small breasts.

"I like this," I say, fingering the trim on the cup, tucking my fingers in.

"Really?" She's so excited I approve that I kiss her, a smile plastered on my face.

"It's almost too pretty to take off."

"Almost?" Her voice is breathy.

I roll on top of her, kissing her neck, her chest. My arm reaches around and unhooks her bra, and I help her take it off, slowly and deliciously.

"Almost," I hum against her skin.

Her perfectly pink nipples are hard as diamonds when I palm them, taking her breast in my hand, she moans, just like in my office when I tasted her.

"Do you like that?" I ask.

"Yes, very much." Her leg kicks up, wrapping around my back.

"What else do you like? I'm out of practice."

"I think you're doing quite alright," Shiloh says. My hand drifts to between her legs, cupping her pussy. That makes Shiloh arch more, biting her lip. Who knew that the sweet and bubbly woman could be such a temptress, making me want to serve her, pleasure her because she deserves it.

"You're doing more than alright," she says, as I rub her.

"Let's get rid of these," I say, unbuttoning her jeans. A sly smile crosses her lips as she wiggles out of them. Matching black underwear still covers her as I peel her jeans off, her little kicks assisting me.

"These are cute," I say, touching the silk.

"It's a matching set," she says. "You're the first one to see them."

She giggles, and I push her legs open and rub the silk against her clit, already plump and hard against my palm. Her panties are damp, and it makes my cock swell knowing I'm the reason for the wetness.

I kiss the silk that covers her pleasure and watch Shiloh's head roll back as I grab a breast, using my thumb to circle her nipple. My finger tucks inside the material, tracing her entrance and she moans loudly and it drives me wild. Shiloh's pleasure is my top priority, and I want her to feel every sensation, feel the strongest orgasm of her life. She deserves more than one tonight. My cock throbs, but I intend to savor this.

We have all the time in the world.

"You are so good at this," she says, breathy as she bites her lip again.

"Thank you," I say, pushing her underwear to the side so her pussy is bare in front of me. I waste no time, leaning in and kissing it, then slowly sucking, licking her from back to front.

Her fingers run through my hair as I eat her out, my fingers flirting with her entrance. When I slowly insert my finger into her, then add a second, she cries out. Now, both of her hands grip my hair, and pride swell in my chest. My cock has settled, momentarily, but it's bucking against my jeans, painful and aching. It will probably be seconds of me inside of her before I feel my own release.

I get her so close, she writhes under me, until she taps my shoulders.

"Stop, stop," she says, and I lift myself to look at her. "I want you inside of me when I come."

A growl settles deep in my throat as I kiss her, and she dips her tongue into my mouth before I reach for my night-stand. I stand to unbutton my jeans.

"I want to help." Her hands replace mine, and she kisses my collarbone, my chest, my shoulder. Her kisses feel like whispers on my skin, her hands so close to my cock, my mind clears, and it's just her and me, in this moment.

When she pushes down my pants and underwear, I groan as she opens the box and pulls out a foil packet. I try to take it from her, but she holds it out of reach.

"I want to do it," she says. She takes my cock in her small, delicate hands and squeezes. I almost come before I even make it inside of her, but she lines up the condom at my tip, squeezing the top and rolling it down, slowly. It's torture to keep my wits about me, not focusing on the stimulation, how much I want this woman.

My cock bobs when she lets go, and she looks up at me. I brush her hair away from her face, gripping the back of her neck before I lower down and lay another kiss on her lips. There's nothing slow about this anymore as I lift her up, my cock between our bodies as I sit down and she takes me in her hand again, lining it up with her entrance as she hovers over me. She sinks down with a satisfying sigh, and we look at each other.

Really look at each other.

This is a monumental moment between us, intense and spectacular. We take it all in. We fit like we were made for each other. When she pulls back to bounce back down, her mouth opens wide as my cock fills her. I sit up to sink my face into the crook of her neck, smelling the vanilla on her skin, and I nip her. She giggles, and then I grab her ass, pressing her body into mine so I can see her all around my cock and sink into her further. I want her to know how much I want this, how special this is.

"This is so good," Shiloh says and lets out a sound. I kiss her neck as she rides my lap.

My hands settle on her hips as I bounce her onto my cock, the giggles morphing into moans. She leans back and I hold her, and I thrust into her quickly, letting her warmth envelop me.

"Tell me what you need," I tell her. I hold it together because she feels so good, I could come at any time, and I want to make sure she comes first.

"I'm so close," she says, and I do not hesitate. I reach between us, my thumb finding her clit. I kiss between her breasts, my lips traveling across her nipple when she throws her head back with eyes closed, her mouth stretching open. She's coming, and her walls pulsing around me pushes me over the edge.

Then I let go too. My orgasm stretches on forever, and I kiss her neck before I collapse on the bed. She lies over me, hearing how fast my heart beats for her.

She wraps her arms around my neck, hugging me close. Her sweat mingles with mine as she pulls me tight.

"I'm glad it was you," I say into her hair. I pat her hair down, wrapping my arms around her back as well, pressing our sweaty bodies together.

"I'm glad I was too," she whispers into my ear.

29

SHILOH

I wake up naked in white sheets, splayed on my stomach. My hair blocks my view as I turn my head, and when I push it out of my eyes, Jackson is sitting there, fully dressed.

"Good morning, Sunny," he says.

I rub my eyes. "What time is it?"

"It's eight."

"Oh my God," I say, exploding out of bed. My clothes are folded in a neat, little pile on a chair after we absentmindedly scattered them all over this apartment.

"What's the rush?" Jackson asks.

"I have to take my grandpa to church. He can't drive."

"Are you going too?" he asks.

"Sometimes I go, but I'm not sure after last night. We sinned. A lot."

"Yeah, we did." He winks at me as he hands me my underwear. "I like these."

I smirk as I pull my underwear on, slightly self-conscious I'm naked in front of Jackson, although he saw all of me last night. We didn't talk about what we are, or what this meant for our relationship, and I'm too nervous to bring it up. Are we dating? Fuck buddies? Is he my boyfriend? We've already skipped lots of the necessary, getting-to-know-you steps.

Better to focus on getting Papa to church. Might be a good idea for me to go after all the pre-marital sex I had last night. Potentially burning in hell was sure worth it for last night, though. I'm sure God would make an exception.

There's a knock at Jackson's door as I pull my sweater over my head. We both freeze, and Jackson's eyebrows collapse into each other.

"Who's at the door?" I whisper.

"I don't know. I'm not expecting anyone."

"Should I hide?" I ask.

"No, that's not necessary," Jackson says, holding out a hand. He walks to his door, looks out the peephole, and then looks at me. "It's my sister."

I pull on my jeans so violently I almost fall over. I pull my hair that looks too much like a rat's nest to a low ponytail and wipe off the smudges from underneath my eyes.

Jackson opens the door, and I make sure I'm out of view.

"You weren't answering your phone, and you know when that happens I need to check on you," Emily says.

"Hi, Uncle Jackson," Olive says. "Mom was worried."

Oh my God. A child is going to catch us.

"We want to know if you want to go to Moe's Diner for brunch," Olive asks. "Mom said I can get strawberry waffles."

"Those are really good," Jackson says. "Give me a sec."

He closes the door and walks over to me. "Do you want to come? After you drop off your grandpa?"

I bite my lip. Having an early meal with my lover (is he my lover if we had sex one night, even if it was multiple times?) is a good sign, but explaining to a child why I'm at Uncle Jackson's apartment in the morning might be more than I'm willing to do.

"I would love to, but I should really go with my grandpa," I say.

"Okay, I'm going to go then." He shoves his hands in his pockets. "I had a great time last night."

This is not a brush-off. He's just talking. You didn't screw it all up. The sex was great. You were there.

"Me too," I say. Great time didn't even begin to cover it. I had strong orgasm after strong orgasm. There were several points where I levitated off the bed in pleasure. We didn't stop after the first time; we kept going until two a.m., and I lost count of how many condoms we used.

"Hey, hey, hey," he says, cradling me in his arms. He brushes my hair from my face and kisses me gently. He whispers, "I don't care if Emily knows you spent the night."

"I do," I say. "Just leave the door unlocked so I can sneak out."

"You don't have to sneak out. I'm not hiding you."

"It's okay. I just can't handle questions right now."

"Okay," he says, kissing me one last, breathless time. "I'll call you."

He opens the door and looks back one last time before closing the door behind him.

Outside, I hear Emily say, "Is that Shiloh's car?" as the steps on his stairwell grow fainter and fainter. Pulling back the curtain, I look out as I see them get into Emily's SUV, backing out from the mini-gravel parking lot in front of the garage.

I'm sore and tired, but euphoric as I leave his apartment and walk down the stairs.

The sex was more than I expected. For someone so out of practice, it was utterly spectacular. I felt cherished and loved, and emotion swells in my throat.

"You can't cry about this," I say out loud to myself as I drive away.

"Girlie, you look tired," Papa says, sitting in my front seat. We usually leave at eight-fifty so he can get a blended coffee drink from the church-run snack bar and then a good seat for the service. I usually don't go because I have to work, and my grandpa has church buddies. Most Sundays, he walks with his friend Joaquin to Moe's Diner for after-church food.

Today, he insists I stay for the service. He glares at me like he knows.

"I didn't sleep well." A lie. Maybe I should go to church.

"You stayed up all night with the Finch boy, didn't you?"

My cheeks must be bright red. I didn't say anything.

"Church might be the best for you."

"I said I would go with you!"

Thinking about where Jackson's tongue was last night, probably not the worst idea. I so rarely have a Sunday off, so it might be nice to spend time with my grandfather.

He looks so happy that he'll have company and that he can show me off. I run into my grandpa's church friends all the time who shake my hand like I'm a celebrity. I know he brags about me, although there's nothing to brag about. I'm twenty-six with no clear career path, but he talks about me like I'm his biggest accomplishment.

I help him out of the car and hold onto him as we walk to the side entrance, where the coffee bar is. The volunteer baristas greet him warmly.

"Is this the famous Shiloh?" a middle-aged man asks, pointing from Papa to me. He must be new. Most of the baristas know me.

"Yes, she is," Papa says, his chest puffing as he puts his hand to the middle of my back. "Shiloh, this is Pastor Williams. He's whipping up the drinks today."

I wonder if he can tell how much I sinned last night. I try not to look guilty as I shake his hand.

"Are you staying for the service?" he asks.

"I think so," I say.

"Wonderful, would love to have you. Mr. Abbott, the usual?"

"Please," he says. The pastor walks to the back bar, grabbing a clean blender and pours milk and scoops powder into it. I order a coffee too. The pastor doesn't look at me when he asks, "I've heard you're friends with Jackson Finch?"

I nod, although it's more complicated than that. "Yes, I am."

"How is he doing?" the pastor asks, scooping ice into the blender and popping the top on.

"He's great, actually," I say.

"I'm glad to hear that."

This town really cares about him. It's so sweet.

"Marla, my wife, would love to talk to you about him. I'm not sure where she is."

That's strange. The pastor blends the drink, coating the cup with mocha sauce like Papa likes it. He pulls his phone out, shooting a quick message, and after pouring the drink, hands it to Papa, who takes a big slurp.

"Fantastic as always, Pastor," Papa says, hoisting up the drink in a one-sided cheers.

"I put a little extra love in there for you," Pastor Williams says. His gaze drifts to me. He looks at me like he's trying to find answers in my face, and I fidget, shifting from one foot to another. He hands me my coffee.

"It's on the house."

"Thanks," I say.

He still studies me. "When you talk to him, let him know we miss him and would love to see him."

"Okay," I say, unsure. Jackson has never mentioned the

Williamses, and so I'm not sure why they look so sad that they can't talk to Jackson, why they're analyzing me like I broke some code.

I honestly don't know how it happened. Loving Jackson happened slowly, that I didn't know I was in it until I was. It happened over days of dog walks, conversations over sandwiches and cookies, New Year's. How I've gotten to know the core of him, and he's gotten to know the core of me. How last night was so special and culminating. It put all my fears to rest.

Now, this man looks at me like Jackson has more secrets that I don't know. Maybe I'll never know him fully. There's dark crevices and spots I may not be able to reach right away. I'm willing to dig.

"Marla, there you are," Pastor Williams says. A woman in her early sixties walks toward us, her hair in a silver bob, wearing a gray cardigan over a floral top. She floats with elegance. There's something familiar about her that I can't place. The pastor wraps his arm around his wife and turns her to me.

"Marla, this is Shiloh, Earl's granddaughter. She's befriended Jackson Finch."

Without warning, she grabs me for a hug, tight and unforgiving. I sense she needs this, so I reciprocate, my arms circling her back. When she pulls back, she looks at me.

"It's so good to meet you. We've heard a lot about you," Marla says, her hands still on my arms.

"What is going on?" My tired brain can't sort this information.

"Jackson was our son-in-law," Marla says. "Amy was our daughter."

The world collapses in on me. I try for a big smile as I let Marla hold my hands. Words are escaping me right now. I'm not sure how to navigate this, what should I say?

Nothing feels right.

I'm sorry for your loss. I'm not replacing your daughter. I never want him to forget her. I respect her so much, and I tried to stay away so long. I'm not sure Jackson will ever love me the same way he loved your daughter, and I'm okay with that.

"Has he mentioned her?" she asks. Her lips press in a line, and I see water pooling in her eyes.

"He has. She sounds like she was a very special woman."

"That's good," Marla says. "That's really good."

I take her hand in mine because this woman deserves comfort. Jackson wasn't the only one who lost Amy.

Pastor Williams walks to his wife's side. "We've been trying to reach him since he moved back. We would love to have him over for dinner. Catch up. You are welcome too."

I feel vulnerable under their gaze. They can tell we're involved, that it's more than friendship, I know it. That I'm the first woman he's been with since her.

"I'll tell him. Hopefully, you can have that dinner." It doesn't feel appropriate to insert myself into their reunion, when they could very well discuss a woman who overshadowed his whole life, while I occupy a small sliver.

"Thank you," Marla says, holding my hands. "Honestly. Jackson feels like a piece of her, in some strange way. We would love to see him. Maybe you can mention it to him?"

"I will do my best." This woman hugs me again, and I smile, crossing my arms across me.

Papa puts his own arm around me, pulling me away. "Rob and Marla, it was so nice to chat. We must find our seats!" He shuffles, hanging onto me, holding his blended coffee in the other hand. He smiles until he's out of sight from the pastor and his wife.

"I worried this would happen," he says.

"Why does everyone assume I have some magical power

over him?" I whisper. I stay out of gossip, but that doesn't mean I'm not the subject of it.

"You do, girlie," Papa says. We walk into the worship room and find comfy, red chairs in an empty row. He pats my knee as I sit down. "Jackson barely left the house prior to meeting you. He's smiling, laughing. People have seen him around town. With Rob and Marla, that's one of the hurdles he hasn't jumped over. They have tried several times to reach out to him, but he doesn't take their calls. It really hurts them. They pray for him all the time."

Why doesn't he talk to them? I remember a couple times we were out, and he would scan each place before we went in, determining if there was someone there he didn't want to see. Has he been avoiding them the whole time? I sip my coffee as I think.

Papa greets several church members and glows when he introduces me to them, and all I can think about Jackson avoiding Amy's sweet parents. Why would he avoid them?

"I have to go to the bathroom," I tell my grandfather five minutes before the service starts.

"Okay, honey." He pats me on the knee before I stand up. I've been to this church once before, on Christmas Eve, so I know where the bathroom is. I didn't notice it the time before, but a portrait of the pastor and his family is hung in the lobby.

I didn't stop last time but I stop now.

The pastor is considerably younger, with a groomed mustache, and his hair is thicker. Marla has not aged at all; the only telling sign is a poofy perm. There's a boy and girl in the picture.

My heart catches in my throat when I recognize her.

Amy Louise Finch.

She's probably sixteen in the photo, the cancer spreading without anyone's knowledge. Her hair is dark and straight, bangs covering her forehead. She has expressive hazel eyes and a warm smile.

I stand there for too long. She was just a girl, but she was Jackson's entire world. To have Jackson's attention like that, it makes an ordinary girl extraordinary in my eyes.

If he can't see these lovely people, is he ready to move on with someone else? Would I be that someone else that he would want to move on with? Would Amy approve? How do I honor her?

Our night together could've been our breaking point, but it might've been just that. Sexual tension that exploded. I'm in love with him, but I'm not sure he is with me.

I'm not sure if he's capable.

I stand at the sink for ages, my hands clipped on the porcelain.

When I go back to my seat, my thoughts are lost the entire service. I don't hear a word the pastor says.

30

JACKSON

My apartment grows darker as I pace in my living room. I switch on a lamp, and look through the blinds again, searching for that head of curly blond hair, walking up my steps.

Her vanilla scent lingers in my apartment. I found three strands of her hair on my floor. I'm counting the minutes until she's back again.

When I hear a knock on my door at six sharp, I open it to find her and my mouth bursts into a huge grin. She doesn't reciprocate. Her gaze focuses on the ground before she lifts her chin to look at me.

I pull her into a hug, kissing the top of her head, swaying her back and forth. When she pulls away, she rubs her face with her cardigan sleeve, a chunky gray knit that reaches her knees.

"How was your day?" I pull her by the hand to the couch.

Shiloh is stiff in my arms. I press my cheek to hers. "What's wrong?"

"I went to church."

"Are there burns anywhere? You didn't burst into flames?" I lift her arm, searching her skin for scorch marks, and she laughs. I go for her side, a spot I discovered was ticklish last night, and she giggles so loud, I laugh too, and I can't stop. Her laughter ceases, and she cranes her neck to look at me. The angle looks awkward, so I take her off my lap and tuck her into my side.

She slaps my knee. "I came out unscathed. I did meet two nice people, though."

"Oh?" I ask.

"Pastor and Marla Williams."

My mouth goes dry. My former in-laws were lovely people; they accepted me with open arms, even though they thought it was crazy to get married so young and delicately questioned if our decision wasn't a knee-jerk reaction to Amy's illness. In the end, they approved. Her dad walked her down the aisle and performed the ceremony, reading from his own Bible and gifting us his late mother's wedding set.

I saw them once after the funeral. That dinner was torture; my head throbbed and emotion wrecked my body like the cancer wrecked hers. After that dinner, I knew it might be my last time seeing them.

It hurt too much.

"How are they?" I ask casually, trying to hide my dread.

"They seem fine. They asked me about you."

I hum a response.

"I said I would pass along a message. They said they've tried to reach out. They want to see you. Why don't you talk to them, Jackson?" Her tone is curious, not accusatory.

"Once Amy passed away, there really wasn't a need to."

"You were married to their daughter."

"I went to Seattle immediately after the funeral so…"

"You've been back for over a year now. Is that why you never left your house?"

She looks at me with her big blue eyes, searching my face for the answers. She assumes I'm a whole person, not this broken man who avoids his former in-laws because they talk about his late wife.

"We really don't have anything to talk about. It's okay, Shiloh. We've moved on."

"Have you, though?" She stands up, tucking her hands in her armpits as she paces. She's never questioned me. Ever.

"You're here."

She flinches like the words were a raised hand. Her eyes terrify me, how round and questioning they are, on the verge of tears. I stand up to hug Shiloh, but she slips from my grasp. Her back is to me when her whispered words leave her mouth like a song. "I love you, you know."

My tongue is heavy. I don't know what to say, how to react. The words are right there, so close, but I can't say them.

She turns, her arms tucked in front of her, tighter now.

"Look, Shiloh...."

She backs away, holding up her hands. Sobs leave her mouth, and my stomach twists, coating my throat with nausea.

I cannot say anything, and Shiloh's shoulders fall while her body heaves with tears. Regret fills my stomach, twisting and rolling it.

"You're not ready for this. For me." Heartbreak is written all over her face.

"I care about you, Shiloh. So much."

She wipes the tears from her cheeks. The red around her blue eyes make them piercing, so vibrant. I want to hold her, but I stay frozen in my stance.

"Are you ready for me? Truly," she asks, placing her hand on her chest.

"I don't know," I say.

She tilts her head when she looks at me, and I know where this is going. I did this. This is my fault.

"I just need some time. I didn't expect you." My voice shakes. "I'm so sorry."

"I am too," she says.

I pull her in for a hug, and she cries against my chest; the tears are about me. I smooth her hair away from her face as she sobs softly. We stand there for seconds or minutes or hours, I don't know, before she pulls away. Her face is red and splotchy, shiny from tears.

"Shiloh, you're my best friend."

She nods and opens the door. I reach for her, but her hand stops my forearm. "I need to go."

"I don't want this to be over."

She places her hand on my cheek, and I lean into it. A single tear rolls down her face. "I want you to find peace. Maybe it's better if I'm not in the picture for a while. I'm just a bandage over a gaping wound."

She kisses me on the cheek and whispers, "I love you."

Then, she's gone.

I don't leave my doorframe until her car leaves. Locking my door, I lean against it, my head throbbing. I sink to the floor, my body hitting the hardwood floor with a thud. It feels like my chest is splitting open; my mind spins like a tilt-a-whirl. Everything about this situation feels impossible.

We will be an uphill battle, and I'm not sure it's fair to put Shiloh through it. She deserves a whole man, and I'm just putting the pieces back together.

This is how I'll always be—a sad man who can't talk about a person he loved very much, who let another person leave without knowing how much she's made his life happier.

In that moment, I don't give a fuck if it's still January.

The bottle of Macallan still sits on the top shelf of my pantry. I rip off the stopper and tilt it over a glass but pause. Biting my lip, I stare at it.

Scotch fixes nothing. Maybe my punishment should be to feel everything tonight.

31

SHILOH

I sit on the floor of the kennel, and Bubba, the brown-and-white pit bull, presses against me. He snorts as he tries to get comfortable, stepping on my legs to curl into my lap. He acts like he's a five-pound chihuahua, not an eighty-pound pittie.

I've unloaded my feelings onto every dog in this animal shelter. They're great therapists. Dogs just listen, give snuggles, and they don't ask for your insurance. Bubba is my main supporter. I've almost taken him home fifteen times, to hell with my grandfather's apartment's ordinances.

It wouldn't be fair to him, though, but anything would be better than this cage.

I might sign adoption papers today, who knows.

"Do you love me, Bubba?" I ask, kissing the lone white spot on his head.

The dog looks up at me, and then lays his head on my chest. I sniffle as the dog listens to my heartbeat.

"I'm afraid." My voice cracks. The dog senses it and burrows his head into me and lets out a huff. I pet Bubba's head. "You're making me feel better."

The dog paws at me as we snuggle. Bubba has a mysterious past, one we don't know the full extent. When he came in, he was neutered and the sweetest boy ever. Volunteers love to love on him, but the visitors don't see how great he is. They just see his breed and his size. They don't see his heart.

In a weird way, I feel like Rory sent Bubba to me because he knew I would be heartbroken. I would be doubting everything I feel.

I pet Bubba's head, and his eyelids droop. It's my favorite when they relax enough to fall asleep in my lap.

I'm staring at a discolored spot on the concrete floor when I hear a voice outside the kennel.

"You're here again?"

I look up. Priscilla stands over me, with her arms crossed. I run into her once in a while here. I'm the first to alert her when a working line dog comes in, and sometimes I do the evaluation onsite to see if the dog is a good fit for the rescue without being asked.

The rescue doesn't take bully breeds, though.

Lately, my heart has shifted to the bully breeds and I'm still the biggest advocate for the senior dogs in danger of living the rest of their live in a cage. Thankfully, we don't have any dogs over six here right now, and that's makes me so happy. I could run for president for how hard I campaign for the seniors.

"Bubba and I are pals," I say, wiping my eyes. Priscilla's eyes soften as she sees my wet and red face, how I've been sobbing to a pittie who has done nothing but snuggle me.

"Dana at the front told me you've been here every day this week."

"I have," I say. Anytime I'm not at the brewery, I'm here. Dogs are my coping mechanism of choice.

"She also says she's never seen you sad, and she's worried."

"I know," I say. In public, I try to keep it together. In private, it's a different story. I sobbed for three hours last night watching dog TikToks and military homecomings. My heart is empty. A little dark cloud follows me as I worked my last few shifts post-Jackson and the customers and employees are noticing. I just smile and shrug it off, and when the door closes to my room, I cry. My grandpa checks on me, but there's nothing he can do.

"Come with me," Priscilla says, opening the kennel door two inches.

"No, Bubba is asleep. This is the best part."

"I need to talk to you without the dogs. They gossip."

"Not this one," I say, pointing down at Bubba. I kiss the top of his head. "He's perfect."

"Come on."

My heart drops that I can't stay in this pile of love mush. I struggle to place Bubba on the floor of the kennel since he is so heavy, and I finally get him on the floor so I can stand up. I follow Priscilla out the kennel and latch the door.

"I'll be back, Bubba." The dog settles his head on the concrete floor and looks up at me with sad eyes. My heart twists.

"Fresh air will be good," she says, leading me outside. It's mild today, probably fifty-something degrees, but I still wrap my zipped hoodie tighter around me. We find a bench in front of the shelter, and she motions for me to sit.

I plop down, resting my elbows on my legs and dropping my head in my hands. My temples throb.

"I have never seen you like this," she says.

"I know," I say.

"What happened?"

"I don't want to talk about it."

"Come on. It will help to talk about it. Is it something with your mom?"

"No, it's not that."

"What is it? I can't handle you sad. If you're sad, something is very, very wrong."

"I got involved with Jackson Finch."

"I figured it was that. Ramon mentioned something," she says, a little too loudly.

"He's not ready." I lower my face to my hands.

"I'm not surprised." Priscilla rubs my back.

"I saw her parents at the church my grandfather goes to. I didn't know they ran that church."

"Rob and Marla Williams. Very nice people."

"I don't mean to gossip." I sit back.

"It's not gossiping if it happened to you. It's just a conversation between friends."

That makes me smile. I've been so focused on Jackson and our friendship that I forgot about others that could be cultivated. Priscilla has been a great mentor to me, and we share lots of values. There's others in my life too. Ramon, her nephew, is my favorite co-worker; I really should hang out with him more. Annie and Whitney, Cameron and Reid's girlfriends, are older than me but have always accepted me. There's Izzie and Tara who have wine nights that I could bring root beer to.

Maybe it's time to spread my energy around. Maybe my heart would hurt less.

"They want to see Jackson. They haven't seen him since right after Amy's funeral."

"I think he left town shortly after that. I don't blame him. This whole town loves their gossip. That man just lost his wife, but women started paying attention to him in a seriously gross way."

My tears dry up instantly. "Wait, am I a gross woman?"

Priscilla waves her hands. "No, no, no. Everyone felt sorry for him, wanted to comfort him. Told him 'everything happens for a reason' and some shit. Sorry, I said that." She covers her mouth.

I giggle. "That's fine."

"What happened with you two?"

I take a deep breath. "I told him I love him, and he didn't say it back. It's more than that, though."

"Oof," she says.

"So, I had to break off our friendship. I have a history of chasing unavailable men." I drop my head again.

"Don't we all?"

I nod and feel the tears building behind my eyes. There's been so many things I've wanted to tell him. How Koda was returned to the rescue again because the adopter received a job offer out of nowhere for a job in Germany. How it broke my heart, and I wished I could take him home, but Papa and I aren't moving to a house anytime soon. How my sister reached a milestone with her business and how proud I am of her.

"I wanted to tell you something," Priscilla says. "It's exciting. I think you'll be happy."

"What?" I ask.

"You know our favorite repeat offender?"

"Koda?" I ask, and Priscilla nods.

"Well, he got adopted again, and I think this time it'll stick."

My heart just went from the pits of my stomach to the absolute highs. "Who is it?"

"Randy Finch."

Jackson's dad. Koda just found his furever home.

I let out a flood of tears, finding it hard to catch my breath since I am so happy.

"Are those happy sobs?"

I nod, although I'm trying to catch my breath and I'm hyperventilating.

"Koda is going to be okay. He's going to be okay."

"That dog will be loved. Always."

I keep crying as Priscilla pulls me into her. I didn't know that my heart can be so full and broken at the same time.

I open the sliding glass door to my parents' house, and I hear barking.

Am I imagining it?

Then, a black-and-tan monster careens around the corner, stopping in the middle of the living room, the tail in a scorpion pose, wagging back and forth.

"Koda?" I ask.

The dog's tongue rolls out of his mouth as he takes a pouncing stance, his butt in the air before he runs toward me, barreling his big head into my kneecaps, almost taking me out.

"I see you've met the dog. Again," my dad says.

My mouth still hangs open. The dog leans on me and looks up, the tongue dangling.

"Come on in." My dad disappears into the kitchen.

The dog wiggles as I pet him, circles my legs, and then pries them open to walk between, the head moving a little too freely, very close to my balls.

"Dad, I thought you weren't ready."

"Now I am."

"How did this happen?" The dog loses interest and walks

towards my dad. Dad gives incredible ear scratches.

Dad shoves his hands into his pockets. "Something about this dog just nagged at me. I couldn't stop thinking about him. So, I called Priscilla and heard that Koda was returned the week prior. I saw it as a sign. No way in hell I'll return a dog like this."

My dad is a happy man, very positive. However, seeing him with a dog, his dog, brings light back to him. It's nice to see.

"So, son, can you tell me why Shiloh Abbott is avoiding you?"

I swallow the lump in my throat. "We were seeing each other. Romantically. It's over."

"What did I say about dating the employees?"

"It just sort of happened. I didn't really plan it. I'm sorry, Dad."

I wait for him to blow up, although I haven't seen him truly angry one day in our life. Dad is reasonable but sentimental, a man who cries at *Field of Dreams*, who cried happy tears when Emily told him and Mom that she was pregnant, although she was twenty. It would be nice to see the type of anger from him that I feel toward myself.

I let the thing with Shiloh go too far and the thing I feared most happened.

I lost her.

"You look like you need a beer. C'mon," he says, motioning for me to join him in the kitchen, the dog trotting after him.

He opens a tall can of our Gold Dust IPA, our most popular beer. He pours it for me, and he pours his own, a hoarded Oktoberfest we do every year. He always insists we make extra so he can keep it through next October.

It is technically February.

We cheers and take a sip.

"What happened, son?" Dad asks, rubbing the dog's head.

"I'm not ready for her."

Dad nods and doesn't say anything. I'm waiting for his words since my dad is the only one whose approval I'm desperate for.

"Has this anything to do with Amy?"

I fold my hands in my lap and look down at my beer.

"Son, I know you loved Amy. Everyone knows that. It's okay to move on."

I know that in my heart. But I've been living a certain way since she died and breaking my way of life feels impossible. I can't move forward, and I don't know why.

"Shiloh deserves so much better than me. I can't give her what she wants."

"Why?" Dad asks. He opens the cupboard to pull out his secret stash of Cheez-Its, a box he hides from Mom after she asked him to. She claims she "blacks out" when she gets her first taste of fake cheese. He offers me some, and I take a few crackers, although my mouth feels like I stuffed one hundred cotton balls in it.

"I'm broken," I admit.

My dad looks down at his beer, giving me a break from seeing the worst parts of me. "I've seen you come alive the past few months you've been seeing Shiloh. It felt like we had the old Jackson back. It was nice."

"I don't want to talk about this," I say, sitting back in my chair.

"Tough shit, son. You've been avoiding this for too long, and I'm tired of it." He smacks the counter, making the dog jump. His voice goes up a couple octaves, as he leans down to the dog. "I'm not mad at you, Koda, it's your brother."

And once again, we're chopped liver to the fur child.

"You know, I kept my mouth shut for a long time. You know how much your mother gets upset about you not coming to events, not participating with the family? How you hid in that closet for months to avoid our employees? I figured you would come around, and you did. For a while."

I open my mouth to speak, and Dad holds up his hand.

"I'm not done. Happiness is a choice. Yes, you had a lot of shitty things happen to you, things that broke my heart as a parent." He sniffles and looks at me.

I look up at him. "I can't force myself into being happy, Dad."

"Happiness is hard work. You have to choose it, every day. Life doesn't make it easy. It was easier for you to lock yourself in your apartment, drink yourself to sleep, and lock yourself in the office. How was that working out for you?"

Blood drains from my face.

"I was a mess after Woody died. A mess. I had to see someone to talk about it."

"Did you see a *therapist*?" My happy-go-lucky dad going to therapy?

"Yes, I went to therapy. I had a lot of guilt about being gone when it happened. That you had to deal with it after all you went through. That's what I feel guilty of most of all."

My dad felt guilty?

"It was okay, Dad. Cameron, Reid, and Emily were here."

"I know that." He instinctually lowers his hand to give the dog scratches on the ears. He leans against his leg, the tongue still dangling. "Woody will always be in my heart. I wasn't ready when I first met Koda, but I became ready because I felt in my heart of hearts that he was the right dog for me.

"Maybe you weren't ready to meet a woman, but Shiloh just crashed into your life before you could become ready. It's just my opinion, but you're never going to find a better woman than her. Amy would approve. I believe that with every fiber of my being." My dad's voice cracks at the end.

To avoid seeing my dad emotional, I study the swirls in marble on the counter. I wasn't ready when I met her. I was back in this town, dealing with all the memories, pulling my parents' flailing business out from the ashes. We're finally in the black, two of my brothers are in serious relationships, my dad has a new dog. It feels like the world is righting itself, but I can't move forward.

"Did you ever get into therapy, son? After Amy died?"

I shake my head.

"Get in therapy. And please for the love of God, go through the boxes in the attic. Your mother has been nagging me forever to bring it up with you."

"I'll get to it. Soon." I stand up from my chair.

"Great. They're all in a corner with a piece of paper with your name on it. If you could figure out what to do with them and get them moved, your mother would be ecstatic. You have time now that you're not with Shiloh every second."

I wish I was. My evenings are completely free now that Shiloh and I aren't speaking, and I need something to do.

I'm almost to the edge of the kitchen when my dad calls out to me. I turn toward my dad, he's still petting that dog. "Mom and I will pay for your therapy. We should've offered a long time ago."

"Thanks Dad, but I can handle it. I'll call."

I surprise myself because it's only three days before I face the boxes.

When I finally walk to the stairs to the attic, I chuckle. We used to think the staircase was haunted when we were kids. The only one brave enough to go was Cameron, and he would mess with us, making up outlandish stories of what was up there. He once convinced us there was a ghost from the gold rush haunting the attic named Mildred and would hide and knock walls to scare us.

I fear for my life since the stairs creak as I climb but then I'm under a low ceiling, with dust particles floating through the air, light fracturing the space. I find my stack of boxes in the corner.

I take a deep breath and inch closer. I know what most of those boxes hold.

My life with Amy.

When I left for Seattle immediately after she died, I left behind most of her stuff. I gave her parents her most important stuff, like her wedding set and her Bible. There were other things shoved into boxes and I didn't give it to them, although they held childhood memories.

I should've returned that too. I just wasn't thinking.

Maybe I should call them.

I stare at the boxes for a while, wondering if now is a good time to see what's in them, whether I'm ready to see what's in there. I could've been standing there for minutes or hours, I'm not sure but I finally take a deep breath and grab the first box.

It's a random assortment of stuff that means nothing. I breathe out, relieved it's an easy one, full of pictures and scratches of paper. I expect to feel emotional looking at pictures of Amy and me, but I'm not. There's ones from Homecoming, standing next to me, both of us giving awkward, closed-mouth smiles.

I remember how my heart fluttered when I saw her in that dress.

I put that picture to the side and look at another one. All I feel is warm nostalgia, not an ounce of sadness.

Amy's diaries are in there, something I was never tempted to read until now. I asked her once why she wrote in journals instead of including it into her prayers and she said with a wink, "God doesn't need to know everything."

I open one with a ballerina on front, the spine cracking.

The dates range from high school to our marriage when she was in remission to the last days before she passed. I flip the last filled page.

The date is exactly one month before she died.

Dear Journal,

Long time no talk!

So, it looks like cancer will get me. I'm so blessed to have the time I had and to find the love of my life. My darling husband is right next to me as I write this, and he's trying to look.

Little did she know I would be looking now.

Sometimes I love him so much it hurts. I worry what he will be like when I'm gone. I want him to be sad, for sure, but I also want him to eventually move on. Maybe after I'm gone ten years he can find someone else.

I shake my head. That's just a coincidence.

I hope after I'm gone he can buy that house with land we always talked about, that he can find a job that makes him happy, and he can be a dad. It kills me (haha I'm so funny) that I can't give him a baby. That we ran out of time. That's my biggest life regret. However, God knows best, and He knew I wouldn't be around forever. Leaving Jackson is the only thing that really sucks about all of this. If I had to leave a child as well, well, that would destroy me.

I reach out to rub my nose and wetness covers my hand. I'm crying as I read this, the tears staining the pages.

I hope I have connections from heaven to find her for him. It's morbid to think of who will take my place, who Jackson will love in the future. I hope Jackson can feel me when he finds her. That it's okay to move on. I hope he continues to grow stronger and keeps going after his dreams. I know he will. He's so much stronger than I am.

"I'm really not," I say out loud, that Amy's spirit is in this attic and not Mildred, the gold Rush ghost. "You were the strong one."

I keep reading although I'm full-on sobbing now.

I've been so lucky in my life. I found the love of my life, even if I may not be the only one of his. I saw the world with him, and we had once-in-a-lifetime experiences together. I just worry that both of our lives will end when I take my last breath.

I put the diary down on my lap. I became my late wife's biggest fear about dying.

I shut everyone out. I escaped from the town we called home. I never bought the house we talked about. All I did was hoard my money and work to avoid the stinging loneliness of my life.

Until I came home.

Until a blond ball of sunshine came into my office, insisting on meeting me, although I was the opposite, a big rain cloud, ready to burst.

It feels like a knife to the gut to know my wife worried this would happen.

That I would stay in this perpetual gray.

That I would meet someone exactly ten years after she's gone.

That I might push this new woman away.

Amy would be so disappointed in me. Most of all, I'm disappointed in myself.

My dad could go to therapy, overcome his sadness, and carry grief like an accessory, not like a five-thousand-pound weight vest.

No matter how much I don't want to do it, it might be time.

I open my phone and search "therapists near goldheart ca."

I scroll through the names and look at their specialties. There's a good one in Auburn who specializes in grief. My thumb hovers over the phone number, and I just do it.

I get a voicemail recording, and I take a deep breath.

"Hi, my name is Jackson Finch. My wife passed away from

33

SHILOH

"Oh my God," I heard Papa say from the door. I'm in the living room, with my current read across my lap, a bowl of grapes within arm's reach. I crane my neck to see who it is, and then I hear a familiar voice.

"Where is my Shiloh girl?"

"Mom?" I say, standing up. I walk into the foyer, and there's my mother with my sister following behind, holding lots and lots of luggage.

I dissolve into tears.

"Oh no," Summer says, walking around Mom, hugging me tightly. I hug my mom too and rub my face when I pull back. I'm not imagining things. My family is here.

"I heard you're having a hard time," Mom says. I nod, still crying, as I wipe my face.

It's been a month of working at the brewery, avoiding Jackson. I love Goldheart, but its townspeople are nosy, and some have started asking me if I'm okay. The Finches all look at me with apologies in their eyes. I was proud of myself that I didn't cry at all this week. I had treated myself to the book I put to the side. Murder is so comforting.

Now my sister and mother reset my streak, but it's all worth it.

Speaking of murder, my sister says, "As soon as I get settled, I'm finding this asshole that didn't want my beautiful, too-good-for-this-earth sister and give him a piece of my mind. Who is he? Where does he live?"

"I appreciate that, Summer, but I'm not telling you." Summer is two years younger than me, but sometimes it feels like she's the big sister. She's told off bullies before and stood up to mean girls. Mark called me one week after we broke up because he received an anonymous glitter bomb with a card.

"He deserved it," Summer told when I confronted her.

I remember covering my eyes with my hand. "What did it say?"

She crossed her arms. "'You didn't deserve her, cunt.'"

Jackson doesn't deserve my sister's wrath.

Summer waits for me to say something about Jackson, but Mom picks up their bags and deflects. "Where should we put our stuff?"

"My room," I say, motioning for them to follow me. The room is small, but I have a queen bed. I'm sure we can all fit, like old times. Growing up, my mom, sister, and I lived in a tiny studio apartment in the middle of midtown Sacramento and owned a beat-up car, and life was wonderful. I learned how to jump a car when I was eight. We all slept in the same bed until I turned thirteen.

"This is so cute," Summer says, looking at my photos tucked under the elastic on a pink board. She scans it, and I forget until the last minute that there's a photo of Jackson and me.

It was a shot that Olive got at the Christmas party—Jackson in that horrible sweater and me laughing at something he said. It was slightly blurry, like most kid photos are, but it was the height of our friendship. When we hadn't screwed it up yet.

My sister is untucking the picture from the elastic as I reach for it.

"Is this him? God, Shiloh, he's *old*."

"He's thirty-six," I say, pulling it out of her hand. My cheeks flame bright red as I walk it to my bureau and open my sock drawer.

"I can see where you're hiding it."

"I know." I move socks to the side so the photo can be flush with the bottom and then cover it. Turning, I rest my arm on the top of the bureau. "So, how long are you and Mom staying?"

"I don't know," Summer says, crashing on my bed. I flop down next to her. "Mom thinks a week would be good. We might move in. Who knows."

I laugh because this is an eight-hundred-square-foot apartment with two tiny rooms and one bathroom. Between my mom and my sister, Papa and I will have to hold our pee more than we're used to.

Grabbing my sister's hand, I say, "Thank you."

"Mom talked about switching places. Taking care of Papa for a few months so you can go back to Sacramento. Mend that broken heart. Again."

I've thought a lot about that in the past month. How so many memories are tucked in so many corners of Goldheart, all of them including Jackson. My workplace is owned by his family. No one would blame me for running away.

Besides what happened with Jackson, I'm happy here. I like working at the brewery. They finally perfected the root beer recipe. I can't just leave.

Still, I'm torturing myself by staying. Every time I see him or hear his name, my stomach flips and nausea coats my throat.

"I like it here."

Summer turns to me. "I have to say something, and I want you to take it the right way."

"Oh no," I say, shifting onto my side so I can look at my sister. "Tell me."

"Just because these bozos don't want you doesn't mean anything, Shi."

"I know," I say. When I met Mark, he wasn't in the head-space to even pay attention to me. Same with Jackson. I knew from the beginning of my relationship with Jackson that I might get nowhere, that I was competing with a perfect ghost. It was an impossible task.

All because I had a couple dreams and the man in them looked like Jackson.

"You can always come home if it gets to be too much."

I fold my hand into my sister's. "This is my home. I can't keep running every time a guy breaks my heart. I need to face it. Maybe it's a sign to really work on myself. Hang out with some puppies. Watch *Blue Bloods* with Papa. Go to sleep at eight-thirty."

Summer laughs, rolling onto her back. "Maybe it's not so weird you dated a guy ten years older than you. There's a grandma in there." She pokes my ticklish side, and I convulse.

"I love my grandma-ness," I say, tickling her back.

"We're still staying a week, though. Mom is going to sleep for two days straight. I intend to eat my weight in carbs and walk around the cute downtown."

"You should," I say. "I'll join you." Maybe eating cookies from Gold Roast will create a new memory, that replaces all those times with Jackson.

"Do they have a year-round Christmas store here?"

"You know it."

"Excellent," she says. "This is technically a vacation so I

can buy an ornament." While my spending habits have been frugal to the point of obsessive, my sister loves knickknacks and workout clothes. She's wearing a long-sleeved shirt and leggings from the store she works for, ISLAY, and she could go three weeks without doing laundry.

I own ten pieces of clothing.

"We'll have fun," Summer says. "Get your mind off that stupid boy. Or an adult man who's close to AARP."

"Stop," I say, shoving her. Then, I grab her into a bed hug as she drapes her leg over me and sneak-attacks my ticklish spot. I groan with impact and squirm away.

"Not fair, Summer."

"I had to."

Our evening together is a balm for my soul. We sit around and laugh, drinking root beer and iced tea and talking about old times, like when Grandma was alive. We played Skip-Bo three times, and my sister won once, Papa won once, and Mom won once. When I walk away from the table and watch my mother laugh with her dad, how she's willing to come back to a town that talked about her behind her back, I know I can stay.

I deserve to stay.

I go to bed before everyone else, snuggling to one side so Mom and Summer can come in whenever they're tired. It's the first time my head hits in the pillow in weeks that I fall asleep instantly, with not a single sad thought entering my mind.

The woman visits me again. When I first had the dream in August, her face was blank, her hair long and brown, motioning me toward something.

This time, she has a face.

It's Amy Finch.

She's wearing a light pink dress, silky and dipping low in the front. We're walking inside the brewery, the mirror ball spinning, casting fragments of light on the hardwood floor. Her fingertips trace the bar top as she walks to the hall. My heart pumps as she glides in front of me. She steps in front of Jackson's office, pointing to a figure hunched over a computer.

Amy takes my hand. I expect coldness, but it's warm, like a spring sun on a cloudless day.

"He's working on it," she says, and with that, I'm ripped from sleep, sitting up. It's twelve-thirty, and my sister squirms in the spot next to me. My mom is not here; she must've taken the couch.

"What's wrong, Shi?" Summer mumbles, turning from her fetal position on the side.

"Nothing," I say, scooching down, pulling the covers back over my shoulder. I expect to stay awake for the rest of the night, but my heart rate slows, and I drift off again, waking up to the golden sunrise peeking through the windows.

When I go into work, I make a beeline to my locker, opening the door.

A scrap of paper floats out.

After pushing my purse in, I lower to the ground and pick it up.

It's a Post-it note, the adhesive barely sticky.

When I turn it over, my heart leaps to my throat.

In horrible handwriting, it says: *Don't give up hope on me. I'm working on it. Jackson.*

My head snaps forward as a tear falls. My gaze scans the breakroom as I check for witnesses.

I read it again. And again.

"Are you okay?" Ramon asks as I walk out front.

"I'm okay, how are you?"

"Great." Ramon takes the only customer in line. I look around the brewery and in the far corner, I see Jackson, standing. He's wearing the Woody Finch polo, with a white long-sleeve underneath, his eyes locked on me. We stare at each other for a long time as another tear slips from my eye.

I hold up my hand, and he raises his.

This isn't over yet.

I just need to take care of myself for a while, while he takes care of himself. I'll cling to the one thing I have.

Hope.

34

JACKSON

THREE MONTHS LATER

"What did you do from our list this week?"

I shift in my seat. I've been seeing Dr. Vernon for three months, and I haven't known a minute of peace since. If I was going to pay for therapy, I was going to work at it. However, every bit is uncomfortable, like wearing too-small shoes. I'm facing things I've been avoiding for ten years. She tells me it won't work overnight, but we keep chipping at it, piece by piece.

She gives me homework every week, and this week's was to go through Amy's boxes and separate what I want to keep and what I want to return to her parents for them to sift through. Ever since that first day I found her journals, I haven't touched that pile of boxes, much to my mother's chagrin.

This week, though, I spent hours up there. I would get derailed by a movie ticket or a note we passed in class. I only cried when I knew I was alone in the house.

Koda joins me, sometimes nuzzling me as I quietly sobbed over Amy's things. That dog may have chewed up my parents' coffee table, but we're cool. He finds me when I need extra support.

My therapist stares me down with a judgmental grip of her pen. I don't tell my therapist I skipped Amy's books, since I ran out of time. She must know.

She knows everything.

Amy was an avid reader, and her books were her prized possessions. Since she loved them so much, it makes sense to return them to her parents. I think Amy's brother might want them for his own kids one day, especially since I've seen him with his wife around town and she's pregnant.

We chatted when I saw him. Frank shook my hand, and I assured him I would see his parents soon. I'm waiting for this week's assignment, which I'm sure is to call Amy's parents.

"I went through all the boxes," I say, telling a white lie. "And I didn't avoid Amy's brother when I saw him. We shook hands."

"Good," Dr. Vernon says, writing something down. *What is she writing? Is she giving me a star?* "How did that feel?"

How did that feel has been a common phrase uttered in therapy. When she first asked it in our first session after I said I was nervous to call a therapist, I blabbed for five minutes. Now, I expect that question I hate so much, but I never answer it eloquently.

It's tough when you're feeling your feelings for the first time in years.

"I feel accomplished," I say. "My mom will get off my dad's case for the boxes in the attic."

"What else?"

Damn it, I'm not going to get away with my cagey answer. My smile drops and I tuck my hands between my knees. "It was bittersweet. Seeing her things...I miss her. Is it normal to miss someone who has been gone for ten years?"

Usually, Dr. Vernon asks roundabout questions, making

me come to my own conclusions on how to approach situations. Rarely does she give me any advice and it's infuriating.

However, Dr. Vernon takes off her glasses and looks at me.

"Yes, it's normal. Amy was a big part of your life."

I nod and stay quiet. Looking up at my therapist, I say, "I don't think I'll ever stop missing her."

"That's fine, Jackson. I would be worried if you didn't." Dr. Vernon tilts her glasses and I brace for the next question. "How do you feel about calling her parents? Returning the stuff?"

I shrug although I'm shitting myself. *Hi Pastor and Mrs. Williams, remember me? Your son-in-law who left town and stopped taking your calls? Yes, hi, here's some of your daughter's belongings that you might want. I kept some notes and her cardigan, but here's all her other stuff that I've been keeping from you for years.*

"I'm nervous," I admit.

"Why?" she asks.

I grind my teeth. "They'll realize I didn't hold up my end of the bargain. With Amy."

"And what was that?"

"That I would be happy. Move on."

A memory overtakes me, one I've avoided for years.

It was right after Christmas, right before New Year's. Amy had lots of energy that day, so she was sitting up, writing in her journal. I came in with flowers, laying them across her lap.

"Oh, thank you, baby," she said, holding the blooms to her nose. She breathed in, the sound raspy. When she placed them down, she caught me looking at her.

Toward the end, I stared at her, trying to force the universe to let her stay. Memorize every inch of her so I could remember little details. So she didn't waste away in front of my eyes and in my memory.

"Why are you looking at me that way?" she asked.

I sat down next to her and took her frail hand in mine. "I just love you. So much."

Amy's expression grew serene as she stared at our hands intertwined. Toward the end, she couldn't wear her wedding ring since it spun on her finger and slipped off constantly. When she looked up, her eyes were glassy. "I want you to be happy."

"I don't know if I can. You're my whole world," I said.

She moved our hands slightly as she looked at them. "I want you to try. Please promise me you will do whatever you can. To be happy without me."

"I promise," I said, although I thought the feat impossible.

I told my therapist this story on the second session, when I mentioned offhandedly that I promised Amy something.

We've talked about Shiloh extensively, how my relationship with her made me realize how broken I was. How I wasn't functioning as well as I should be. I told my therapist I asked her to essentially wait for me and whether that was fair.

Dr. Vernon forgets nothing so she says, "Do you think Shiloh could make you happy? Like Amy wanted?"

"Yes." Two lumps growing in my throat.

"How is she doing?"

I shrug one shoulder. "She still works at the brewery. We've been giving each other space. My sister says she's doing well. She's been building her dog-walking business."

"That's great," Dr. Vernon says. "We talked about missing Amy. Do you miss Shiloh too?"

"Yes," I say, without hesitation. My time with her was the first time in ten years I felt true joy. She helped me integrate back into life. I started hanging out with my family more because of her.

I went from being so lonely to having a best friend.

"You mentioned you became romantic with Shiloh before you decided to take a break. How did that make you feel?"

"Wonderful," I say. Once in a while Dr. Vernon digs like she's an archaeologist, picking at me, looking for the bone.

"You never told me why you decided to take a break."

I know, lady. I rub my knuckles and then cough into my hand. My skin feels too tight as I sit there, my pits are sweating. Her gaze is too much.

What happened was I was a coward. I feel things for Shiloh—deep, raw emotions that feel similar but different to what I felt with Amy. What Shiloh did to me, pulling me out of the abyss I didn't know I was in—I'll never be able to repay her.

Amy will always be my first love. The love of my life. Until now.

"Do you think you can love two people in a lifetime?" I ask.

I brace for the "What do you think," but Dr. Vernon takes off her glasses again. "Yes, absolutely."

"How?"

"You've been coming to me for three months, Jackson, and I can tell you loved your wife. It's not wrong or cheating to fall in love with a new person. If that's what you want, you deserve to find love again."

"What if I screwed it up?"

"Do you care about Shiloh?"

"Yes."

"Do you love her?"

I concentrate on a spot of discoloration on the carpet. What I feel for Shiloh does not fit in the box I called love. It's calm, peaceful. Every time I was around her, I felt comfort and support. She made me laugh unlike anyone else. I could say anything to her, and I was accepted for exactly who I was.

I am so attracted to her too. Last week, we almost ran into each other at the hallway at work, and she looked so beautiful, with her blond hair tied back in a ponytail and wearing our brewery's awful green polo. She smiled up at me like I didn't break her heart, and her smile told me everything I needed to know.

"I love her. I'm *in* love with her."

It feels like a brick released from my chest.

"Good." A small smile curls Dr. Vernon's lips. "When are you going to tell her?"

"There's things I need to do first," I say, pulling out my phone. I hold it up, opening to my contacts. I find Marla Williams, and my thumb hovers over her name. "Do you mind if I call Amy's mom to arrange a time to drop off the boxes?"

"If you need me here to do that, I don't mind."

"Well, when you put it like that," I say, dropping my phone down into my lap.

"It's fine, Jackson. If that's the only way you'll do it…"

I press the phone to my ear. My heart is in my throat. The phone rings three times, and then a voice that sounds like a mature version of Amy says, "Hello?"

"Hi, Marla? It's me."

All I hear is a sob on the other end.

"Jackson Finch."

Marla pauses before saying, "I would know your voice anywhere."

35

JACKSON

Marla hugs me like I came back from war.

When she pulls away, tears are streaming down her face, creating skin-colored rivulets mixing with her makeup. She sandwiches my face between her hands and looks at me.

Really looks at me.

When I see her, I see a version of Amy that will never exist. They have the same brown eyes and the same nose, but her eyes crinkle at the sides. Her smile reminds me of Amy's.

This is why I didn't call them earlier. It's not because we have nothing in common anymore.

It's because I knew it would hurt.

It does hurt, a little bit. But this feels healing too.

"I prayed that you would call us," she says.

"I have the stuff in my car," I say. I consolidated Amy's stuff into six heavy boxes. The books take up two of them.

"We'll get that later. Please come in."

When I step inside the door, I'm brought back to the time when I was their son-in-law. The carpet is still brown, the ceilings are still popcorn. It even has the same smell of faint lemon.

They invited me over for dinner when I told them I finally went through Amy's stuff. Marla said she would make whatever I wanted, and I specifically requested shepherd's pie. My mouth watered the second I mentioned it, and I've been looking forward to it all day.

"Do you want something to drink?" Marla asks.

"Yes, whatever you have," I say. I sit down on the couch, resting my hands on my knees.

Marla reappears with a glass of wine for me. She has a matching one.

"Rob is in the other room, let me get him." She disappears down the hallway, and I look around, sipping the wine.

My eyes scan the mantel and there in the middle is my wedding photo with Amy.

With the help of my therapist, I now feel a twinge in my heart, not the soul-crushing weight that I felt. I honor her by moving forward.

I'm ready to do what Amy wanted me to.

To live. To love.

To beg the woman I'm in love with to take me back.

I just need to tell my former in-laws.

Pastor Williams rounds the corner with a big smile, outstretching his hand.

"I'm so glad you've come," he says. He hesitates before he pulls me in for a hug and we slap each other's backs.

We talk about our families, the weather. The upcoming event at the brewery, a companion to our nineties-themed party we had last year. It's Y2K, and I'm expecting lots of boy band costumes.

I wheel in the boxes on the dolly I brought, and Marla goes for the books immediately. Marla cries again.

"When Amy was a little girl, we used to go to the library twice a week. It was an obsession."

She pulls out all sorts of books. Hardback books, paperbacks. When she got to the bottom with the childhood books, Marla pulls out a small paperback.

"Amy loved this one. So much. She asked us to get a beagle constantly. We always said no dogs because we weren't home a lot, but we really should've gotten one."

She shows me the book, and my stomach drops.

The book is called *Shiloh*.

There's a dog on the front.

Amy has been trying to tell me all along. Shiloh is the one.

I spent so long trying to ignore what I was feeling, thinking it wasn't right, that I was disrespecting Amy. I wasn't.

There were signs all along.

"Isn't that the name of Earl Abbott's granddaughter?" Rob asks. "The one you're friends with?"

"Yes," I answer before they can.

"When we met her, she said you two have become close."

"We had," I say, rubbing my hands together. I look up and I say, "I'm in love with her."

Bracing for their reactions, my eyes flick from Marla to Rob and back again. I want to say so much more, but the fact I'm in love with Shiloh is the full truth.

It doesn't cancel the love I had for Amy.

I feel her presence more than ever.

Marla covers her chest with her hand. "That's lovely, my dear."

Rob stands by his wife, wrapping his arm around her. "She seems like a wonderful person."

"It doesn't mean I didn't love Amy. I did. Very much."

"We know that, dear," Marla says, leaning forward to pat my knee. "You loved our daughter so well, and Shiloh is a lucky woman that she gets your love. We would love to get to know her."

There are so many things I need to do to earn her trust again. To convince her that I have healed, that I'm ready to move forward in life. With her.

Like my list with Dr. Vernon, my list for Shiloh is long.

But tonight, I will hang out with Amy's parents.

We continue to drink wine and eat Marla's delicious shepherd's pie with green salads and crusty French bread. We tell stories about Amy, how she and Frank pranked each other as kids. I double over laughing at the story of her brother hiding in another room at night when he knew she went to the bathroom and charged her with the vacuum that lit up in front. It scared Amy so badly, she spooked the cat, who knocked over three ceramic pots holding fake flowers.

I spend the evening mad at myself that I wasted so many years avoiding these people when I feel like I'm finally alive again. Being stuck in misery was comfortable, but this moment is scary and magnetic and dynamic.

I want this feeling forever.

All because of Shiloh.

She began this for me. I hope she's there with me in the end.

The next day, around five o'clock, I park my car in the Goldheart Cemetery parking lot and grab the bouquet of lilies I bought that morning. I walk along the path, pretty much alone in this cemetery, as I step onto the grass, careful not to walk directly over graves.

When I find her headstone, a beautiful granite piece with *Amy Louise Williams Finch* etched into it, I drop to my knees.

When I first came home, I visited her grave once, but I didn't feel her presence. To me, she's not here, not really.

However, it feels different today. Like she's been waiting for me to return.

The headstone has a small holder for flowers, so I replace the crispy ones with my bouquet, removing the wrapping and fluffing them. Once I'm done, I lean back and just look at it. I press my hands to the grass.

"Hey, baby." I grumble and cough, and then continue. "I haven't really kept my promise to you. That I would live. I love you so much. I will never stop loving you. But I know now that the best way to honor you is to live well, when your time was cut so short."

I cough again, my throat thickening as I sit here to tell her. "I met someone. Her name is Shiloh. She even has the same middle name as you. She's wonderful—sweet, kind, warm, and she makes me feel like you made me feel. I can't help but feel like you sent her to me."

The wind hits me, and I sneeze. An instant smile crosses my face. I wonder if that's her.

"I screwed up, Amy. I was so scared to give her everything because of what happened to you. I don't want to be scared anymore, but I am. I can't lose another person I love."

A shiver runs down my shoulder, and I flinch, looking behind me, expecting a person to be standing there, but there's no one.

"I know you wanted me to find someone. It took me ten years, but I did. I just hope that she still loves me."

The wind picks up again, and a rush of calm floods my system. It tells me this is right. That Shiloh is the one.

"Thank you," I say, pressing my hand again to the ground. What I loved about her, her spirit, is not in the ground, it's not in the things I went through. She lives in my memories, and I will always love her.

However, I can't live in the past anymore.

Shiloh is my future. Shiloh is everything.

36

SHILOH

"How do I look?" I ask, spreading my arms wide.

"You look wonderful. Who are you supposed to be?" Papa asks from his recliner.

"I'm Mandy Moore from the 'Candy' video, Papa," I say with a big smile. I straight-ironed my hair, which reaches my waist with no curls in it. I weaved it into two space buns in the back with a fan of hair. I layered two tank tops, one yellow, one red, and sewed a turquoise skirt from material I found while thrifting. I also bought a vintage Walkman with headphones of questionable cleanliness from eBay as a prop.

I've been ridiculously excited for the Second Annual Woody Finch Brewery Adult Prom and this year's Y2K theme. I've never gotten to dress up like Mandy Moore, so this was the perfect opportunity.

I plan to play "Candy" all the way to the brewery.

"Are you sure you don't want to go? We can make you look like Justin Timberlake."

Papa chuckles. "That's fine, girlie. I want you to have a good time with your friends."

I check the time on my phone. "I should get going."

"Okay. I think your date's here."

"Date?"

"A fine strapping lad." Papa stands up and shuffles to the door. When he opens it, there stands Jackson. My mouth falls open, and my eyelashes flutter.

He looks so handsome—his beard neatly trimmed, his black-wired-rimmed glasses. He's wearing a black suit over a white shirt, holding flowers. Tulips, my favorite. I could cry, he's so attractive.

I've done my best to forget him, but whenever I catch a glimpse of him, everything stops.

I heard he started therapy, and I suspected that he finally saw his in-laws because the pastor gave a cryptic sermon at church the day I happened to go with Papa. I also thought Pastor Williams looked straight at me and gave a smile, but I shook it off. Coincidence.

Papa checks his bare wrist and says, "Oh man, *Jeopardy!* is on. I'm going to catch it in the other room."

There's no TV in the other room.

He shuffles off, and we smile awkwardly at each other.

"Hi," I say.

"Hey." Jackson hands me the flowers. I bury my nose into the flowers, inhaling his scent.

"You look great. Mandy Moore?"

I pick up some of my handmade skirt and swish from side to side. "I had to."

We stand quietly, and I know he can hear my heart because it's in my ears, beating so loudly at his presence. I don't know what to do so I turn and walk to the kitchen and find our one vase, dusty and abandoned on the top shelf. I can't reach it without jumping onto the counter, so Jackson uses his height to get it down.

Our hands brush, and I flinch.

Is this the moment he told me to wait for? Everything I've

rehearsed is gone like the wind. My brain can't form a coherent thought about him.

"So," I say after I put the flowers in water.

"So." Jackson shoves his hands in his pockets. "I want to apologize."

I force myself to look at him, give him my attention. I nod once, and he continues.

"I wasn't ready for you when I met you. I do think I would've lived my life like that for the rest of my life if you didn't come into it. I was barely functioning when you came into my office that day. Shiloh, you brought me back to life."

My heart flutters. *Don't cry*, I tell myself. *You can cry later, alone.*

"I didn't want to say this until I could come to you as a whole man. I feel like it's time now. I'm so sorry this is late, Shiloh, but I love you. I love you so much."

Okay, now I'm crying. My lip quivers, and I can't stop it. I wipe my cheek, but tears are rolling.

"Amy might've been the first one I fell in love with, but I want you to be my last. You're my best friend. There's been a Shiloh-shaped hole in my life, but I needed to become the man you deserved. A man who really, really wants to take you on a date tonight. Finally."

The butterflies in my stomach are manic, my heart pounding. I tuck my hands tightly around me because if I don't, I will flail my arms. I've been dreaming of this.

I know it was Amy who visited me before my first day. I knew to never give up hope. A small part of me knew that he would come back to me.

Holding up one finger, though, I want to make him sweat. He made me wait four months; I can make him wait a little bit.

"Jackson, this is a lot to process," I say.

"Okay," he says. He turns to leave, his hand reaching for the door.

"Wait!" I yell, and he turns around, his grin huge.

"I would love to go on that date," I say. He fans out his elbow, and I take it. He covers my hand with his. "Papa, I'm leaving for the party!"

"Okay, girlie, have fun with Jackson!"

He sounds closer than the other room. I see him hiding in the faint shadow of the hallway, fifteen feet from where Jackson and I reconciled. We'll have to have a talk later about eavesdropping.

"He was listening the whole time, wasn't he?" Jackson asks.

"Yes, he was. I think he deserved it, though. He's heard enough about you the last few months."

"Does he want to fight me?"

"No," I say. "But he might need to have a few words."

"I get that," Jackson says, pulling me closer. "I have one more surprise for you. Well, it counts as two."

My stomach drops, and I get giddy at the same time.

"I love surprises."

"Well, I really hope you like this one. Since they're both kind of permanent and cost me a lot of money. Consider them both peace offerings."

The light has settled into a golden glow as we drive some narrow roads through the wheat-colored hills to the outskirts of town, into the rural areas of Goldheart backing up into Nevada County. I'm so excited, I bounce in my chair, anxious to see the surprise.

I have no idea what it is.

Jackson holding my hand over the console is enough.

When we got into the car, I hoped I would be cool enough to pull my hand away, be an ice queen. Play a little hard to get for the months we did not talk.

That's not how I function though.

I never fell out of love with this man. I am his, in every way possible. I really hoped with the passing time that the ache in my heart would dull to a manageable twinge, but it never did. Every day going into Woody Finch was torture, my hope to see him high. He always looked at me like he was begging for my patience.

Now, he's here. He told me he loved me. He's holding my hand and looking over at me, like I'm a dream that is not real.

"Here we are," he says as we pull onto a gravel driveway, a property surrounded with tall trees and bushes. When we drive closer, I see a sign, and I blink several times.

It can't be.

"Rory's Rescue" is etched into the sign, nailed to two round posts in front of a log cabin-inspired, single-story home.

"What is this?" I ask, tears already filling my eyes.

"I bought this." His grin is big as he turns off the engine and sprints around to my side to open the door. He points to the house and beyond. "It's four acres, so there's plenty of room for the dogs to run…"

"What?" I ask.

"Your rescue. You told me you wanted to save as many senior dogs as possible, so I got this place. I talked to my family and Dan, and we agreed that all the proceeds made from Rory's Root Beer will go toward the rescue."

I don't know how I sink to the ground because the skirt is so tight, but my butt hits the ground, and my hands cover my mouth. Too many dreams are coming true. He picks me up so we can walk to the porch, one that wraps all around the house, with a swing, a perfect place to sit in the evenings, talking about everything and nothing.

"I can't wait for you to see this," he says, as he sticks the key in the door. When he opens it, the living room is bare, but the focal piece, the brick-laden fireplace, stands like it was waiting for me. It's roomy, but not too big.

Imagine all the dogs I can save. All the dogs that will have a chance to live out the rest of their lives in this house, on this property, not in a cage on a concrete floor.

"I know it's fast, that I need to earn your trust back, but I was thinking you and your grandfather could move in when you're ready."

What?

He leads me by the hand to a small room off the laundry room with an en suite bathroom, perfect for Papa so he can have his personal space, but also be part of the house. I can imagine his memorabilia on the walls, a picture of my grandmother on a nightstand.

I'm still crying, but a huge smile is on my face.

He takes me out of the room and to another area, where our room would be. It's larger and has a bathroom, and it overlooks the backyard with trees and a small hill.

He's holding my hand in silence, as we look out the window, in this empty room that's so full of possibilities.

"I talked to Priscilla, and she gave me some basic pointers for setting up the rescue. I did get the sign made, but we can change the name…"

"No, it's perfect." I imagine my soul dog Rory up in heaven, looking down on me, proud that I'll be able to help dogs just like him. Dogs that wouldn't get a second chance otherwise.

"I have one more surprise," he says. We walk to the other

bedroom, right next to the master. The door is closed, but when I open it, I let out a wail.

There, standing in the middle of the room, is a brown and white pit bull, my buddy.

Bubba.

The dog wiggles as he walks toward me, and I go to my knees. The dog licks my face, like he's thanking me. Jackson looks down at me with a big smile, and there's some mistiness in his eyes.

"I told Priscilla that I wanted to surprise you, and she told me to adopt this dog and I will be forgiven. So, if the house and the rescue didn't work, I'm keeping him because we bonded on the way home."

"You adopted Bubba?" I ask, standing up, as the dog leans against me, his little tail thumping.

I can't hold back with Jackson; I wrap my arms around his neck and kiss his cheek, his eyelids, his nose. When our lips meet, calmness courses through my body. We just kiss as he holds me, squeezing a bit before he lets me go.

Bubba nudges my hip, and I laugh when he knocks me into Jackson.

Jackson holds me, kissing my throat, my ear, my head.

"I don't want to leave Bubba now." I point to him.

"Don't worry. I got him a dog sitter."

The doorbell rings, and my eyes widen. I walk to the door, and Priscilla is standing there with my grandpa on her arm.

"Are you going to give this boy another chance? Because this house is great and I want to live here. I'm tired of living in an apartment," Papa says. I hug both of them.

"Were you in on this?" I ask Priscilla.

She nods. "I was. I had to make sure he properly apologized to you. However, I think you'll just have to get back together with him because Bubba loves him."

I turn around to find all eighty pounds of Bubba in Jackson's arms.

My boys. Together.

A girl couldn't dream up a better future.

The brewery is full of streamers and glitter, mimicking an early 2000s teen romantic comedy.

I walk into it, still dressed as Mandy Moore but without a stitch of makeup on. I cried it all off.

The best part is Jackson is holding my hand, and he kisses it as we stand there, looking at the crowd.

"I'll let the piranhas get you," Jackson says, leaning in to kiss my neck. Emily, Annie, and Whitney descend on me, their eyes curious.

"He bought you a house," Emily says. "I assume you took him back."

I nod. "Thank you for agreeing to the proceeds from the root beer."

Emily flips her hand. "Don't worry about it. We wouldn't have the root beer without you, and obviously we love dogs here."

They all hug me, and when Whitney pulls me in, she says, "I want to be your first donor. I have a check for you. To help you get started."

"You don't have to, Whitney, I have more than enough."

"You're helping me out. I'm gonna get murdered in taxes this year." She hands me a check, and I put it in my crossbody Mandy Moore bag. Whitney plays off her generosity, but she is one of the most giving people I know.

Jackson returns to me with a smile and hands me a root beer, and we clink our glasses together.

"It's weird seeing you happy, brother," Emily says.

"She does it to me," he says, kissing the top of my head. The women cooed, and Annie's eyes leak as she rubs her swollen stomach.

"I can't handle this," Annie says.

The opening beat of "It's Gonna Be Me" by NSYNC booms through the speakers and the sparse crowd takes notice.

It's tough not to dance to this song.

Whitney turns to Emily. "Let's go."

"I'm going to sit down," Annie says. "Congratulations."

"Thanks," we say in unison.

Thumper is the DJ tonight. He's wearing a clean baseball cap, while his girlfriend, Izzie, stands by the stage. They're laughing about something, and he grabs her by the waist, kissing her neck.

"What Mandy Moore song should I request?" Jackson asks, leaning in.

I shuffle through her catalog until I land on the right one.

"'Cry'," I say.

"'Cry'." He looks at me with a lifted eyebrow. "Why that one?"

"That's when I knew I was falling for you. That night at the lake. You cried."

He laughs as he takes me in his arms. "I did."

He walks to the stage and talks to Thumper as the song winds down.

"This one goes out to the sweetest person we all know. Shiloh, here's your Mandy Moore."

"I'll always remember..." starts playing over the speakers, and Jackson walks to me, offering his hand.

I take it and he pulls me onto the dance floor, wrapping an arm around my back, pulling me close. I rest my head on his chest as he holds me.

"This feels right," I say. "I always knew it was."

"I'm sorry it took me so long to get here."

"It doesn't matter. You're here now."

"I love you, Shiloh."

I will never get tired of hearing that.

"I love you too."

EPILOGUE

JACKSON

Two Months Later

"Jackson Rollins, I swear if you don't right now..." Shiloh says, her eyes squeezed close, her mouth open as I pull away from her. My fingers have teased her on and off for the last few minutes as I drive her slowly mad, applying pressure and removing it from her clit with my tongue. Hearing my name on my girlfriend's lips drives me wild, so I giggle against her breast, and I take a taste, sucking her into my mouth.

"Oh my God," she says, as I slip a finger in, then two. She's so ready for me, but I hear slight whining at the door.

We have about five minutes before Bubba busts in like the Kool-Aid Man.

I roll onto my back and pull Shiloh onto me, as she slowly lowers onto my cock, her hands on my chest.

"Is that better, honey?"

"Much," she says as she starts to ride me. The whining at the door doesn't faze her as she takes what she wants, bouncing up and down on me. I press my thumb into her clit as she rides me, feeling so tight and hot that I have to focus on the dog's whining so I can last longer than five seconds.

We have a birthday party to be at in about thirty minutes, but we couldn't help ourselves. It all started with some playful butt-smacking in the kitchen as Shiloh wrapped my sister's present. Then, we checked that Earl was deeply engrossed in old episodes of *The Honeymooners* before we snuck off to our bedroom for a quickie.

It turned into anything but, and now we're both sweaty, trying to beat the clock of a dog obsessed with us.

"Oh my God," she moans, and I try to shush her. Papa Earl might be old, but his hearing is still great. When Shiloh comes, her walls pulse around my cock and I finish shortly after, pumping my load into her, filling her up. She kisses me hard before tucking in beside me. "The dog really wants in."

"I know. You're so loud for being in the same house as your grandfather."

"He doesn't have to pay rent. He's fine."

Shiloh and Earl moved in a week after we reconciled. Some people thought it was quick, but it felt like I wasted time getting over my own shit. Once I was ready, I was ready for the huge things and so was she. She's busy between her hours at the brewery and setting up the rescue with the help of Priscilla. Dan made his own donation to Rory's Rescue. My love has a hard time accepting help, but with the money she received from Whitney and Dan, the rescue can take in senior dogs for years to come.

We're so close to starting her mission. She's ready to pull dogs from the shelters now, but we have to be patient.

I fall more in love with her every day.

When Shiloh pops into the shower to freshen up, I open the door to Bubba.

He likes both of us, but it's shocking that he picked me as

his favorite when I live with the dog whisperer. Everywhere I go, Bubba must go. He's my buddy, and Shiloh has joked that she should step out of the room when we're together.

Bubba likes Earl too, and sometimes he sleeps in his room. He's an equal opportunist lovebug.

When my girlfriend walks out of the shower, her hair down and fluffy, wearing a cute, stripped dress, I want to devour her all over again.

"Honey, this dress is not fair," I say, grabbing some of her butt as I lean in to smell the vanilla in her hair.

"Behave yourself," she says. "We need to get to your sister's birthday."

I pout, but I kiss her head as we get into the car to go to the brewery.

We're opening the brewery later to do a breakfast brunch for my sister's thirtieth birthday. She just started seeing the chef who owns Bistro 530, Burke, and he's catering. My sister has been freaking about turning thirty, when our brothers and I have been in our thirties for some time.

When we arrive, the same decorations are up from the Y2K party, but there's a new banner hung: "Thirty, Flirty, and Thriving." Someone told me that was from a movie, I think.

"Happy birthday, Emily!" Shiloh says, wrapping her arms around her.

Emily smiles, but I know she's feeling anxious. I take her in for a hug as well.

"So, your boyfriend is here," I say, looking for him. Emily hasn't dated anyone since Olive was born so we all are taking shots at her and teasing her for it. Burke seems nice enough. He came to one family dinner and stayed quiet for most of it.

I don't blame him. It's becoming more and more chaotic.

Reid and Whitney got engaged two weeks ago, and now they're planning their wedding. Cameron's wife Annie will be giving birth any day now. She's forty weeks today and is doing everything in her power to get the baby out. Annie even joined Shiloh on a five-mile hike with Bubba, and still nothing. My brother and Annie got married just in time for their baby's birth. My mother got bent out of shape they went to the courthouse. I mentioned she was there for my first one.

It won't be my last.

Shiloh says that the rescue and adopting Bubba is more than enough to profess my commitment to her, but I want to marry her. I want her to have my last name. I want to fill our house full of dogs and children, including her desire to adopt through the foster care system.

These last two months, I got a glimpse of forever, and I've seen enough. I've loved Shiloh for less than a year, but I know I want to love her for the rest of the years that we're alive.

I'm still going to therapy. Still working through my issues. With Shiloh by my side, we can conquer everything. We can save dogs. We can make the best kids. We can give kids the best home. Overall, we will have the best life.

That just leaves Emily.

I hope Burke can make her happy. She deserves it. Olive deserves it.

There's a knock at the door, and we look back.

"Don't they see the sign on the door?" Emily scoffs as she walks away and heads over to Burke in a white chef's jacket, stirring something in a big bowl.

The knocking grows more and more insistent as I kiss Shiloh on the head and walk to the door of the barn. I look through the window to see a man with his head down.

When I open the door, he looks up.

He looks so damn familiar. He's blond, with short hair and flat cheeks. His eyes are bright blue. He's a little taller than I am, and it's driving me mad I can't place him.

"Can I help you?" I ask. "We're closed for a private event."

"Hi," he says, smiling. "You're one of the brothers, right?"

I've never seen this man before in my life.

"Yeah, but we're closed..."

"Is Emily here?"

"Yes, but..." I peer at him closer, and my heart stops. It can't be.

"I was wondering if I could see her," he asks. "Just for a second."

This can't be him. I never met him, I only heard about him. So, I'm still trying to figure out what to say when I hear my sister's voice behind me. She stops talking, and I know she's seen him.

It's all happening in slow motion as I turn to look at her. Emily's face is pale white, her green eyes large while her lips part.

"Hey, Martini," the man says. "It's been a long time."

THE END

WANT MORE?

To keep up to date with Jenny and be the first to hear about new releases and sales, please go to jennybuntingbooks.com to subscribe to her newsletter!

Loved *Golden Hour*? Please consider reviewing on Amazon! It helps others find and enjoy this book.

Curious about Cameron and Annie or Reid and Whitney? Their books, *Fool's Gold* and *Gold Rush*, are available in ebook and paperback!

Come find Jenny on socials! She has a readers' group on Facebook called Jenny Bunting's Adultish Readers, a Facebook page called Author Jenny Bunting, and she's on Instagram at @jennybuntingbooks. She adores connecting with readers.

ACKNOWLEDGMENTS

A huge thank you to my Finch Family team—Sarah from Lopt & Cropt Editing and Kari from Kari March Designs. What can I say that I haven't said already? You both are the best.

My beta readers—Candice, Erica, Julie and Ava. Thank you for saving me from my own audacity. I'm always grateful that you're willing to take time to help this book be the best it can be. An extra special thank you to Candice and Erica who read early copies to catch typos and goofs. You both are gems.

Thank you to the ShepHeroes rescue for our precious baby Booker and for opening your hearts to this work. German shepherds are unbelievably special and I'm so thankful you save them. A special shout-out to my husband for answering questions on owner surrenders and what it's like to be a dog rescue volunteer. Another big thank you to Nick from Consistent K9 who helped turn our velociraptor into an actual dog. We're still working on the whole "Respect Jenny" thing, but we're getting there.

Lastly, I want to thank you, the reader. Some of you I will never hear from, but if you've ever purchased my ebooks, read them on Kindle Unlimited, or displayed my books on your shelves—thank you. I mean that from the bottom of my heart. I write for me, but I also write for you. I hope this book filled you with joy and hope and I hope you loved Shiloh and Jackson as much as I love them.

ABOUT THE AUTHOR

Jenny Bunting is the author of seven full-length romantic novels and four romantic comedy novella titles, all self-published. Jenny dabbles in spreadsheets for her day job so she can do this on the side, as her passion. Her current ranking of favorite dog breeds are as follows: German shepherd, Newfoundland, and Samoyed. She once was attacked with love kisses by three dogs at a group dog training class while her actual dog didn't display one ounce of jealousy. Jenny lives with her husband and their German shepherd in the suburbs of Sacramento, California.

www.ingramcontent.com/pod-product-compliance
Lightning Source LLC
Chambersburg PA
CBHW052039240626
47153CB00006B/2158